DOCTOR
TAYLOR

SHARON WOODS

To everyone starting something new. Trust the magic of the beginning.

CHAPTER 1

ALICE

"READY TO PRETEND YOU'RE a millionaire?" Blake says as we exit the Uber.

My heels click on the concrete pavement as we take a few steps toward the entry for Luxe, the hottest new club in the city. Blake, from my course at college, has been begging me to join him for weeks, and I finally caved. It's been a really long week of finishing my final exams, and though my eyes feel heavy, and I have a constant throbbing pain in my temples from the constant late nights, nothing will stop me from celebrating the completion of my nursing degree with my three best friends.

I'm so excited I'm bouncing on my toes while waiting to get inside. I love the light-hearted pleasure of a club. The mix of dancing and drinking gets me feeling more relaxed and self-confident. Tonight's club is even better; it's a club I haven't been to before, but I'm now a member of.

Luxe is a club for the elite. Only the most successful and disgustingly rich men and women secure a membership to Luxe. It's a secret club where you must earn a minimum of a million dollars a year—with proof—in order to get a membership. But Blake scored us all one from his dad's work connections. His dad worked on the construction of this club, which has allowed us to take advantage of the perks of a lifetime membership.

They hid the club off the main road, and you wouldn't know it's here unless you're a member, as only members get the address. Shuffling up to the front of the line, I rub my hands together, trying to warm myself up, but it's not working. The fresh air on my skin raises goosebumps all over my body. I stopped by the local department store to pick up a new dress on my way home from work today. It's different from my usual style of jeans and a top. My wardrobe is usually a mixture of sweats or jeans, along with the occasional dress. I have my regular clubbing dresses, but I needed a statement dress for Luxe.

I feel super sexy for a change, and I love the way I am feeling tonight. I have been getting a few eyes raking over my body, just while standing in the line, so I know it was the right choice of outfit—the little black dress, paired with black strappy heels that wrap delicately around my calf, adding height to my small frame. Smoky gray eye shadow makes my blue eyes pop, and pinning all my hair back in a sleek high pony completes the outfit.

I never wear this much makeup; I'm usually a mascara-only girl. But thanks to YouTube, I have slain my makeup game tonight and look older than my twenty-three years. We strut past the two suited bouncers and step through the doors into the moodiest club I have ever been to. I take in the packed crowd. There are men in three-piece suits and a woman for every man, who are all dressed in designer gowns. I tug nervously at my dress, wishing it was an inch longer after seeing all the elegantly dressed women in the room.

Blake grabs my upper arm with his soft fingers. "Leave it, Alice. You look hot as fuck. If you had a dick, I'd totally fuck you."

I bring my hand up to stifle my giggles.

I had a few vodka, lemon, and lime drinks with Blake back at my house, so we already have a warm buzz coursing through our veins. The alcoholic drinks at clubs are too pricey for us students, and I barely make enough money at the coffee shop to pay my share of the rent.

Blake's hand drops from my arm. "My treat. Let's find the bar!" he shouts above the loud music blaring all around us.

On the right, just behind the crowd, the abstract gunmetal bar with servers in suits comes into clear view. We amble over the white stone floor to the front of the bar to order.

"This is incredible, Blake. I have never seen a club like this. Check out this bar. It's so luxurious." I skim my hands along the smooth surface. It's cool to the touch and completely opposite to how the alcohol is warming me.

Blake orders our drinks while I finally take in the whole club. It's a lot bigger than I had imagined. The dark-gray walls are softly lit by down lights; 3D sculptures are popping from the ceiling, and there are white couches lining the walls, leaving a large dance floor in the middle. Men and women already occupy every seat, so we have no choice but to stand. There are no fluorescent lights or nasty sticky floors in sight. Everything here is in immaculate condition.

When I turn back to the bar, the server is putting a peach-colored shot in front of each of us. I frown, touching the glass between my fingers, and shout, "Blake, what is this shot?"

"Just shoot it." And with that, he taps the shot on the bar and downs it.

Without giving it a second thought, I lift the cold shot glass to my bottom lip, and closing my eyes, I chase mine back. The shot burns my throat, making my eyes pop open, reminding me why I detest shots, but the aftertaste from this one is scrumptious. I lick my lips to pick up any remaining residue.

"Oh, peach. Yummy. What are these, Blake?" I question.

Before Blake can answer, the bartender speaks up. "Wet pussies." He winks and I flush, but he collects our empty glasses from the bar and takes them away before I can respond.

I turn to Blake. "Let's wait until the girls get here to order more drinks. I've got a good buzz going already, and I don't want to be drunk too early, especially since we had a few at home." I hiccup. We're waiting on my two roommates, Maddison and Tahlia, to get here. Tahlia had to work later than usual today, so they should join us soon.

He shakes his head. "No chance. They take forever getting ready. We are ordering now."

I giggle at his impatience. He swivels slowly on his heel and orders another round of our favorite—vodka, lemon, and lime. Blake hands his credit card across the bar to the flirty bartender to pay for our drinks.

The bartender shakes his head. "A fellow patron has already paid for these. Enjoy."

My lips shut into a flat, thin line. *What?* "By whom?" I ask.

Blake and I stand frozen before spinning around, trying to find the person responsible for paying for our drinks and, more importantly, why? The bar is full, and everyone is either in groups chatting among themselves, dancing on the crowded dance floor, or waiting in lines at the bar to be served. None of them are by themselves or seem to be paying attention to Blake and me. *Weird.*

"Who the fuck cares? Thank you to whoever paid for these." He picks up his drink and toasts the air.

I shake my head, reaching for the glass. Clutching it in one hand, I stir the alcohol with the black straw in the other. Wild doesn't begin to describe Blake. Meeting Blake three years ago was like finding another sibling. He sat down in the empty chair next to me in our first biology class for our nursing degree, and he kept distracting me with his constant outbursts. We both got warnings that very first day for disrupting the class, but we still achieved the top marks out of the entire class by the end of the three years. He always keeps the girls and me laughing at his weekend antics. It's like living in a real-life episode of *The Bold and the Beautiful.*

"You're crazy. We can't accept them. The person could be a weirdo."

"Honey, have you looked around the club? He would be a rich, successful weirdo. Drink his money. I'm sure he's swimming in it." He drinks it without a care and pushes off the bar, nodding to the dance floor. "Come on."

I peer down at the drink, thinking and watching the lemon bob around on the surface. *No one has ever bought me a drink before.* It sends a slight chill through me, but I shake off the feeling and walk over to stand beside Blake, taking a swig of my drink. No words leave either of our mouths, both of us happy just to peer at the patrons dancing on the floor in front of us. We have a good view of the entire dance floor from where we are standing. The music blaring from the speakers is R&B and the latest pop.

I take my last sip and drain the glass. My stare lands on a man standing across the dance floor directly opposite us, leaning his large frame against the arm of a white couch full of men. My gaze meets his and I let out a shocked gasp. My grip on the glass loosens and the smooth surface slides straight through my fingers to land on the stone floor, where it smashes into tiny fragments with a popping sound.

"Shit." I crouch down, but Blake pulls my arm, preventing me from picking up the glass.

"Alice, don't. You will cut yourself. The cleaners are heading over now."

Allowing Blake to help me up, I push up on my heels to straighten myself out. I spot a cleaner in a suit holding a dustpan and brush strolling over in our direction. I swallow and glance down at my twisted hands.

Remembering why I dropped the glass, I raise my head and look around for the handsome man with scorching blue eyes, but he's no longer standing there. I close my eyes, squeezing them shut for a moment, wishing I hadn't been so clumsy in front of him. He is probably used to elegant women, not a clumsy mess like me.

I have never had a reaction like that to a man. His eyes and the way he stared at me set my whole body on fire. Then the sexy smirk at the corner of his lip that rose when I dropped my glass sent chills down my spine. He must have seen what effect he had on me. I open my eyes, grimace, and hurry to the bathroom to clear my head. I need to forget about that man and focus on having a good night.

I hurry through the crowd of people, weaving in and out as I make my way toward the ladies' room. Not paying attention and keeping my gaze on the sign above the door with the word 'bathroom,' I collide with a hard chest. I bounce backward, stumbling on my heels. The stranger reaches out, grabbing on to the back of my arms to steady me, saving me from falling flat on my ass.

"Shit, I'm so sorry." The voice is smooth and rich, making me take a step back.

My eyes flick up and I meet the same magnificent blue eyes from before. I smile to myself as he stares, feeling heat spread across my cheeks. He stands there, devilishly handsome, his brown hair gleaming in the club lights. His lips part in a dazzling display of straight white teeth. He holds an air of authority and has the appearance of one who demands instant obedience.

I nod, fighting the overwhelming need to be close to him, to feel his tongue tangled with mine.

My tongue slides out between my lips, and I skim it across the lower one, moistening it. He makes no attempt to hide the fact that he's watching me with a heated stare. The air around us crackles with electricity.

"Can I buy you a drink?" The double meaning in his gaze is obvious.

I stand frozen, and my heart jolts inside my chest.

But as I stand there staring into his glowing eyes, I give in, and I lean forward and kiss him. He kisses me back, and it's a slow, all-consuming kiss. Not the hungry kiss I expected. I can taste the liquor on his tongue and the delicious sensation of the touch of his lips. When we pull away, I'm panting, staring up at him under heavy, hooded eyes.

The air becomes thick, overwhelming me. Clearing my constricting throat, I try to suck some much-needed air into my lungs. "I have to go to the bathroom. I'll catch up with you later," I whisper before I rush off to the ladies' room.

After using the bathroom, I collect myself. My breathing is now regulated, and my body temperature seems to be returning to normal. I wander back out and stand by the entrance to the bathroom. Scanning the club, I can't see him in the sea of faces. My heart constricts as I look around a few minutes more before giving up and walking to meet Blake. I spot him, so I quicken my pace. I notice my roommates, Tahlia and Maddison, have arrived, and they are standing around talking.

"Hey, girls," I yell, moving between them. Draping one arm around each of their shoulders, I squeeze them closer in a hug.

Chuckling at my affection, Maddison asks, "Where did you go? You sound happy."

"That's because you girls are finally here, so we can dance now." Just as I finish the sentence, my skin prickles. I glance toward the spot the man had been standing in before, and he is back in the exact same position. He's staring at me, but this time he is clutching a glass of amber liquid that he brings to his lips. I watch his Adam's apple bob when he takes a sip. His eyes don't falter; they drink me down with it. A delicious shudder heats my body, and before I can register what's happening, Maddison squeals.

"O.M.G. Yes! I love this song! Come on, let's go dance!"

"This Is How We Do It" by Montell Jordan plays, and I lose eye contact with him when Maddison drags me by the hand to the dance floor, pushing through the crowd of people to get to the middle. I'm almost tripping over my feet, trying to keep up with her. My tight dress only allows me to take short, quick steps.

Maddison, Tahlia, and I met during high school. Tahlia and I were working in a local coffee shop as waitresses after school. Maddison would come every day after lessons to have coffee and study. After a few months, I began talking to Maddison about college applications and she offered to assist me in the research and also with applying to my top three preferences—which I accepted. We hung out every weekend, all becoming fast friends before moving to the city and renting a house together. Blake was the final piece that completed our friendship group.

"Maddy, slow down. I'm going to break my neck in these stupid heels!" I shout.

She stops suddenly in the center of the dance floor, and, spinning my body to face her, she dances. The entire floor is packed with sweaty bodies touching and grinding against each other. I can't see past the people dancing to see if the man has moved or if he is still standing there. I'm strangely flattered and intrigued by his interest.

A few songs later, the crowd surrounding us has thinned. I'm having a blast. My knees ache and the balls of my feet are burning with pain from all our dancing, but I'm too buzzed to care. Tahlia and Blake join us, and we all dance together. I can't remember the last time I had this much fun. Recently, my life has consisted only of work or study. To be so carefree in this moment makes my heart sing. I sway my hips from side to side to the beat. I look around again for the sexy stranger and I note he is standing near the bar. A woman with rich, long brown hair, and wearing a black sequined dress, is engaged in conversation with him, her fingers wrapped around his bicep. They are standing relatively close to each other, and she is whispering in his ear.

My heart sinks at the sight of them, so I tear my gaze away. I'm about to ask if the others want to call an Uber soon, when I feel a body slide up behind me. A masculine arm snakes around my waist to pull me back flush against his hard torso, and he rocks our hips slowly to the beat.

The body hugging mine is tall and seems to be built of solid muscle. I can smell his deep sandalwood and caramel scent, which is intoxicating. I sigh audibly at the memory of when I was last being held in a man's embrace. I feel his breath tickle the tip of my ear, pulling me from the memory as we continue to sway into the next song. I close my eyes and get lost in this moment, forgetting everything and just enjoying his warmth.

He whispers, "You're incredible. I couldn't resist." His tone is soft and sensual, totally different from the smooth, rich voice of the man I kissed earlier in the night. I grin from ear to ear at the memory. The warm embrace is pulling a deep longing from me that I don't want to lose. I don't reply, but I continue to dance with him.

"Turn around, beautiful." I stop and turn in a circle, curious to see what this man looks like. Raising my arms, I lay them on his shoulders and step back, leaving a decent gap.

His eyes close and his hands are on my hips, moving them to the sound of the beat. I seize the opportunity to take him in—he has short brown hair, tanned skin, and his jeans, t-shirt, and blazer are all black. My lips lift at his classically handsome features. As I finish scanning him from head to toe, his eyes suddenly pop open and his blue eyes meet mine.

He is beaming, which makes me grin back. However, his beauty and presence don't hold the same power and control over me as the other man's did. It doesn't stroke the deep desires and feelings that have awoken in me. My gaze drops to his solid chest. And I sigh. *I'm not feeling it.*

Before I have the chance to speak, he leans forward, closing the gap until his lips meet mine. I gently push on his chest and take a step back, which breaks the seal of our lips.

I swallow hard, with a soft shake of my head. "I'm sorry," I whisper.

Then, in the corner of my eye, I see *him*. His fine tailored suit and crisp white shirt with no tie stand out in the crowd of dark clothes. He stands motionless, a dark, angry expression on his face, his hands deep in his pockets. The brunette is still talking to him, but his icy gaze is focused entirely on me. My eyes widen and I turn away to gaze back at the man in front of me. An easy smile plays at the corners of his mouth. He hasn't noticed the other man or my sudden loss of focus.

"I didn't intro—" he begins.

Tahlia comes over, her presence cutting into his speech. "Hey, Alice, can we head home soon? I'm pretty tanked and I have work in the morning." Her smile widens in approval as she glances between me and the man I had just been dancing with. A lump forms in my throat because my mind was elsewhere, and I couldn't get into him.

I twist to face her. "Sure, T." I swing back to face the man in front of me. "We have to go. Thanks, err, nice to meet you, I guess."

His posture is relaxed as he stands there, chuckling. "Yes, and I'm Alex, by the way. It was my pleasure. Are you going to be okay getting home, or do you need me to call you girls a cab or an Uber?" He is being so nice, making me feel a twinge of guilt in the pit of my stomach. I almost wish I had felt a small connection to Alex, but I shouldn't be surprised at my lack of interest. After all, I was with my ex for two years without feeling real love for him.

"No, thank you. I already called an Uber, and there are another two people coming with us. Thanks anyway."

"Okay. Well, if you're sure. It was lovely to meet you both. I'd better head off now to find my group of friends before I'm left here. Hope to see you here again sometime. Bye." He nods at Tahlia, and the beginning of a smile tips the corners of his mouth before he moves away.

I let out a shaky breath. I was petrified he was going to ask for my number, and I would have had to turn him down in front of Tahlia, but he didn't, so maybe he read the same signals I did. Even though he was nice, there was no spark.

Oh well. I won't have to see him ever again, except maybe when I come back here, so I don't have anything to worry about.

Linking my arm through Tahlia's, we slowly wander off the dance floor. "Let's find the other two and get out of here. My feet are killing me," I moan.

"Me too. What a great night, though, celebrating the end of your studies."

My smile widens. "The *best* night. Thank you."

CHAPTER 2

ALICE

SIX MONTHS LATER

It's midmorning and Blake is driving me into the city. Both of us need to pick up our parking passes for our graduate year. We decided to do it together and make a day of it. Neither of us has work today and we want to do a test run of driving into work to see how long it will take. Blake didn't get placed at the same hospital, but he is around the corner, within walking distance.

I gaze down at my Google Maps, noticing the hospitals are close by. "Let's park here," I say and point to the parking spots along the curb.

"Good idea," he mutters as he pulls in and parks.

I dressed in my comfortable clothes—jeans, a cream crewneck, and sneakers. My hair is thrown up in a sleek pony, opting to pin all my fringe back. We exit the car and peer around before I throw my phone inside my bag, then walk up to read the sign. "It's free all-day parking and we can walk up. Your building is farther away, so let's do yours first and then mine."

"Sweet. Let's get to it. I just need to find the information desk. They should have the pass ready."

I nod and we walk along the sidewalk. I link my arm through his, and we walk in sync as I peer around, admiring the trees and tall city buildings. The buzz of the people and cars surrounding us has me grinning wide.

"I still can't get over the fact we have finished our studies. All that hard work is finally paying off," I exclaim.

"I know, right? No more exams or studying, thank fuck. Here we are." He motions to the entry to his glass building.

I scale my eyes up and down the tall building, noting people standing outside smoking and others talking on their phones.

"You go inside. I will wait here." I point over to a spare bench outside the building.

"I'll just be a minute."

I watch him enter the doors before I walk over and take a seat, then I take out my phone to send a picture to Mom.

My phone vibrates after I hit send.

I smile and answer. "Mom."

"Hi, love. Are you at work today?"

"No. Blake and I are picking up our parking passes."

"Oh, how nice. Say hi to Blake for me."

I watch as Blake comes out, waving his pass in victory. I laugh loudly.

"Mom, I gotta run. I will call you tonight. Love you."

"Okay, have fun. I love you too."

I end the call and stand up.

"Ready?" Blake asks, nudging his head in the direction of my building.

"Yeah, let's go." We link arms and wander slowly down the path. "Mom called to see what I was doing. I sent her a picture. She said hi."

He throws his spare hand on his heart. "Aw, I love her. Let's go get your pass now before we find somewhere for a drink—I'm parched."

I giggle. "Okay."

Blake waits outside on the sidewalk while I enter the building, locating the information desk on my phone.

It takes me a minute to get mine, and when I exit the building, Blake jumps up.

"Drink time?" I ask.

"Are you talking alcohol?" He winks.

"No chance." I look around us and locate a shop across the road. "Hey, there is a smoothie bar across the road. Let's go there."

"This could be dangerous. I could waste all my money here when I'm working so close."

I nod in agreement and loop my arm through his. We cross at the lights and enter the smoothie shop. It is surprisingly quiet, with only a few patrons inside.

"Let's sit there in the booth," Blake says, motioning toward the brown leather booth in the corner. We walk over and slide into the seats, across from each other. I shiver from the cold leather before I pick up the menu and scan it.

"What are you thinking?" I ask Blake.

"Mango dream."

"Oh, that sounds good. I'll order them. Stay here. I will only be a minute."

Blake smiles and pulls out his phone. I round the booth and walk to the counter, then order two mango dreams.

I stand to the side and wait for them to be ready.

The door chimes, signaling people entering. I peer up and watch as a group of four men in tailored suits walk through.

But it's the last one that walks through the door that catches my eye. *Fuck.* He is taller and broader than the others, but that's not what captures my breath. It's the eyes I haven't been able to forget and the lips. His gaze holds mine and his jaw is tight from him clenching.

The black suit, fit to perfection, shows off his large shoulders and lean body. I shudder at the memory of his soft, controlled lips on mine and the taste. How I would love a taste again. My mouth dries. *Where the hell is my order? Did they pick the mangos off a tree themselves?*

He owns the room and I stare after him as he takes a seat opposite me. The guys around him are talking, clearly oblivious to his distraction.

He leans on the table, brows furrowed, rubbing his jaw—staring at me. The electricity in the room crackles, and the heat level makes my crewneck sweater feel restrictive. I bring my finger up and pull on the neck of it, trying to get more air.

"Two mango dreams."

I jump with a squeak. I spin around, breaking my intense eye contact with the sexy suit guy, and scoop up the drinks. I turn to see him still watching me. I dip my head with a flush and suck the drink up through the straw immediately, and his eyes darken. The cold sweet drink hitting my tongue helps to cool me down.

I reach our table and peer at Blake as I slide his drink to him.

"Thanks, hon."

I nod, just sucking the drink as I squeeze back in the booth. I peek over. He is still staring. I tear my gaze away again, overwhelmed by his presence.

"What's the plan tonight?" Blake asks.

"Let's grab something for—" I lose my train of thought as I hear the screech of a chair dragging on the floor. I look over and watch *him* on the phone, practically running out of the shop. Once he is out of my sight, I drop my head, sadness washing over me.

Twice I have missed out on finding out *his* name.

CHAPTER 3

ALICE

ONE MONTH LATER

I come to an abrupt stop, my heart jumping inside my chest as I arrive at the hospital for the first day of my new career in nursing. It's impossible to steady my erratic pulse as I walk through the doors on shaky feet.

The advisor was the one to find the rotation and thought I should apply. I didn't think I had a hope being young and fresh out of college, but the advisor said that is exactly what they wanted.

I managed to not give up on mine or Dad's dream. He would have been so proud to hear about this. My stomach knots at the memory. I've worked hard these last few years, sacrificing nights out, having fun, or traveling the world, like most women my age. Instead of doing any of those things, I kept my head stuck in my books. The sacrifices were worth it because I got the top grades out of the entire class and then was accepted for this once-in-a-lifetime opportunity.

I remember playing "doctors and nurses" with my family all the time when I was growing up. My mom constantly reminds me how I used to bandage my sister up and tend to her care. Claire, my younger sister by eighteen months, let me do whatever I wanted. I used to be the nurse and make her play the patient. I would bandage her arm or leg, and she would happily let me, often lying like that for over an hour. I'm so lucky to have always had the most supportive and loving family.

Just thinking of them makes me feel lighter, so I inhale deeply and step through the doors of the hospital. My jaw drops and my heart quickens inside my chest as I look around. The size of the hospital is bigger than I remember, making me feel bewildered at the sheer size. I dressed with a confidence I don't feel, but at least I can look it. I smooth down the scratchy fabric of my black-and-white-checked skirt with my hands, straighten my spine, and pop out my chest before taking off down the hall.

I open my handbag to grab the directions and the name of the person I need to meet today. As I pull the papers out, a few other pages fall to the floor. When I crouch down to pick them up, a pair of large masculine hands reach in to help me. I lift my head too quickly, and my head hits the chin of the helper. *Ouch.* I reach for my head to rub the painful area.

"Oh, shit. I'm so sorry," I say.

My eyes meet with a familiar pair of soft blues—Alex, the guy I danced with at the club. Recognizing him immediately, I drop my gaze to the papers on the floor and begin fixing the ones in front of me. *Shit, shit, shit.* Hopefully, he doesn't recognize me. I know I look different, so if I can make this conversation short, I'll be fine.

I quickly notice an overdue phone bill lying on the floor that I don't want him to see, and I panic. Quickly grabbing it, I stuff it in my handbag and stand back up. He follows.

"It's okay," he says. "I noticed the papers falling and wanted to help, but maybe next time I should talk to give you warning." His cheeky smile and words make my lips turn up.

"Thank you. You really didn't have to. I'm sorry I hurt you. It was unintentional." I watch him rub his chin with his hand.

"I know," he replies.

Standing here gazing properly at him, I take my time, noticing how different he looks compared to when we met at the club. Today he is dressed in a tailored, pin-striped suit with no tie, and he has a slight five-o'clock shadow across his jaw. He is still handsome and charming, looking more like he belongs in a catalog of a magazine than at a hospital, but slightly rougher. I can't see any recognition in his face, so I need to leave right now before he works out who I am.

"I must be going. I am so sorry about your chin," I apologize.

Alex's lips turn up. "Don't worry about it. I hope you have a good day."

He is still staring at me, but before he can put two and two together, I spin and take off down the hall, quickly waving at him as I call out, "Bye."

I quicken my pace to put some much-needed distance between us. My breathing has increased in pace, and I feel tightening in my chest. I ride the elevator up and pull the paper with directions out and concentrate on where I need to go, counting to ten to calm my heart rate down.

I exit the elevator and arrive at a set of doors marked Fracture and Emergency. They are ID swipe access only, so I stand and wait to grab a passerby, because I don't have any ID yet. I will need to ask about that today.

The doors open, and I turn when a nurse pops out. She doesn't stop me when I walk straight in through the same doors. Down the corridor, I find the row of offices I'm looking for, just before I reach the nurses' desk. I focus on finding the door with the name "Kate Irwin." After I locate her door, I stand directly in front of it and take a few deep breaths. My hand trembles, and my throat gets dry before I raise my fist and knock..

Waiting for an answer to my knock feels like years when it's only been a few minutes.

The door flies open, and a middle-aged woman, wearing a bright-red shade of lipstick and the warmest of smiles, greets me. "Hi there. You must be Alice Winters."

"Hi." My voice cracks so I clear my throat and start again. "Sorry about that, and yes. Hello, Kate. I am Alice Winters. It's very nice to meet you." I hold out my hand for her to shake. She looks at my hand and smiles, clearly impressed with my manners.

She shakes my hand, and it's a nice, soft shake. She lets go and opens the door wider, waving her arm in the direction of her office. "Come in."

I step into the office, which is light and airy, with neat bookshelves lining both sides of the room. Kate treads over to a white desk, which sits in front of a large window. Following close behind, I wander directly over to the leather chair in front of the desk and take a seat. Kate then sits down directly opposite me.

"So, Alice, first, I would like to formally welcome you to The Chicago Hospital. I hope you will enjoy your graduate year here in the fracture and emergency department. I can tell you that I, for one, am excited for the year ahead. This is an exciting opportunity we have never offered before."

My mouth hangs open, and I shift my body forward in my seat with delight. I feel so honored to have been chosen for this role. I don't know if it was my application letter or my test scores that made her choose me, but I am forever grateful for the opportunity.

"The role will involve you working part time on the ward, and part time with our top orthopedic surgeon. You will have the opportunity to watch him perform surgeries, assist him with notes, attend interstate conferences, and do a little bit of PA work. He was awarded the Best Surgeon in the Country award this month. This year will have lots of new opportunities for both you and him. But pick his brain, because he is one intelligent man. Please don't tell him that. I am sure he has a big enough head as it is with that award." We both laugh. Kate is so kind; she gives me the feeling of being wrapped in a warm blanket. I am so glad she is the manager. I will work hard to impress Kate and the surgeon to show them my gratitude.

Wow. I rub my hands together. He sounds impressive with all his high credentials, and I start feeling as though the walls are closing in on me again. Her eyebrows rise a fraction, waiting for my answer.

"I'm still shocked, to be honest, Kate, but I'm so grateful for the opportunity. I won't let you down."

"I have no doubt, Alice. I'll organize your roster and ID today. Now, just to let you know, the contract is fixed for the three-month rotation, so neither you nor he can change it. After three months, I will decide if we should continue or change your rotation. Does that make sense?"

I nod. "Yes, it does, thank you." Three months is a short amount of time, so I'm sure there will be no issues. Working with the middle-aged doctor won't be difficult. *At least, I hope it won't.*

"Dr. Taylor is running late, so I'll show you around the ward and let you grab a tea or coffee. I'll come find you when he arrives."

I nod, and she stands, then walks around her desk toward her door. I get up and follow her out of the office. On the way to the break room, she gives me a tour of the ward. I take in all my surroundings, trying to memorize the layout. She passes the nurses' desk and ushers me into the empty break room. I see a coffee station, which I instantly gravitate to.

"Have a tea or coffee and relax for a bit. I will be back as soon as he arrives. Do you have any questions for now?"

"Umm, not right now. Thank you, Kate. But I will let you know if I do. I will make a coffee and sit here," I say as I move toward an empty table near the window.

"Okay, I'll come grab you soon. You know where my office is if you need me."

Kate exits the break room. After five minutes, I finally figure out how to use the fancy coffee machine to make my drink and sit down at the table to enjoy it. I'm savoring the peace and quiet of the room while hugging the warm cup between my palms, when two nurses come barging in, talking loudly as if I don't exist.

"Did you see Mike arrive? He was rushing to his office in his gym gear."

"Oh, no, I didn't. No way. What a sight that would have been. He is so hot. Did you hear he kissed Monica in the elevator the other day?"

"What? No, no way. You have to be kidding."

"Yes, way. I overheard the mechanic telling Kate there was nothing wrong with the elevator, so he must have stopped it midway to make out with her in the elevator or fuck her." *Whoa!*

The girl gasps. "How lucky is she? Maybe I should head into his office now and see if he is keen for a quickie. Do I look okay?"

My eyes nearly pop out of their sockets, and my jaw hits the floor as I watch her flick her long, blond hair over her shoulder and straight her uniform with the palms of her hands.

"You're a bombshell, Rachel. As if he could say no."

I watch the exchange out of the corner of my eye. One is a brunette whose back is to me, so I cannot get a good view of her, but I can see Rachel clearly, and I'm speechless. I have to agree that Rachel is a bombshell—tall, probably about my age, slim but with killer curves, and green eyes.

Keeping my head down, I busy myself with drinking my coffee. I cradle the mug tighter in my hands and stare down at the milky brown liquid. After a few minutes, the girls exit, leaving me to melt back into the chair in the room by myself again. My brain is ticking over and absorbing what I just heard, and I make a mental note to stay clear of that doctor.

After a while, Kate comes hurrying back through the doors, out of breath. "Hi, I'm so sorry, Alice. I had an emergency conference call that overran. Let's go to my office and we can call Dr. Taylor in."

I rise from my chair, put my paper cup in the trash and follow her out. My pulse has picked up and my palms sweat.

When we arrive at her office, I expect to find him sitting in one of the chairs, but the room is empty. I sigh and take a deep breath, waiting for direction from her.

"Please take a seat." She points to the same chair as before. I nod and sink back into the cold leather seat. It feels good against my back and thighs that are now burning hot. She picks up her desk phone and dials a number. "We are ready," she says into the phone before carefully hanging up.

A knock on the timber door sounds behind me less than a minute later, and then it creaks open. I turn in my seat, twisting my body to see the doctor as he enters. When he comes into view, the air is knocked out of my lungs, and I'm grateful that I am sitting. I grip the arms of the chair tightly and mentally count to ten to calm my breathing down.

Staring back at me are a startlingly familiar pair of piercing blue eyes that send chills down my spine.

CHAPTER 4

MIKE

MY HEART STOPS IN my chest, and I turn to stone when I see the same set of blue eyes peeking up at me behind her thick black lashes. I inhale the rich vanilla scent that is wafting toward me and my lips purse into a thin line.

I'm taken aback by her. She looks so youthful today. My eyes roam up and down her body, taking in all her natural beauty and stamping it in my brain for later when I'm alone. She has minimal makeup on, her hair is down, fanning over her shoulders, and she now has a cute fringe covering her forehead.

She's sitting there peeking up at me so innocently, which I know is far from the truth. Her eyes still have the power to destroy me, to bring me to my knees, and I can clearly see the recognition written across her face, answering the question that's circling in my head. *She kissed my brother Alex at Luxe seven months ago.*

"Dr. Mike Taylor, please meet the graduate nurse, Miss Alice Winters." Kate's voice cuts through my thoughts, and I shake my head to clear it.

"Hi." I nod at Alice and take the seat beside her, clenching my jaw. *Alice.*

Her jaw drops at my name, and her mouth hangs wide open.

"You're drooling," I mumble so only she can hear. I wink at her, and her eyes pop further out of her head, making me chuckle out loud.

"Now that you're both here, let's get started," Kate begins.

I lean back in the chair and keep my eyes firmly on Kate. I'm trying not to make any glances in Alice's direction, but her sweet scent is so strong now that I'm this close. So, I breathe through my mouth and just listen to Kate.

"First, I'd like to congratulate you, Alice, on your placement here. As you both are aware, this is a new role that we have only introduced this year. You've both signed your contracts, so here is your ID and your uniform that we had ordered prior to today." Kate leans forward, holding out a bag for Alice to take.

"Thank you," Alice replies and reaches forward to collect the bag before settling back into the chair.

Her voice is angelic, sending goosebumps rising all over my body. I have had dreams about her and how she sounds, and upon hearing her voice again, it is even better now than in my memory. It makes all the hair on my body stand up.

I'm regretting signing that contract right now. *It's going to be a really long three months.*

"Your time will be split, so half the week is spent with Mike, and then the other half will be on the ward. And your pay will be double the standard rate." I notice she sits up in her seat and I stare at her, noting her eyes have lightened up at the mention of pay. She nods at Kate but doesn't say a word. Kate continues. "There is ample opportunity for overtime, as I'm sure you know emergency surgeries happen at all hours, and once Mike starts an operation, he can't leave until it's finished. And Mike, I expect you to call Alice with any exciting surgeries. She is here to learn and observe everything."

"Understood," I grunt.

"There will be opportunities for you to attend interstate conferences, but I don't plan to send you on too many, as one or two would be enough. Now, I must get to my next meeting, so I will have to cut this off here."

"Thank you," Alice responds.

"Okay, well, you two go and get started now. Tomorrow will be another day with Mike, but then the rest of the week you will be on the ward. And, Alice, I'm here anytime you need me. I will catch up with you soon to see how you're settling in."

My body has tensed up. I now have to go into my office and work with her, like right fucking now. I stand. "Thanks, Kate."

I round the chair, passing Alice and not bothering to glance her way. I walk out and march straight to my office, closing my door behind me. I just need a second to collect myself. *Fuck!* I rake my hands through my hair and drop myself into my office chair and thump my arms on the desk with my head in my arms. I'm royally fucked. To work this close to her is going to test me.

A tap on the door has my head whipping back up. "What?" I bark loudly. It comes out a little more harshly than I meant.

I sit up and the door slowly opens. Alice is standing there, her chest rising and falling quickly, and I take my time to take another good look at her. She hasn't moved an inch. She is still standing in my office doorway, nervously grasping the handle. She looks like every man's wet dream...and my fucking nightmare.

CHAPTER 5

ALICE

THE ICY LOOK IN Dr. Taylor's eyes stops me in my tracks. I stand still, unable to move.

My breathing is becoming more rapid, and I count down in my head to calm myself. *Ten, nine, eight, seven... I do not want to pass out in front of him.* His elbows are on his desk, his hands clasped together, and his eyes haven't moved. Neither of us speaks.

I clear my throat. "Hi, Dr. Taylor. I'm sorry to interrupt, but Kate said I'm with you for the rest of today." He doesn't reply; he just continues to stare. I wish he would just speak because the anger rolling off him is confusing me. I decide to try again. "What would you like me to do?"

Letting go of the door handle, I step inside and shut the door. I shake my hand to get the blood flowing properly again and then clasp them in front of me. I stand close to the door and wait for his instructions.

"Just... get me a coffee and it will give me some time to think of a task for you." He stands abruptly, reminding me how tall he is. His hand dives into his pocket and I watch as he grabs his wallet, opens it to pull out a bill, and thrusts it in my direction. "Get me a long black and buy whatever you want," he snaps.

He shakes it at me again, his eyebrows raised, so I quickly move forward and grab the bill, nodding my understanding as I can't seem to speak. My words are stuck in my throat. He drops back down in his chair and carries on shuffling the papers in front of him, silently dismissing me. My mind races, searching for an explanation for his cold demeanor, but coming up empty, I shrug and spin around to leave. I exit his office, giving him the time that he requested. However, he didn't give a specific time to return by, so I roam my way through the corridors, taking in the old building and all the areas I haven't yet had the chance to explore.

I notice up ahead the elevator doors have opened, and as people begin to enter, I rush forward and just make it before the doors close. I arrive on the ground floor and follow everyone out. Spotting a few shops, I mosey around until I arrive at the important one—the coffee shop.

I had a coffee back in the break room earlier, so I don't order anything for myself. I just order the long black for Dr. Taylor. It only takes them a few minutes to make his scorching hot coffee, so I trek back upstairs carrying his takeaway cup. On the ride back up, I think about how he was acting. He has had a giant stick up his ass since he met me in Kate's office and has been nothing but a cold prick to me. He barely knows me. I have been through worse than this at other jobs, and I didn't come this far to let him scare me off. I reach his closed door, and after a moment of staring at the timber barrier, I inhale a large breath and knock with my free hand before pushing the door open.

I let out a shaky breath, and my shoulders relax because he isn't here. I walk over to his desk, inspecting the room. Dr. Taylor's office is laid out in the same way as Kate's, except with dark furnishings—*dark and moody, just like him*. The bookshelves on either side of the room are full of books and his dark wood desk is piled high with papers. Unlike Kate's office, there is no window. I sniff the air, breathing in his intoxicating, musky spice scent. I smelled it briefly in Kate's office, but in here it's everywhere and it's almost suffocating, reminding me of the first time I met him. I will never forget a single detail about that night.

I wander over to the desk, moving some papers aside so I can find a coaster to place the coffee on, adding his change beside it. Wringing my hands together, I wonder what I should do next, since he's not here. I'm unsure, so I decide to sit in the chair opposite his desk and wait. A few minutes later, I hear the door creak open. I jerk my head around to peer over my shoulder and see him entering with a file hooked under his armpit. I turn away without a word.

He walks past the desk to sink into his black leather chair. He doesn't acknowledge me, just picks up the coffee and sips it. "You took your sweet time. Did you get lost?" he asks in a mocking tone.

I stare at him, baffled how I've earned such anger from him. I bite my tongue until I taste the metallic tang of blood. *He isn't worth it.* The connection I had with Mike has vanished. This man in front of me is obnoxious.

"No, I didn't get lost," I reply sweetly, refusing to bite back and enable his smart mouth.

"Right, well, I need to get home. I have just come back from an interstate conference and I'm exhausted. I don't have the energy for this shit today. You can sort out all of this until the end of your shift." He flaps his hands over the papers covering the desk. I blink rapidly at his attitude, watching in shock as he picks up his coffee and a briefcase that was tucked underneath the desk and storms out.

Sitting still, I try to absorb what's just occurred in this office. He clearly doesn't remember me, so I'll have to act like I don't either. On a positive note, day one is done. I hurtle back to earth as reality strikes, and pushing up out of my chair, I step around his desk, pondering.

I contemplate where these papers should belong, opening cupboards only to find them mostly bare, besides a few golf products and a family picture. The most impressive thing about his office is the book collection.

I browse along the spines of the books and notice a mix of true stories, fiction, and medical books. After a lot of snooping, I decide to see what the paperwork consists of so I can then plan a system for filing them—clearly, he needs one. I pile them up in one neat stack, then sit down in his office chair and sort them into categories. I realize there are a few different types. I also think he would benefit from a desk planner and diary. I decide to finish up for the day and head to the store to grab the supplies I need. I'll finish the organizing tomorrow.

In the car on the way home, I dial Blake.

"Hey, love, how was your first day?" he exclaims.

"A fucking disaster." I sigh. "Can you come over for dinner tonight, so I can fill you in?"

"Of course, I'll bring wine."

I chuckle. "Okay, I'll catch you later." I hang up and drive to the store to buy the stationery for Mike's office before driving home.

Blake, Tahlia, Maddison, and I are sitting around the dinner table enjoying pizza and wine. I haven't said much yet. I'm still trying to process my day. Hopefully, they can shed some light on my situation.

"Are you going to tell us what made you call me over midweek?" Blake questions.

Inspecting my half-eaten Margherita pizza, I inhale deeply and decide to speak before finishing the rest. "Where do I start? It was awful."

"From the beginning. It's okay, just tell us. I'm sure it's not that bad."

I laugh at Maddison's comment. "Okay, well, you know that first night we went to Luxe?"

"Mm-hmm." They all nod and murmur.

"Well, there was something I never told you." I shuffle in my seat, poking my pizza around on my plate. "I dropped my glass because I was sharing this weird eye fuck with a guy across the room."

Cutlery falls with a loud bang on a plate, making me jump, and I glance up at Tahlia.

"Sorry," she mouths.

"Then, when I was heading to the bathroom, I bumped into him and had the hottest kiss of my life. I got flustered and ran off to the bathroom." I swallow the lump that's formed in my throat, as they all laugh. When they recover, I continue with the story. "Then when we were all dancing, I spotted him talking with this tall, stunning brunette. She was draped on his arm. So, when that random guy came up to me grinding, and he pecked me, I let him, but when I stopped, I saw *him* staring at me again. It was so weird. I have never had a connection like that before, especially not with a stranger." I pick my pizza back up and take a large bite.

"Sounds hot," Blake says.

"I agree." Maddison's fanning herself with her hand, which turns my mouth up mid-chew.

"Well, I saw him again when we went to the smoothie bar, but he ran out on his phone."

"Okay, but what's that got to do with the problem you had today?" Tahlia frowns, looking at me for answers.

"Well, it started when I overheard two nurses describing a doctor called Mike, and how he had stopped the elevator to make out with another nurse."

"No fucking way," Blake says.

"You're kidding, how?" Maddison asks mid-chew.

"I don't know, but then I go into my meeting to meet the surgeon I'll be working with and guess who the doctor is?"

"The doctor from the elevator, surely," Maddison chirps, bouncing up and down in her chair.

I laugh at her enthusiasm. "Well, partially correct, the nightclub guy, the doctor, and now my supervisor is the exact same person."

"You're pulling my leg here, right?" Blake's mouth is hanging open.

I shake my head. "I wish. It was bad. He barely acknowledged me, so I don't think he remembers the moment we shared at the club. And then when we were alone in his office, he sent me to get him coffee so he could think. When I returned, he proceeded to leave me to clean his office while he went home for the day!" I huff.

"Oh, hopefully the hot doc pulls the stick out of his ass," Blake states.

"I'm sorry your first day wasn't better," Tahlia says.

"He is a piece of shit. You're not a damn cleaner," Maddison spits.

"Now I'm stuck with him for a minimum of three months because of our contract. But the money is too good. I can't say no." I glance down at my plate, wishing I knew what to do.

"Just keep turning up and do your best. You know what doctors are like. They always think they are above you," Blake reassures.

I sigh. "Thanks for listening to me complain. I guess I just needed to vent."

For the rest of the evening, Blake and the girls discuss their days at work and school. I can't concentrate on anything they are saying, because my mind is still racing with thoughts of Mike. Why do I have to be attracted to him? Why, when he is around, do I want to feel his lips on mine again?

I yawn and rub my heavy eyes, tired from the eventful first day. Excusing myself from the table, I plod to my room and throw my body down and drift off into a state of unconsciousness.

CHAPTER 6

ALICE

THE DOOR BURSTS OPEN as I hum a tune to myself. I'm sorting through the piles of paperwork in his chair. When I hear the thump of footsteps as Dr. Taylor approaches. I glance up and abruptly stand, stepping back around his desk so I am out of his way. I watch his face as he inspects his office, taking in what I have done. His eyes roam the room as he continues his walk around. His jaw is tight, but his eyes are brighter than they were yesterday. The cupboards are all open and the shelves lined with trays that I have labeled, and most of the piles of paperwork now have a home.

"Have you had a break?" he asks gruffly, walking toward his desk. He puts his case underneath and presses the button to turn his computer on before he drops down in his office chair.

"No, I haven't yet," I say directly to his face, but he doesn't bother to meet my gaze. My gaze travels over his outfit choice today, and I am unable to tear my eyes away. I notice it's another suit, but this time without the jacket and tie, and his shirt sleeves are pushed up to his elbows, showing off his toned, tanned forearms.

There is something about him. I can't help it; my heart beats faster. *What am I doing?*

I glance away before he notices me checking him out and I get back to filing the papers into their assigned trays. The space feels like it's ten times smaller whenever he is in the room with me. The sexual tension is evident. We work in comfortable silence, the typing of his keyboard, the clicking of his mouse, and the rustling of paper being the only sounds in the room. When I'm finished filing the last paper and softly close the cupboard, I turn around to face him.

"I'll have my break now. See you in half an hour."

He nods at me, but otherwise doesn't respond, just continues to type away on his computer. Retrieving my handbag from the floor, I amble out the door and head toward the break room. When I enter, I halt in the doorway and stare at the back of Rachel. *Great! Just who I need.*

She spins with a cup handle in one hand and bobbing a tea bag in and out with the other. Even when making tea, the woman is a knockout. *So unfair!*

When she spots me, she offers me a dazzling smile. "Hi there. Who are you?"

"Uh, hi. I'm Alice, a new nurse graduate."

"Oh, nice! Well, I'm Rachel. It's nice to meet you. I work on this ward full time." She tilts her head in the direction of the ward.

"Oh, that's great. I'll be there part time."

"Have you met Dr. Taylor yet? Some lucky nurse is getting to work up close and personal with him. I wonder when she will start. I'll be trying to steal her job." She laughs, but I know she isn't kidding. "Why did *she* get it anyway?" My eyes bulge and my mouth drops open at her brash comment and bitter tone.

"Yeah, no idea." My stomach drops at the lie, but I don't want to get into it with her when it's only my second day. I decide to ignore her and stroll over to the fridge to retrieve my lunch, sitting down in the same chair as yesterday and focusing on eating my sandwich. When I've finished my half-hour break, I drag myself slowly back to Dr. Taylor's office. As I open the door, I see him speaking on the phone in the middle of a conversation. I've got no idea to whom, but it sounds like he is being as abrupt to them as he's been with me. I can't wrap my head around his cold attitude, but what really baffles me is that for some reason Rachel wants to fight for this role. I can't understand why she would want to. *What am I missing?*

"I'm not interested in hearing what you have to say. Just stop calling. I'll see you Sunday," he barks, slamming down the phone, and I'm sure the ears of the person on the other end will be ringing afterward. He cradles his head in his hands and stares down at his desk. My heart cracks at the sight. He clearly hasn't noticed me come in.

I clear my throat. "Hi. I'm back."

He whips his head up and his gaze meets mine. The pure hatred in his expression makes me take a step back. Then the look settles a bit. When he glances back at his monitor, I realize it wasn't being directed at me. "Okay."

What the hell am I going to do? This is bullshit. I march over to the cupboard underneath one of the bookshelves, yanking it open. "I have organized the paperwork into categories. Each tray is labeled with what each one is... like here." I point at one of the trays I've labeled. "This contains patient notes..." Then I move my finger to the tray beside it. "Correspondence..." I move my finger again to the next tray. "Bills... I'm sure you get the point." I straighten up, wrapping my fingers around the door that's open for something to lean on. I don't glance in his direction, instead keeping my gaze focused on my handiwork.

I don't know if he was even watching as I was explaining or whether he kept his gaze fixed to his monitor, but then he speaks, letting me know he was listening. "Right."

My lips purse up into a thin line. It wouldn't hurt him to say a simple "thanks," but I guess I would be asking for a miracle. *Asshole.*

"What's the plan for this afternoon?" I ask through gritted teeth. Closing the door, I swivel around to face him. I'm still standing near the bookshelf, not really knowing if I should sit or stand. I cross my arms over my chest to keep from fidgeting.

He eyes me suspiciously. "I need to discuss basics with you, and I'm assuming you don't know anything about orthopedics?" His brow raises in question.

"I have studied procedures, but no, I haven't physically worked on this type of ward."

"Right, okay then," he mumbles, scanning around for something. "Come, sit." He demands, before returning his gaze to the computer. He gestures for me to sit down in front of him.

I can't be bothered arguing with him, so I walk over, pull the chair out, and sit down.

He finds a spare notepad and a pen, passing both to me, and then pushes his chair back and stands and strolls over to the bookshelf. I watch as he grabs one from the top shelf, allowing my eyes to roam over his body. His shirt is tucked into his suit pants, which I'm sure are expensive by the way they are tailored to show off his fit, muscular body. His pants are so tight around his ass, I shift in my seat to try and ease the sudden throb.

He pulls it down, and I spin around, quickly glancing away, hoping to not get caught checking him out. I bite my lip and he steps over to stand next to me and I freeze. As if sensing his body near mine, the throb turns into an ache and I shuffle again in my seat.

He places the book down next to me with a heavy thud. I lift my gaze up, meeting his, and I notice that his jaw is clenched, but he doesn't utter a word.

CHAPTER 7

MIKE

STATIC IS BOUNCING BETWEEN us, so I move back quickly to my office chair, putting some much-needed distance between us.

Looking around my office, I can see that it isn't going to be an easy ride. Alice has completely organized my mess. I can actually see my mahogany desk now that there are no papers scattered on it. After her break, she begins explaining her filing system to me, showing me how she has filed and labeled where everything is. All my paperwork is inside the cupboards and will be completely out of sight. I notice there are multiple new trays, which she must have purchased herself. How is she this organized for someone so young? Normally, women her age are more worried about their social media, clubbing, and getting drunk. Working and careers always seem to be the last thing on their minds... but clearly that's not the case for Alice. It's refreshing and a huge turn-on.

Her passion for being a nurse was evident from her application letter and test scores. However, when I agreed to offer this position to a graduate, I didn't expect to be attracted to the applicant.

She is keen to help and eager to learn, so I decide to help prepare her for surgery. I step over to the books I keep in my office for teaching. Feeling heat on my back, I can tell she is staring at me, and when I turn around from grabbing the book from the shelf, I catch her checking me out. My lip twitches. I don't want her to know she's been caught, so I say nothing, instead acting as if I didn't notice. My cock gets excited at the prospect of her liking what she saw. It may be fun to torture her for a few months; it may even make this nightmare more bearable to know she's suffering too. *Let's see how she does.*

She is in her uniform today, and not the sexy little clothes that show off her body, but the ill-fitting scrubs. I'm not complaining, though. I would struggle to concentrate on my job if her tight body was in my face every day. Most people wouldn't realize how sexy Alice really is unless they have seen her out of this navy uniform. Thinking of her has made my workouts at the gym intense, and I'm so wound up I feel like I want to snap all the time. Every time she is near me, I stiffen and am forced to put a mental wall up to hide my attraction to her. The more she is around me, though, the harder it is to hold up.

I need to focus on the work at hand, and today I'm tasked with giving her a glimpse into nursing from an orthopedic perspective. I found a new notebook and pen and grabbed my old Tabner's book. I'm sure she'll already have a copy, but I would like to expand on certain areas while she is here. Knowledge is power, and she'll need a recap on some basics before entering an operating room with me.

I stare at her intently, but she hardly glances my way, so I just get on with what I have to say. "I assume you have this book at home, probably the newer release?"

She nods. "Yes."

"Don't you mean, 'Yes, Doctor Taylor'?" My voice commands her attention.

She lifts her head immediately, her eyes widening with surprise, and I watch as she swallows before mimicking, "Yes, Doctor Taylor." *Better.*

"I will list a few surgeries I do in my position, and what I want you to study. After that we will run through them. I need your basic knowledge to be immaculate. I need to help you get up to speed, ready for surgery next week."

I scan her critically. I see no expression on her face. *Should I be concerned?* "Are you okay with that?" I ask, raising a brow.

Her gaze meets mine and the glow of appreciation in them makes me glance away to the computer, pretending to be distracted by something other than her.

"Yes, Doctor Taylor," she repeats in a low composed voice.

I watch her from the corner of my eye as she opens the notepad with a shaky hand and grabs the pen, ready to take notes.

"Obviously, the main surgeries I perform are arthroscopy, knee replacement, specifically ACL repair, as well as shoulder and hip repairs. There are a few more, but I'd like you to focus on those first. I need you to study these in detail today, make notes, and write down any questions you have, and I will answer them next week when I see you. I have a patient booked for surgery next week, so you will be able to see one of these performed. It will help you understand what I do and will give you an idea what before and aftercare the nurses carry out. It should benefit you and your future patients. I have a good relationship with everyone on this floor because they understand exactly what I like and how I like things done."

A frown begins to form between her eyebrows, and her mouth tightens.

My jaw ticks and I thrust my hand through my hair. I shift, staring at her closely, trying to understand why she has reacted that way. I can't shake it off, so I ask her, "I assumed going into surgery would make you happy, not make you angry. Why are you angry?"

Her head snaps up to face me and she stares at me with wide eyes, her mouth falling open. My eyebrow lifts with interest, waiting for her to reply.

"No, it's an amazing opportunity, thank you. I'm not angry. I'm just..." She glances away.

"Just what?" I snap back. I'm so over the way she constantly talks in riddles, and I don't trust her responses. *Three months is going to seem like an awfully long time.*

Her gaze flies back to mine. "Nothing. I'm happy."

Her dull eyes tell a different story.

"I don't believe you, but I don't care enough to continue this conversation. I need to write some notes on here and see some patients, so you may as well study at home." I dismiss her and continue scanning through my notes on the monitor, not glancing in her direction again even though I sense her glare on my face.

"Why are you being like this? I know you know who I am. Why are you so rude to me? I just don't get it?" she huffs.

My jaw ticks. I knew this would come up at some point. The electricity in the room is messing with my head. I don't look away from my computer as I respond tiredly, "Yes, I'm aware. Just go home and study. I will see you next week."

She stands up, grabs her bag and the book, and walks out the door, closing it behind her. As soon as I hear the door click, a deep sigh leaves my chest and I sit back in my chair and close my eyes for a moment. *She can't know how fucking attracted to her I am or how much I want her.*

I finish my ward round and arrive in my office, then I shut down my computer before I leave the hospital to drive home. Just as I am pulling my briefcase out, my phone rings. I remove it from my pocket, dump the briefcase on the desk, and check the screen. It's Ryan.

"Hey, what's up?" I answer.

"Not much. Driving home from the office and just checking in. You still at work?"

"Yeah, still here, but I'm just about to head home and watch the game. You want to come over to watch it?"

"I'm going to my parents' for dinner, so I can't, but did you want to come to Luxe again this weekend?"

"I would because it's been a hell of a week, but I'm on call," I groan.

"No big deal. Is everything okay? Just work shit? Or are we talking about your dad or your ex Amanda?"

Laughing, I answer, "Nah, none of them this time. However, my old man keeps blowing up my phone on a regular basis."

"Hear him out. It's been years."

"Maybe." I give him the same answer I always do. I zone out and stare at where the young and beautiful Alice sat today. I take a deep breath, clearing my thoughts. "I've got to go, man. I'll give you a call soon. Enjoy Luxe."

"I will. Let me know if anything changes and you can come."

"Will do." I hang up, stuffing the phone in my suit pocket, then open my briefcase and toss my unfinished papers inside before closing it and walking out. I take the elevator down to the staff parking lot. I've just exited the elevator and started walking to my car when I spot Alice. She's sitting on the hood of her car, slumped over, talking on her phone. *Shit.* I wish I could pretend I hadn't seen her, but I can't, and after what she did with my office, I owe it to her to ask if she is okay.

I turn and march toward her, and when she hears my shoes thundering along the concrete approaching, she leans back and lifts her eyes from the phone in her hand. Her eyes bulge as I stand over her, one hand clenching the briefcase and the other on my hip.

I tilt my head. "Alice, are you okay? Shouldn't you be home already?"

She hangs up the phone, shoving it inside her pocket. Pushing off the hood, she spins on her heel to face me, adjusting the bag on her shoulder. She slowly shakes her head. "Yeah, I know. I went and studied for a bit in the cafeteria and then came down here, but Lady here decided she didn't want to start. So, here I am, waiting until one of my friends answers their damn phone, so I can ask if they'll come pick me up."

I smirk and raise my eyebrows. "Your car has a name?" Her cheeks flush and it reminds me of how she looked at the club, so pretty and youthful.

"Yes, I named her Lady, like ladybug-red car. Please tell me you get what I mean because I'm rambling now." Her eyes drop down toward the concrete and my stomach clenches.

"Let me take a quick look. Give me your keys." Her head whips up in my direction and her face is etched with a perplexed expression. I hold my palm out in front of me and repeat, louder, "Keys?"

She examines my palm then snaps out of her daze, sliding her handbag from her shoulder and fishing in the bag to find the keys. When she finally finds them, she pulls them out and places them in my waiting hand. I grip the cold metal, place my briefcase down on the concrete, and walk over to the door. I rip the heavy beat-up door wide open, and leaning over, I push the lever down that controls the chair so I can slide it as far back as it can go, making room for my long legs. I climb in her car, noticing that it's a very old Toyota Corolla. Putting the keys in the ignition, I turn the key to try to start it. It doesn't work so I repeat, but it still doesn't work. I pop the hood lever and exit the car.

I stalk over to the front of the car, and once I've located the latch, I click it and lift up the hood with my other hand. I hook up the stand to keep it open while I inspect the motor. I check the oil and water levels, which are both full, then inspect the engine itself, but I'm unable to pinpoint any obvious issues. She is standing off to the side, giving me space to inspect, and as I close the hood, I notice she is chewing her lip and shuffling her feet, but I shrug it off.

"Nothing is sticking out to me; your oil and water levels look good. It's going to need a mechanic to look over it. I will take you home. Get all your stuff and let's go."

She stiffens momentarily before answering, "No, it's fine. I'm sure one of my friends will call me back soon."

"And how long have you already been waiting?" Her cheeks turn crimson. "Don't bother answering. Come on, I'll take you home," I fire back.

"Are you sure?" she whispers.

"Please hurry up. I'd like to get home tonight too."

Without waiting to see if she's following, I swing around, pick up my case, and take off in the direction of my car.

I hear her hurried footsteps on the pavement behind me as she tries to catch up. I stiffen as soon as she is near me, but don't say a word. When we arrive at my car, I open her door and her brows crease, but she hops in. I close it gently behind her and walk around to the driver's side. Yanking it open, I throw my briefcase in the back and climb in. I watch as she examines the car. Her mouth opens wide as she reaches out and touches the dash with her hands.

"Wow," she whispers.

I chuckle at her reaction with a knowing grin. *I do love this car.*

"What type of car is this?" she asks, still checking it out. Her eyes fill with awe as I turn the car on.

"Aston Martin, but it doesn't have a name," I cheekily mock.

"Marty," she whispers under her breath; I manage to just catch it. She has gone back to stroking the dash and I turn away, laughing and shaking my head.

I point to the monitor that's set into the dash between us. "Marty needs your address, so type it in here, please." I hear her small gasp, and then watch as she proceeds to enter her details into the GPS. When it has mapped out the route, I reverse out of my spot and drive out of the parking lot onto the main road.

We drive in comfortable silence with only the radio playing tunes through the car speakers, and her phone rings, startling us. She arches her back, trying to dig inside her pocket to retrieve her phone. I watch her from the corner of my eye as heat floods through me. She manages to pull it free.

"Ah-ha!" She waves it in the air.

An easy smile plays at the corners of my mouth as she answers it. I move my heated gaze to the road.

"Hi. I was just ringing about Lady. She wouldn't start after work today, and I just wanted to see if you could pick me up from work, but I'm on my way home now... Yes, I'm fine... I will see you soon," she whispers and hangs up.

"One of your friends, I take it?" I blurt. I don't know why that just came out, but I want to know more about her.

"Yeah, it was one of my roommates." She shrugs.

"So, you don't live with your parents?" My nose wrinkles. I know I shouldn't pry, but I can't help it.

"No, I live with my two of my best friends," she answers matter-of-factly.

Nodding slowly, I process the information. She didn't say anything about having a boyfriend and didn't say she was waiting for him to call her back, so I assume that she must be single. I really don't know why the fuck I even care. She is far too young for me. I'm her supervisor, and she danced with my brother shortly after we shared an intense kiss. I don't speak another word during the remainder of the drive. I pull up outside her house, which is a nice, white, weathered, older-looking home. The manicured front garden is full of blooming roses and luscious green grass. I park at the end of the driveway, behind another car, which I assume belongs to the roommate who called earlier.

She turns to me in her seat, her hands twisting in front of her. "Thanks for the drive home. I really appreciate it. You didn't have to do this. I know you're busy."

I shake my head. "It's fine. I was heading home anyway, so it's not a big deal. Would you like me to arrange a tow truck?"

"Oh no, I'll figure it out. Thanks for the offer, though."

"Let me know if you change your mind. I'll see you next week," I add.

She nods and reaches for the handle, pushing the door wide open, and steps out, closing the door after her. I watch her trek up the path, and as she reaches the front porch, she pauses, spins around, and waves at me with a small smile curving her lips. My jaw clenches, and as I continue to watch her, she swivels back around and heads into her house.

When she is safely inside, I take off down the road, deciding to drive back to the hospital to finish the last bit of paperwork. It's not like anyone is waiting for me at home. I dial a tow truck service to tow Alice's car back to her house. Money pays when it comes to service, so Alice should have her car back at her house by the time I get home tonight. Then she can figure out what to do with it. Although, if you ask me, it deserves to go straight to the scrap yard, but I didn't get the feeling she was willing to part with it.

CHAPTER 8

ALICE

I STEP INSIDE AFTER waving like a dickhead. *Sometimes I could just kick myself.* I walk into the kitchen, dump my handbag on the countertop, and go to the fridge to grab the bottle of Moscato. Pouring myself a glass, I fill it all the way to the top, then take a large sip. *Ahh, so good.*

Standing here in the kitchen, my hand on the cold stone counter, my other hand clutching the wineglass, I stare out the window and my thoughts drift over the day I've spent with the insufferable Mike. I hear light footsteps hit the tiles and I glance over as Maddison joins me in the kitchen with a towel wrapped around her hair and wearing her sleepwear. She drags out a stool and plops down on it. Her eyebrows draw together as she inspects my beverage choice.

"Whoa, Alice. It's only a Monday." Her eyes are wide as she looks me over.

"I had the worst day today. My head is all over the place, and I'm officially fucked." I sigh, enjoying another sip of the sweet wine.

"It can't be that bad. What happened?"

"The doctor I am working with is still being a moody asshole. It's like he barely wants me around, and ugh, I really don't know what to do. He hardly talks to me, but then when I tried to call you for a lift—"

She cuts me off. "I'm so sorry about that. I was stuck at school."

I shake my head. "Don't be sorry. It's fine, really. Here is the weird part. So, I'm waiting on top of Lady when *he* comes walking over to *help* me." My chest burns at the memory.

"No way. And then what?"

I lift my glass of wine and take another sip before I continue. "Well, I don't know if he knows much about cars, but he tried to see if he could start her. She wouldn't start for him, obviously, but then he popped the hood, and I nearly had a fit. He is leaning over in his suit pants and shirt, looking at my oil and water levels, or at least that's what he said he checked. He is so hot, Maddy, like his body is crazy fit. He must work out—a lot."

"Oh, that's so fucking hot." She starts fanning herself with her hand, and I chuckle.

"You have no idea. That image is seared into my brain forever. And that's not the only thing. Then he insisted on dropping me home. He drives this sexy gray sports car—I can't remember what model—but I named it Marty." I rub my brow, trying to think of the model, my mind coming up blank.

Her mouth drops open, and she shakes her head in denial. "No! You didn't name his car?"

My brows pinch together. "Err, why? Is that bad?"

She nods her head. "Oh, God, you make me laugh."

"I'm guessing I should be embarrassed based on your reaction, but he really didn't seem to mind. Anyway, back to my story. So, when he dropped me home, he asked if I wanted him to arrange towing Lady. I said no, of course. How embarrassing would it be to have him paying for that? He's my boss. I would never ask him that. Could you imagine? I plan to ask T when she gets home from work. When did she say she would be home?"

Glancing down at her wristwatch, she mumbles, "She should be here any minute."

"Oh, okay. I will start dinner then." I push off the counter, lift my drink, and down the rest of the wine. I don't usually drink during the week, but I just felt like one tonight. Moving to the sink, I lower the empty glass before roaming over to the fridge and scanning it for ingredients. I spot hamburger and decide to make tacos.

Tahlia arrives a little while later as I'm about to serve dinner. "Hey, girls. What a day." She blows out an audible breath.

Both Maddison and I laugh at her passing comment before I ask her, "What happened?"

She sighs, standing near the table. "It was just so busy. I barely managed to squeeze in a break."

Tahlia still works in the coffee shop, much to her parents' disgust. She is still trying to figure out what she wants to study, and the shop gives her the money she needs to not depend on her parents.

"Oh, one of those shit shifts. At least the time passes quickly. Well, dinner is almost ready. Did you want to have a quick shower and I'll dish it up?"

She lets out an appreciative moan. "That would be amazing. I won't be long." She saunters off in the direction of her room.

A little while later, she joins us at the table. Maddy and I have already begun to eat. I peer over at Tahlia, who starts to prepare her own taco. I clear the lump that's formed in my throat.

"T, would you mind if I borrowed some money until I get my first paycheck?"

Her gaze flicks to mine. "Of course not. What do you need it for, and how much?"

I glance over to Maddison, who is grinning like a Cheshire cat, and I roll my eyes before moving my gaze back to Tahlia. "Well, let's say I had a very interesting day with—"

"Doctor Dreamy!" Maddy yells out, cutting me off.

My eyes widen in horror, and I glare at Maddison. "Don't call him that!"

"Did you not describe him as hot to me earlier?" She smirks. *Bitch got me there!*

"Hey, is someone going to fill me in here?" Tahlia questions.

I laugh, shaking my head. I reach out to take a sip of water, needing something to soothe my dry throat. "I'm trying. It's Maddy's fault."

Maddison scoffs in the background, but I ignore her and keep my gaze on Tahlia. "So, the doctor was being his moody-ass self at work today, and at the end of the day, when it was time to drive home, Lady wouldn't start. So,

I was sitting on the hood of the car, messing about on my phone, when he must have spotted me. He came over to check why I was still there and not at home already. I explained my car wouldn't start. So, he insisted on looking at the engine, oil, and water, but couldn't work it out, so he offered to take me home and wouldn't take no for an answer."

"And she named his car," Maddy adds.

I shoot her a hard glare. *Shut the fuck up!*

Her face splits into a knowing grin before I look back at Tahlia, who has an arched eyebrow in surprise.

"Hey! What is so wrong with that? He didn't laugh at me," I protest.

"I'm sure he did, just not out loud or openly like we are." She smirks.

I groan and slide down in my chair. "I need the money for a tow truck. I need to arrange one tomorrow."

A flash of humor crosses her face.

"What?" I ask.

"Lady is out front." She rolls her lips, suppressing a smile.

"What are you talking about?" I furrow my brows and peek over at Maddy. I don't understand, so I slide my chair back and march over to the front door, reaching the metal handle and yanking the wooden door wide open. My eyes blink rapidly. Sure enough, Lady is sitting outside of our house. *What. The. Fuck!*

"I told you," I hear her say from behind me.

I can't respond to Tahlia. My body is frozen in place, my hand still gripping the metal handle, my mouth hanging open.

"Now what will you do?" Maddy asks.

"I don't know," I whisper.

I hear the light patter of footsteps fading away. I'm alone at the door when a cool breeze hits my skin, causing goose-bumps to rise on my body. It wakes me from my trance. I close the door, cross my arms over my chest, and wander back to the kitchen. My mind is racing. I don't understand what this means or what I should do.

The girls are packing the dishes away as I re-enter the kitchen. Uncrossing my arms, I slump over the counter and drop my head into my hands, massaging my temples.

"T, I definitely need the money now. I just need to figure out how much it cost to have her towed. I can't believe he did that." I groan.

"Yeah, of course. I think it's thoughtful. What a great boss," Tahlia coos.

My forearms slap down on the counter as I drop my hands to flick my tired gaze to her. "Oh, you don't know the whole story. He keeps fucking with my head. One minute I'm to call him Doctor Taylor, next he helps tow my car. I can't keep up. But this conversation is bringing on a headache. Can we go chill out and watch some Netflix?" I ask as I press my hands onto the counter to straighten up and begin to wander over to the living room. Curling up in one of the chairs, I'm more than ready to relax for the evening.

I managed to drift off to sleep last night easier than I thought I would. I dreamed of Mike—well, more about Mike's hands on my body and his smart mouth consuming mine. Maddison offered me a lift into work today, and as we sit in silence for the drive, I stare out the window in a daze. My mind is on the ward and how I'll manage working there with the constant need between my legs that doesn't seem to want to let up, reminding me constantly of Mike's attractiveness.

I sink my teeth into my bottom lip as the hospital comes into view. Maddison pulls over into the loading zone so I can climb out. I hesitate for a second before I shove open the car door, and as I'm about to shut it, she barks, "Wait."

Reaching out with my hand, I stop the door from closing and peer down into the car. "Yeah?"

"I didn't say good luck on your first day on the ward. Knock 'em dead." She beams.

I chuckle. "Maybe not the greatest term to use near a hospital, Mads, but I get you. Thanks." I lean back and thrust the door the rest of the way shut with a bang. I roll my shoulders back, draw in a breath, and take off inside.

I arrive on the ward and store my bag in my assigned locker and arrive for morning handover. I'm assigned to follow a fellow nurse named Sarah.

Unlike Rachel, Sarah is very similar to me, wearing only minimal makeup, her hair tied up in a high ponytail, and wearing navy-blue scrubs. I watch Sarah work, from the beginning of the shift, when she's writing up her day plan, to her finishing the day handing over to the next member of staff. I'll be following nurses for the first two weeks before I'm on my own.

I'm standing next to Sarah at the nurses' station while she is completing some patient notes before filing them away.

Closing the folder, she spins to face me. "You ready to eat lunch now?"

I nod. "I'm starving."

She giggles. "Me too. It's all the walking we do."

We move away from the desk and walk toward the break room. We don't get far when Sarah gets stuck chatting with another nurse, so I walk ahead. When I spot a male doctor in scrubs leaning over a patient's bed talking, I pause outside the doorway to watch. The patient is an elderly woman with wild gray hair. Her face is flushed, and she is grinning widely at him in awe. I can see him shaking his head and his shoulders bouncing from a laugh. A warm tingle runs up my spine as I watch their exchange. I sigh, wishing Mike was as warm as this guy. Unable to see his face, I step forward and lean my shoulder against the frame to get a better view. It's nice to see a doctor who cares, but when the doctor rotates and gapes directly at me, I gasp in recognition. *Oh my, it's the god himself—Mike. Fuck.*

I thrust myself off the frame, suddenly feeling hot and flustered. I step back, bumping into Sarah, whom I didn't hear approach. Sarah's cheeks turn red.

"Sorry," I mumble, trying to focus anywhere but him, wishing my body would calm down. My heart is beating erratically in my chest, and I get a buzzing sensation before

I hear the heavy footsteps of *him* approaching. I jerk my chin up, my gaze landing on his brilliant blues as he comes to stand right in front of us.

"Hi, Doctor Taylor, how are you?" Sarah speaks with a slight hitch in her voice.

His gaze briefly lands on hers as he answers, "I'm wonderful. Thanks for asking." His voice is seductive, and for once, his mouth is turned upward and his cold demeanor is nowhere in sight. I cross my arms tightly over my chest.

His gaze flicks back to mine. "Good morning, Alice."

I meet his stare, frowning at how brightly his eyes are shining. "Err, hi, Doctor Taylor."

Sarah looks between Mike and I, arching a brow, but not saying a word.

"Are you caring for Mary in room five?" He inclines his head to the room we are outside of.

"Yes, we are, Doctor. Did you want something for Mary?" Sarah is beaming, eagerly waiting for his reply.

He gives her a curt nod. "I just wrote up her discharge papers, her prescription, and explained them all to her. I'll be calling her daughter to give her an update, but it looks like she can go home. If you don't mind, could you please organize her medications from the pharmacy and file the release paperwork? I'll be in my office if you need me." He steps toward me and thrusts me the file.

As I reach out to take the file, our hands touch, sending a violent rush of heat between my thighs and a warm flush to my cheeks. I clutch the file tight, slamming it into my chest. As I watch him pivot and walk in the direction of his office, I have to restrain myself to keep from following him in there and demanding to find out. Shaking my head in dismay, I scold myself for my reaction toward him. I need to be acting professional, not like a schoolgirl with a crush.

Sarah and I begin speaking at the exact same time. "Go for it," I say, smiling at Sarah. I don't want to ask first, in case she didn't notice anything. But of course, I'm not that lucky.

"You two seem familiar with each other. I can tell that he already knows you because he knew your name." She moseys slowly over to Mary's room so we can have a quick chat before getting there.

A flush creeps across my cheeks. "I'm the selected graduate student this year chosen to work closely with him. This is the first time they have offered this, but I spend half the week with him and the other half here on the ward."

Tugging my arm gently, she stops me before we get too close to Mary. "No way. I'm so jealous."

"Yes, way." I laugh and continue, shrugging it off. "I applied while at college last year, and between the letter and test scores, I got it."

"That's amazing! He is the best surgeon, very intelligent, and you will learn so much. Plus, he is great eye candy." She wiggles her brows suggestively.

I chuckle. "I hope so. Is he... umm... is he that nice to everyone?"

"Oh, yeah. He is well respected around here. The patients love him, and the staff idolizes him. Just watch out for a few of the gold diggers. They've been throwing themselves at him since he became single a little over a year ago." My eyebrows shoot up in surprise as she tips her head toward me and begins whispering into my ear. "Rachel, for example, wants to bag a doctor so she can keep up her expensive lifestyle. It's so blatantly obvious, and most of them won't go near her because she reeks of desperation."

My mouth hangs open at her confession. "Ohhh, okay. Yeah, I can see what you mean. I haven't had much to do with her, but I have overheard her conversations, and I did get that vibe from her."

"Well, we better get Mary sorted so she can go home." She starts to wander off and I follow behind.

I want to go and talk to Mike about my car, but I'll be taking my lunch break next, so I'll do it after work.

After Mary leaves an hour later, we have only three patients left, so I take the opportunity to study from Mike's list and book. I haven't seen Mike on the ward again, which disappoints me as I enjoy catching glimpses of him without him realizing. Now that my shift is over, I walk up to his office with my stomach in knots, my heart rate up and my palms sweating.

I stand at his door, shuffling my feet, delaying knocking because I don't know which version of Mike I will get, but I need to pay him back. I pray for the warm Mike I witnessed earlier on the ward today. I suck in a breath and knock hard, mentally preparing myself with a pep talk. *You've got this. Just go in and do what you need to do.*

"Come in!" I hear him call out.

I gently push open the door and see him sitting at his desk, writing on papers that are once again sprawled out over his desk. When he peers up and sees me, he smirks, leaning back in his chair. *Beautiful bastard.*

The air in the room feels as though it's been sucked out and replaced with fireworks and steam, and I don't know if I want to slap him or fuck him more in this moment. I step in and close the door, and as I make my way toward his desk, he watches my every move. His eyes seem darker and his eyelids heavy, sending a shiver running down my spine from his intense scrutiny.

He pops a brow. "And to what do I owe this pleasure?" His tone holds a note of mockery.

"You arranged the towing of my car, didn't you?" I ask, my body vibrating with tension.

"Maybe." His smirk turns to a grin that reaches his eyes and shows off his stunning white teeth.

He moves one of his hands from the arm of the chair to under his chin and stares directly at me for a change. *He is actually really looking at me.* I feel my sex throb, so I switch feet, trying to discreetly rub it out. It doesn't work, which only annoys me more. *Fuck!*

"Please, Doctor Taylor. I know you did and thank you for the lift and the tow, but... It's too much and I need to pay you back. Could you tell me how much it was so I can give you the money for it?" I plead.

"No." His eyes don't move from mine, and he doesn't say anything else.

I take a deep breath and try again. "Please, tell me how much."

He shakes his head. "You brought the trays, planner, and the files." His hand thrusts in the direction of the newly organized system.

"Yeah, but... it's not the same," I huff.

"It's fine, I can afford it."

Excuse me? "And so can I!" I snap, raising my voice in frustration from the combination of the aching between my legs and the annoyance at him not telling me. I don't want to feel like a charity case. I try to keep my personal issues to myself and work hard.

"Alice, I know you can. But I have more than enough—"

"Knock, knock," I hear a woman say as she walks in, so I turn to put a face to the voice, and I recognize her straightaway at just one glance. *The woman from the club.*

"Amanda, I'm busy, so you need to leave!" he shouts, pointing to the hall and glaring at her with curled lips and a crease in his brows.

I didn't realize she would be older than me. She's a lot closer to his age of late thirties than I am. Sucker punch to the stomach, I'm just the young dumb student. I'm mortified that I was so close to jumping him, and now? Now, I just want to get away from here, to put some distance between us, give myself some time to think and sort out my head and heart. There's a mindfuck of emotions running through my body. All the sexual tension evaporates, and I'm left empty and heavyhearted.

"No, it's fine, I'm leaving." I storm out of the room.

"Alice, wait!" he shouts urgently, and I hear the thud of his chair hitting the wall as he stands.

Without looking back, I leave through the open door, slamming it shut behind me. Leaning back on it, I close my eyes, taking some much-needed deep breaths to slow down my speeding heart. *Him and all these girls. Paying for my tow, what is he into?* Thank God, I don't have to see him for a whole week.

CHAPTER 9

ALICE

I LEFT HIS OFFICE shaking and emotionally spent, wanting to get home as soon as possible. These mixed signals of his are giving me whiplash. The worst part is I want him; my body and mind crave him like a drug, but there are so many reasons why it can't work. Plus, I don't even know if he genuinely wants me, or if he is playing with me like every other nurse that he fucked around here.

Clearly, he doesn't take me seriously because he keeps treating me with disrespect and insisting on not telling me how much the tow service is. *I'm not a charity case for fuck's sake.*

I'm frustrated by his kindness. It feels like I'm struggling to breathe; it's too much—besides, he hardly knows me. The only people who know about my financial struggles are Tahlia, Blake, and Maddison. I don't need the world knowing how my family has struggled paying the bills since my dad passed away. I'm still visibly shaking from being so wound up, but thankfully I have two days off away from the hospital. I have homework to do, which is handy because I will have something *other* than Mike to stimulate and occupy my brain with.

I call Blake who is waiting to pick me up after my shift. "Hey, I'm ready. I'm just coming down now," I huff. I move quickly in case Mike decides to follow me... or am I just hoping he does? I know he won't, but I can't seem to convince my heart of that.

"Yeah, perfect. I'm just down in the loading zone," he answers.

I hang up the phone and ride the elevator. When the doors open, I rush out of the hospital. I spot Blake's car and walk up, tugging the car door open when I reach it. Climbing inside his car, I sink into the seat as Blake pulls out into the traffic and drives off in the direction of my house before I've had the chance to buckle up.

"What a day. Seriously, Blake, I have the worst headache starting and I hope it doesn't turn into a migraine. I cannot wait to get home, order some takeout, and chill out on the couch," I groan, closing my eyes and lying back onto the headrest.

"Sounds perfect, hon. Did you have a bad day with sex-on-legs?" My eyes pop open, and I tilt my head as he turns to face me, a wicked grin on his lips.

I choke out a laugh at his nickname for Mike. "Ha! Nice, but seriously. I went to chat with him in his office about paying him back for the tow, but he insists on not telling me how much it is, saying he has enough money to pay for it. Like, ugh, he fucking annoys me. I hate when people insinuate that I'm poor. It pisses me off. He doesn't know me."

He shrugs. "Yeah, but who cares. If he has the money and he is happy to pay for it, then I say, fuck it. Let him pay." His tone is nonchalant.

I sit forward, rotating to face him. "No, Blake. I just don't want to owe him anything. I want to be treated like we are on a level playing field. Could you imagine the rumors?"

"Yeah, I get you. And it's hard if he is a known player at the hospital. Do you think he is trying to say that he's sorry for being a dick?"

"Hmm, I doubt it. But as I'm talking to him, this woman walked in, and I recognized her straightaway. It was the woman from the nightclub."

His eyebrows shoot up in surprise. "I don't remember there being a woman."

"So, after using the bathroom at Luxe, I came out. Don't you remember, he had a brunette draped over his arm?"

He shakes his head. "No, sorry, I don't, but continue on."

I take a deep breath. "Well, in the middle of me arguing about him telling me how much I owe him, she walks in."

"Oh, shit." He sucks in and whistles.

My shoulders drop. "Yeah, he was shouting at her, trying to kick her out. Her name is Amanda."

"Ahh, so you think that she's a woman he is seeing?"

"No idea. He is a man-whore, so I'm sure she may be one of many. All of his female colleagues at work gush about him nonstop. They think he is smart, rich, and gorgeous." I roll my eyes.

"Well, hon, he is all that, but in your own words, he is a massive player. Clearly you don't want a fling. That's what you're saying."

"I don't want him at all. I think I'm just really sexually attracted to him, like I want to fuck him. He *is* hot, I can't deny that. But I work with him, and he doesn't really give me any vibes he is keen on me."

"I wish I had this problem on my ward. Seriously, all the hot doctors are straight. I just wish one was interested. I would be in heaven having these issues." He sighs.

We turn off the main road and start approaching my street. "You could have anyone you want. Your looks and personality are killer, Blake. I really wish I were you right now. I don't need this drama. I want a quiet life."

"Aww, honey, I love you. You're a beautiful person. Don't let those other girls make you forget that." I know Blake genuinely means that and I feel so lucky to have my friend's support.

"Thanks, Blake." I sit quietly for the last few minutes of the drive, deep in thought. I have two days off before I have to see Mike again. I have *got* to calm down and figure this out—and also study my ass off so I am ready for next week. *Bring it on.*

CHAPTER 10

MIKE

IT'S A MONDAY MORNING and I'm sitting in my office organizing the day ahead. I'm working with Alice, so I have decided to prepare all the patient notes prior to her arrival. I have just finished answering the few emails that arrived overnight—being on call all weekend enabled me to keep up to date with them.

My stomach has been in knots since Friday afternoon after the way Amanda barged in last week, right in the middle of Alice getting upset over the tow service money. I can tell there was more irritability from her than that. I just didn't get the time to figure out exactly what. It seems I really offended her, which was never my intent. I really can afford it, and I want to help her, like she helped me here in this office. I get a nagging suspicion that she needs it, but doesn't want to feel like I'm buying her, or that she didn't earn it.

Amanda can't seem to get the message that I don't want anything to do with her. She barges into my life when it suits her, disregarding all my feelings. It pisses me off, and it doesn't seem to matter how long it has been. She still insists on trying to talk to me. *Like I will ever forgive her and magically want her back after what she did to me.*

I'm not mentally or physically attracted to her anymore, and I wish she would understand that. No apology can make me forget the past. My feelings toward her will not change, and the way I feel toward Alice, with how strong the pull and desire for her when she is around, I know that Amanda did me a favor.

I click send with the mouse for the final email and am just twisting to file the paperwork in a neat pile when I hear tapping on my office door.

I bite my lips together to suppress a smile and answer, "Come in." Even though I know it has to be Alice, I inhale deeply as I peer up from my papers at her as she gently pushes the door open. Our gazes lock. "Good morning."

"Good morning, Doctor Taylor," she mumbles softly, barely louder than a whisper, clicking the door closed behind her.

My body instantly warms at her voice and her calling me "Doctor Taylor" stirs something inside of me. It makes me hard, and I'm glad for now that I'm sitting behind my desk so she can't see what she does to me. I run my fingers through my hair, and I try to keep my cold attitude down and replace it with a professional one. She begins to walk toward my desk, her eyes staring with purpose.

I stare back. "Did you want to join me for a coffee? I thought we could discuss the morning's surgery."

"Sure." She sounds a little hesitant, but still agrees.

Knowing how important work is to her, I guessed correctly that she would find it hard to turn down my offer. I think the fact that I'm only going to discuss work with her, not the topic of her car again, only helped her decision. I need her to be warm and calm around me. I need to be my softer, gentle self to get her to open up to me more.

"Okay, then, let's go." I step around the desk and reach for the door, holding it open for her to pass me, and when she does, her rich vanilla scent wafts through my nostrils causing them to flare. I swallow hard, closing the door, and walk with her to the elevator. While we wait for it to arrive, I decide to probe her with questions to break the awkwardness that is swirling around us.

"How was your weekend, Alice?" I ask.

I hear her audible intake of breath. "Pretty quiet really. I just studied and hung out with friends. What about you?"

My brows crease at her answer. "Studied?" I question.

"Just the topics you gave me." She is looking down at her joined hands, and I see her cheeks turn slightly pink.

She is so serious for someone so young, and her maturity is very alluring. "Wow, if we had more dedicated nurses like you, the hospital would run so much smoother."

Her cheeks deepen in color as she shyly peeks up at me from under her dark lashes. "Thanks... I guess."

"Considering that you spent the weekend studying, I should quiz you. Let's see if all your studying paid off." I wink at her, trying to be playful in an attempt to get Alice to relax around me.

"Okay," she replies, unimpressed by my teasing.

We arrive at the cafeteria and line up to order our coffees from the barista. I order a long black for myself while Alice orders herself a latte. I hand over my card to pay, and get no resistance from Alice, and I raise my eyebrows when she doesn't complain about it.

"I'm shocked."

"Why, what happened?" She looks around to see if something has happened.

I chuckle out loud. "No, nothing has happened. You just didn't fight me about paying." I smirk at her. I have to resist the urge to touch her, even though I really want to hold her against me. While we wait for our drinks, she shuffles from side to side.

"You're weird, and I'm not keen on having another disagreement with you. Start quizzing, mister."

I find myself smiling broadly at her cheeky attitude.

Her cheeks glow, and a small smirk forms on her lips. I enjoy the more relaxed side to this work relationship she seems to be bringing out of me. Hopefully, it will be a good few days, with no further arguments.

I use my index finger to point to my temple, and I ask, "Hmm, where should I start? Do you want it easy or hard?"

She clears her throat, and the blush is returning to her cheeks. Realizing what I said and why she is blushing, I smile back at her with a knowing look. *Such a dirty mind.*

"Start with hard," she says with no hesitation, and I instantly harden.

To drive this direction to where it's going, I reply, "Just how I like it." My eyes bore into hers and I watch her swallow as she processes my words.

She doesn't say anything back, though, just watches and waits for the question. Our order is called, and she dives for it, breaking our intense eye contact, which makes me laugh.

I quickly and subtly rearrange myself in my pants, so she doesn't notice. I don't need to scare her away just yet. We are only just warming up.

She hands over my coffee without looking at me, and our fingers brush. The spark of electricity hits me hard and my dick strains in my pants further, almost to the point of pain. She bites her lip, clearly nervous, so I continue in my attempt to get her to relax and feel more at ease with me as we walk back to the elevator, by redirecting the questions back to her comfort zone.

"You've studied ACL surgery. Can you tell me who I'm most likely to perform this surgery on?" I question.

"I wouldn't say that's hard, but to answer your question: women over forty and people who play sports."

I nod. "Correct. And what does the general recovery look like?" I ask.

"Patients should be able to walk unassisted between two to four weeks, and after ten to twelve weeks, they can return to brisk walking or light jogging, but the full recovery takes approximately six to twelve months with the help of physiotherapy."

I sip my coffee, listening to her and nodding in approval. I could listen to her all day. She spent her weekend studying and not partying—what young woman does that? I'm in awe of her.

"Seriously, Alice, you have shocked me with your dedication. Thank you for caring enough to learn what I set out for you. I hope you're aware it's all for your benefit and I'm glad you're doing it. Your hard work and diligence will pay off."

Her eyes flick to mine and they are filled with an inner glow. "Thank you. I'm actually enjoying it, I never thought orthopedics would pique my interest, but it has."

A jolt is felt in my chest at hearing those words. "I'm glad to hear that. Well, we need to drink these, and then I have paperwork on my desk we need to read through, and then it's surgery time."

"Sounds great. I'm looking forward to witnessing a surgery. I have never seen one before," she gushes, offering me a shy smile.

"Well, I look forward to breaking you in." There is heat behind my words. All this talk is like foreplay in my brain. I'm going to have to straighten myself out before surgery so I can fully concentrate on the patient.

There her cheeks go again, pink rising to the surface.

Back at the office, we read through the papers concerning the patient. I answer any questions I can for Alice before we must leave to arrive in the operating room at the scheduled time.

In the operating room, I show Alice around before I leave her with Sarah to introduce herself to the patient, get into operating room scrubs, and meet me inside the operating suite. She won't be scrubbed in as she will only be observing today, but she will get a good view of what I am doing. I plan to teach her step by step of how things are done in my world.

I approach the sinks after getting into scrubs, and I begin the handwashing process. My usual flutters appear in my stomach and my heartbeat accelerates from the adrenaline that will not ease until after the completion of the surgery.

I have Doctor Paul Jenkins assisting me in the operating room today. He's five years older than me, making him forty-three, but he's still a great surgeon—although I'm more skilled in this area, despite being younger.

I exit the washroom, keeping my hands up and using my back to push open the door to protect my sterile hands. When I enter my OR, I pivot, scanning the room until my gaze lands on Alice. My lips turn up in acknowledgment before stepping slowly up to my sterile field. Paul is scrubbing up and will be inside the OR at any moment to join me, so I slowly begin the double-glove process.

When I'm ready, I peer across the room at Alice. I can see her wide grin and her eyes shining brightly with interest. I can already feel the air getting thicker and my desire returning.

Paul enters the operating room, the squeaking of the door breaking the silence of the room. I introduce Paul and Alice, and I notice how Paul takes her in, his eyes lighting up with interest as he studies her. I shake off the feelings the sight raises and refocus my concentration on the patient who needs my help.

As I perform the surgery, I talk Alice through the process of repairing the ACL. The patient is a forty-seven-year-old woman who played long-term netball, which has resulted in this injury. During the operation, Paul is talking and flirting constantly with Alice, and I wish he would stop. My annoyance is creeping back up the longer he continues. *She is mine, so he better fucking stop.* I feel my body growing more and more tense, and I need to relax in order to finish this surgery successfully. I can't afford for my hands to be tight.

I can feel the sweat dripping down my back from trying to hold inside all the anger I'm feeling toward Paul. *I need to concentrate.* When I glance up, she is watching me intently with her wide, bright eyes, and I notice she is looking only at me and not at Paul. I feel my shoulders relaxing, and with a slight perk of my lip, I finish the rest of the surgery with ease.

The patient heads to recovery, and I wash up with Paul. Paul finishes first and when I turn around, he is flirting with Alice again.

My body starts burning with rage and I can't stop myself from snapping. "Alice, what are you doing? We need to go and check on our patient," I huff.

I storm off without turning around to check if Alice has followed. I run my hand through my hair and smile when I hear the steady pattering of her light footsteps behind me. *Take that, Paul.*

CHAPTER 11

ALICE

I FOLLOW MIKE DOWN the hall, watching his tense body radiating with rage. His hands are balled into fists down beside him. I don't know what his issues are, but if I had to guess... I would say he is jealous. Which makes me smile.

When I catch up to him, I'm breathless and my lungs are burning. I tug on his arm, and he spins. His cold stare is back.

"Not now," he spits through clenched teeth.

"Yes. Now!"

"No, we need to work," he argues, walking off to the recovery room.

I watch his broad back leave before I follow. Walking into the room, I watch as he approaches the patient's husband. He offers his hand, and the husband slips his hand in his and shakes it. After the handshake, Mike guides him to take a seat, and he drags a chair to sit in front of him.

I quietly tiptoe toward them and stand behind Mike, my mouth hanging open as I watch him speak.

"Your wife's operation was successful. She is very healthy. She should have a quick recovery. I will check on her tomorrow before she can go home. Do you have any questions?" He is so humble and caring.

"No questions, but thank you for taking care of my wife, Doctor Taylor." His eyes are bright with relief and awe.

Mike pushes off the chair to stand, offering a warm smile back. "I'll see you tomorrow." He nods and strolls out of recovery, and I trail behind.

"Get changed and meet me back in the office," he orders. Without waiting for a response, he takes off into the male changing rooms.

I change back into my uniform and walk inside his office. I step slowly up to the desk and drop down into the chair opposite him. He is slumped over, writing, and I note that the earlier tension has gone from his posture.

When he finishes writing, he glances up and pops a brow. "Did you want to have a go at the ward notes?" he asks nonchalantly.

I nod. "Yes, please."

He scoops two pages and hands them over the desk. I take them and scan through the details as he talks.

"Just write what you can next to each heading. Any you don't understand leave blank, and I'll run through them with you at the end."

"Okay."

I take a pen off the desk and begin filling in notes as he completes the medical bill claims. When I finish, I sit back and admiring how I left no blank spaces, pleased with how I managed it all on my own.

I glance up and Mike is staring at me, the beginning of a smile tipped at the corners of his mouth. His hand is stretched out to take my papers. I hand them over and watch as his smile widens with approval.

He nods. "Well done. Let's take the notes to the ward. The patient should be back there now. And afterward we need to do a ward round. I'll get you to write the notes into each of their files as I talk to the patients."

"Yep. Got it."

We walk out of the office and when we arrive at the ward, I follow behind Mike as he places the notes in the recent patient's folder and wanders off to visit his other patients. Visiting all his patients takes us an hour, but I managed to write in each of their files while he talked to the patients. It's an easy and enjoyable task. We seem to have a good system going.

Back in the office, I reach for my bag when Mike speaks. "So, how are you getting home today?"

I freeze and glance up. "My friend Blake is picking me up."

I watch his body stiffen and his lips press into a thin line. I can't help but laugh at the way he is looking at me with hurt and confusion before I quickly reassure him. "Blake is gay."

I watch as his shoulders sag, and he relaxes, all the tension leaving his solid body. I grin. *Maybe my feelings aren't one-sided.* His jealousy today is next level, and I secretly love every minute of his protectiveness.

Throwing my bag onto my shoulder, I yawn and roll my neck as we wander out of the office and walk silently to the elevator.

To fill the quiet, I ask, "What are your plans tonight?"

His walk falters, and it seems I've caught him off guard. "Huh? I'm just... ugh... heading home to watch football. Nothing exciting, really. What about you?"

I shuffle my feet from side to side while we wait for the elevator to reach our floor. I hold my handbag with both hands at the strap on my shoulder, feeling the fabric rub against my skin. "Probably just watch Netflix with my roommates. Nothing exciting either, to be honest."

The doors slide open, and it's empty. He waits, letting me step in first. I gaze down at the elevator floor when Mike reaches over in front of me to press the button for the ground floor. I completely forgot to press it. Standing inside the elevator with just him is intense. The air is crackling between us, warmth is building, and my stomach is on fire with the desire swirling around inside me.

I hear the words "Fuck it" leave his lips, and I lift my head just in time to catch the onslaught of Mike as he grabs my head with both of his hands, kissing me with enough passion to make me dizzy.

His kiss is so hungry, like he has been starved for days. I lose all sense of control and I can't stop him. My will just caves in, and I simply enjoy the moment, meeting his kiss with my own furious passion for him. His powerful, toned body presses against me as he walks me backward until my back hits the wall. This is enough to shake some sense into me.

"Mike, what are you doing?"

I shove at his chest with both hands, and he stumbles back until he grips the rail to steady himself. We are both panting heavily, trying to catch our breath after our shared moment of weakness. Mike's captivating gaze is sparkling blue under his heavily hooded lids.

My mouth opens and closes, but just then the elevator doors open, breaking the moment, and for a brief second, neither of us moves. Mike steps over to me, staring at me seductively, and I watch as he peels my hand off my swollen lip and lays his large hand on top of mine and links our fingers together. My heart flips in response, but before I can stop him, he stalks out of the elevator onto the ground floor, dragging me along behind him.

"Mike. No!" I have to fight my overwhelming urge to be close to him. I scan around, looking for any familiar faces, and not seeing any, I sigh in relief before my gaze lands back on him.

I tug my hand from his, unlinking our fingers. My hand feels cold and empty, so I cross my arms over my chest to prevent me from snatching his hand back. His eyebrows raise and his mouth forms an *O* at my move.

After clearing my throat, I speak up. "We can't do this here. I can't. I'm sorry."

Tears well within my eyes, and swallowing hard, I smother a sob and flee. Once I'm outside, I peer around for Blake's car. Eventually I spot it, and I move on shaky legs as I dive for the door, tearing the handle open with force and flopping into the seat before opening the dam to the flood of tears. The deep sobs violently rack my body, and the hot tears slip down my cheeks. The last week's emotions pour out of me, and when my sobs ease and I resettle, I look up to see Blake stroking my hair as he peers at me with a quiet concern.

"What happened, hon? Am I going to have to fuck up that pretty fucker's face?"

I snort, trying to laugh during a sob, so I shake my head vigorously. My voice breaks as I say, "No, please don't."

"Let's get you home so you can tell us what happened and what has got you in this state." His tone is cool and authoritative.

Inclining my head in a small gesture of thanks, I close my eyes, settling into the seat for the drive home.

I walk inside the house, heading straight to the pantry and tearing the door open to scan the contents for comfort food. Pulling the fresh block of milk chocolate out and ripping it open, I shove a few pieces inside my mouth. The chocolate melts on my tongue and I blink my eyes closed at the sweet taste. When I exit the kitchen, Blake, Maddison, and Tahlia are all sitting at the table waiting and staring at me.

"Is this an intervention?" The amusement quickly dies when none of them react. I let out a shaky breath before dragging a chair out and sitting down, dumping the chocolate on the table with a thud. "It's really not that bad. I-I think there have been a lot of new feelings—good and bad—and I didn't have enough time to process."

Tahlia reaches over and places her dainty hands over mine and tightens for reassurance. "Talk to us, please."

I lean my head back to gaze into her green eyes, and I take a deep breath. "He kissed me in the elevator at work today."

"Holy shit!" Maddison says.

"Fuck me!" Blake shouts.

"If it's not wanted, then you need to report—" Tahlia begins to say before I rip my hand out from under hers and wave my arms in front of me.

"No, no, no, it's not that! I want it. Trust me! That's one of the issues. I feel overwhelmed. I have never had this compelling reaction. It's like he has unlocked something inside me." I reach over and snap off another piece of chocolate and stuff it in my mouth.

"I'm confused. What's the issue? Go jump his bones." Blake shrugs.

"Now he wants me, and even though I want him badly... my job. I worked so fucking hard to get that position. I'm not losing it over him, or to a meaningless office hook-up. I love it, I really do. My dad would be so proud."

"But I am sure you can have both, if that's what you want," Maddison says.

"How? And the other problem is, he sleeps with every nurse. I'm not going to be just another nurse on his bedpost." I sigh, shaking my head.

"Just take it one day at a time. I'm certain you won't lose your position, but you should tread carefully and don't do anything at work," Blake suggests.

I shiver at the memory of his mouth on mine. I lean on the table with my elbows and touch my lips with my fingers.

"Find out his motives for wanting you before you do anything," Tahlia cautiously offers.

"So, what was the kiss like?" Blake asks.

My cheeks flush a deep crimson. I bite my lip between my teeth before gazing at Blake. "Honestly? Hungry and dominating."

"Fucking hell, just from a kiss?" He pops a brow, and he drags his chair out. "I need some water. It's hot in here. You lucky bitch." I stare at him and then burst out laughing.

I feel so light and open after the cry and the discussion with my friends. I manage to have a deep, solid sleep that night and wake up the next day with a spring in my step.

I march into the hospital corridors with a determination that I haven't felt before. I stand straight with my shoulders back, ready to hash it out with Mike. My shoulders drop when I find his office empty, but shaking the disappointment off, I march over to his desk and throw my bag underneath it and go about starting the day.

I have my head buried in the planner, ticking off items on my to-do list, when my stomach grumbles. I glance at the clock. Nine a.m. My brows crease with worry. *Where is Mike?*

My stomach growls again, and I decide to get our usual coffees and some food from the downstairs cafeteria. I'm sure he will be here when I get back. I squat down to retrieve my wallet from my bag and wander down the hall to the elevator. When I step inside, a spark of excitement courses through me as I think back to yesterday. If this is the effect the slightest kiss has on me, I would love to know what would happen if he touched me properly. I'm pretty sure I would melt into a puddle.

I walk in the direction of the barista and restrain myself from contemplating acting on the urge that's demanding me to find out.

I carry the two scalding hot coffees in each hand, a bag with blueberry muffins, and my wallet tucked under my arm as I wait for the elevator back up to Mike's office. The bell dings and I watch the doors slide open. My skin prickles and my gaze lands on Mike's compelling blue eyes, the firm features of his handsome face, and the confident set of his broad shoulders.

I swallow hard and set my shoulders back and saunter into the elevator and stand beside him. *You can do this. Show him you are not like every other nurse.*

"Good morning, Mike," I say eagerly.

"Good morning," he mumbles before his mouth sets in a firm, straight line.

"Here you go, your long black."

His head tilts to the side and with his free hand he reaches out to grab the coffee. His hand grazes mine, causing the skin on my arms to shudder and the scalding coffee to leak on my hand.

"Shit," I yell as the burn sinks in.

His other hand immediately drops his briefcase with a thud on the floor, and he takes the coffee cup from my grip.

I draw my hand to my mouth and wrap my lips around the skin, wetting the skin with saliva from my tongue. It calms the burning sensation somewhat. He watches intently with his lips parted and his eyes shining.

"Are you okay, Alice?" he grunts in a strained tone.

I remove my hand from my mouth with a pop and saliva coats the slight red mark on my skin, but thankfully the burn was superficial and hardly stings now. "Yes." My voice comes out breathy, and I stare down at my own coffee, embarrassed by my response, and take a large sip. The ache between my legs becomes a heavy throb. I need some distance to clear my head.

When the elevator doors open, I burst through the door and rush to his office. I suck in the fresh air, trying to cleanse his spicy masculine scent out of my nose. I hear his heavy footsteps becoming louder, signaling his approach. My back is on fire from his gaze. I pause at the door, but then enter, walking to his desk to dump my coffee cup and muffins, and then ease into the chair in front of his desk.

He inhales deeply before stepping around his desk and setting his coffee down, then he sits directly across from me in his chair. He stares at me as I reach out for my cup and take a long sip before putting it back on the desk. We both begin talking at the same time.

He laughs and waves. "You first." His stare is uncomfortably intense.

I twitch in my seat, trying to rub the ache out. It's not helping. If anything, it is adding friction and causing an even deeper throb in my core.

The attraction between us is palpable. Am I attracted to him? *Yes.* Do I want him right now? *Yes.* Does he want me? *I don't know.* Or is he playing with me like all of the other nurses he's fucked around with at the hospital?

Spit it out, Alice.

"We need to talk about yesterday. That cannot happen between us under any circumstances. This job is everything to me. I worked too hard for you to fuck it up!" I yell. He slumps back in his chair and crosses his arms as I continue my rant. "I refuse to lose my job because of you. I'm not just another nurse you can fuck, and I will not be a toy in a sick and twisted game to get me into bed." I point at him. The frustration of my longing and the gratification of my honesty is leaving me breathless.

"Are you done?" His voice is tight, and there is an expression I haven't seen on his face before. I refuse to apologize for my outburst, because it needed to be addressed.

I lean back in the chair and offer a curt nod.

"Do you want to attend a conference in New York next week, or would that be part of some sick game?" His expression is mocking.

I cross my leg over my knee. "Mike, I am serious about this. It's important to me. And to answer your question, I would love to. I saw that on your planner, but I didn't think I was included," I say.

He sits up straight and swivels to face his computer, banging on his keyboard and clicking on his mouse. "Did you forget about the contract? Kate will have my balls if I leave you here. I'll print our booking passes now."

I smirk and peer up at him from under my thick, dark lashes. I rake my assessing gaze over his blue tailored suit, white shirt, and his matching blue tie. The suit against his blue eyes and brown hair is intoxicating. I finish my coffee that's gone cold, which is refreshing rather than disgusting, and the complete opposite to the warmth that is tingling between my thighs.

A Week Later

Sitting in the back of the car on the way to the airport, my leg is bouncing on the spot and I get an empty feeling in the pit of my stomach as the car parks along the curb.

The door opens and Mike climbs out first. I remove my seat belt and slide myself across and gaze up at Mike's hand. Without thinking, I clasp it and step out. I don't let go of his hand. His brow arches and I quickly yank my hand back to my side, gripping my bag handle. My hand starts to sweat as my gaze takes in the enormity of the airport. It's larger than I imagined.

"Is everything okay, Alice?" he questions, gazing down at me.

I clear my throat. "Ah, well, confession time... I have never been on a plane before."

An irresistible grin of amusement lights his face. "Well, I'm honored to be the first to take you and break you in." His double meaning lightens some of my tension.

"Come on, you'll be fine. I promise to look after you." He spins and saunters inside, and I trail behind, taking the chance to openly study him. Wearing his tailored suit, he looks like a hunky model. Looking down at my plain uniform, I cringe, wishing I didn't have to wear this ugly navy attire.

"Alice, you look great. No matter how shitty the clothes are," he drawls.

I didn't notice him pause. I must have been too slow for him, so he decided to wait for me. My muscles tense and my nipples harden. This is going to be a torturous day. *Why did I have to work with him?*

The flight is smooth, helped by being in business class for the two-hour-and-two-minute flight from Chicago to New York. The leg room and service were a dream. I have never felt so spoiled. They even offered me a warm wash-cloth to wash my hands when I boarded. I must admit, the downfall of flying was on takeoff and landing. I held on to the arms of the seat in a vise-like grip, and the way my stomach dropped felt so unnatural I was close to being sick on the plane.

Mike warned me on the plane that we weren't visiting New York, and that as soon as the conference was over, we would need to leave to catch the flight home. Entering the enormous red brick building, Mike is stopped every five minutes for a "congratulations" or a surgery discussion. He would ask how their wives or children are, but I notice that not one person has asked how Mike is, or anything about his personal life.

What is in Mike's personal life? He has never mentioned a family or after-work activities apart from watching football. All I really know about him is his work. My chest becomes tight, and I bite my lip as I stare at his profile. *Who is the real Mike?*

We enter the large hall lined with chairs, and a mic is positioned on the stage in front. We take our allocated seats and the middle-aged gentleman seated next to Mike sparks up a conversation. He asks question after question. Mike, as always, is proper and polite. He has never once been disinterested or rude.

I watch in fascination as the speakers come on stage and discuss a surgery or a case study.

The announcement of the next speaker is called. "I would like to call to the stage, Doctor Mike Taylor."

My lips part in surprise, and I straighten in my seat, swiveling around to gape at him. Mike grins and places his hand on my knee, squeezing it gently before he stands up, taking long strides up the steps and onto the stage. After introducing himself to the crowd, he discusses the new techniques he has been using, including the robotic machine. Images of him using the robots to perform surgeries appear on the screen behind him, and I'm in awe. His talent is moving and inspiring, and his passion for orthopedics radiates through him with every word he speaks while on the stage.

I take a peek around and everyone's gazes are fixated on Mike. The respect circulating is evident. I settle my eyes back on Mike who is roaming the stage, demonstrating different techniques, and the power radiating off him and the way he owns the stage is breathtaking.

He thanks the crowd, who erupts in an onslaught of cheers and clapping, and I beam. I feel like I'm a spectator at a football game and we've won. I rise on shaky legs and watch Mike closely. His eyes find mine in the sea of faces and he winks before sauntering off the stage. I feel a flush of warmth enter my body.

A tug on my upper arm has me tearing my eyes from the stage, and I tilt my head to see a middle-aged man trying to gain my attention. "You're a very lucky woman." His lips turn up in a smile.

I open and close my mouth. The words, *He is just my boss*, don't seem to want to leave my throat. The man walks off, and I stand frozen on the spot. *What just happened?*

"You ready, Alice?" Mike's tone is gentle and breaks my trance. I didn't even hear him approach.

"Yes." I spin and follow him out of the room. It takes a long time because he is stopped multiple times and engaged in conversation. I grin, enjoying the chance to catch glimpses of him without him realizing.

When we reach the taxi, he collapses inside, and I break into a wide smile. "Mike, that was incredible! The robotic system was cool, but I admire the way you spoke in the room. You owned that stage. You are the most hardworking person I have ever met, and you still managed to stop and kindly speak to every single person with a genuine smile. You make them feel so comfortable. I'm in awe of you."

He stares at me intently, the smoldering flame I see in his eyes startling me. My cheeks glow with an almost uncomfortable heat.

"I'm so sorry. I should shut up. How embarrassing," I mutter under my breath and tear my gaze away to my clasped hands in my lap.

I see a movement out of the corner of my eye, and he reaches out, caressing my joined hands. My gaze lands on his face, where an unreadable expression is etched.

"Alice." He shakes his head, so I tear my gaze back to my lap. "That means everything to me. Thank you. No one has ever said such kind and thoughtful words to me." His voice cracks.

My brows furrow and I stay silent, waiting for him to finish.

"Yes, they compliment my work, but they have never, not once, complimented me as a person. You just complimented *me*." His voice is strained, and his hand leaves mine to run through his hair.

My heart drops at his admission and I shuffle closer, my body aching for his touch again. His gaze travels over my face and he searches my eyes.

"You're different, Alice. You're not some toy, and I'm not playing any game with you," he admits honestly.

Wetting my lips with my tongue, I'm unable to hold back my craving for him. I tilt my head, my heated gaze focused on his darkened blues. My hand reaches out and thrusts roughly into his hair, tugging his head down toward mine. I hear him growl as I plant my lips on top of his and our mouths move together in a slow and sensual kiss. My lips part in a sigh, and he takes the opportunity to explore my mouth with his tongue. My nipples harden and I wish the hand he's resting on my thigh would move toward my sex, or the hand holding my head in place would drift down over my breast.

The car suddenly stops, and I pull back, breaking the seal of our lips. I glance out the window. We've arrived at the airport. We fly back in silence and when we arrive at the employee parking lot. The sight of it feels like someone just poured a bucket of ice over us, instantly cooling the heated exchange we shared earlier.

Mike grabs my hand and guides me out of the car toward Marty.

"Alice, you're coming to my house."

"Mike—"

"No, Alice, I cannot handle another second of this. I need you. I want you, and I crave you. I want to pull you apart and put you back together. I want to destroy you so no other man will please you like I can, ever again. No one will ever compare to me. You will only crave me, my touch, my kiss, my *fuck*."

Decision time. I stare up at him with lust-filled eyes that are begging me to accept. Exposing my heart, I give him my blessing with a nod.

He rushes to open the passenger door of his car, so I climb in. After buckling up, I quickly get my phone out of my pocket and send Blake a text.

> **Alice:** *Change of plans. No need to pick me up tonight. I'm hanging out with Mike. I will fill you in tomorrow.*

> **Blake:** *Get it, girl! Enjoy that fine as hell man.*

I stuff the phone back in my pocket as we drive in silence. I should be scared by Mike's words, but I'm not. I'm just intrigued, and so turned on... I need more of the intense passion and connection shared back in the cab.

Before we can arrive at his house, he drives his car at a crawl through a set of automatic gates, which slowly open to reveal a modern house. Mike's house is a concrete gray two-story, with four rectangle windows at the top and bottom. An attached garage with a simple green garden and lots of trees surrounding it.

"This is your house?" My eyes bulge at the sight.

"Yes, it is. Is it a problem?" He turns to me with a look of concern etched on his face.

"No, it's just... Wow, Mike, I have never seen anything so nice."

I hear him sigh in relief. "Oh, well, thank you."

He parks in the garage and then steps around the car to open my door. He grabs my hand to pull me out of the car and pecks me on the lips before locking the car and leading me down the path to the front door. Once we get to the front door, my legs start to wobble and my heartbeat picks up. I'm less experienced than him. He is older and most likely way more experienced with women. I doubt I can please him. I'm probably going to embarrass myself, so I should just ask to go home.

But before I can say anything, he has opened the front door, and as he leads me inside to what I presume is the kitchen, he asks, "Would you like a glass of water or wine or a cup of tea?"

"No, I am okay, thanks. Maybe I should just go..." I glance at him and then down to the floor sheepishly.

He walks over to me and stands directly in front of me, and putting his finger under my chin, he lifts my face up so I'm staring directly into his blue eyes.

"What's going on in that pretty little head of yours? You're pulling away, I can feel it." He is gazing down at me with a worried expression on his face.

I need to tell him my fears, but I don't want to sound like a whiny schoolgirl. The way he is looking at me makes my stomach feel as though it is full of butterflies. "Mike, how do I say this... I'm not experienced like you..." I bite my lip.

"Fuck, are you a virgin?" His eyes widen and he looks mortified.

"No! But I have only done it a few times, and it's been ages since my last..." *God, this is embarrassing.*

He instantly relaxes and takes a deep breath. "It doesn't matter about our previous experiences. All that matters is what happens now and how you feel about me. I want to please you. There will be no comparing scorecards."

I sigh and while my heart is still beating fast inside my chest, at least I'm feeling less flustered. "Okay."

He grabs my hand, moving me into the kitchen. Before I can take a good look around, he wraps his hands around my waist and lifts me up onto the kitchen island, spreading my legs wide to stand in between them. My jaw goes slack with shock, but I'm also instantly aroused, feeling my apex thud and my sex getting wet.

"Are you sure you don't want a drink?" I shake my head and grab his jacket lapels, pulling him down to me so I can kiss him. I don't know when I became so bold, but I like it. *Maybe it's because I'm so aroused.*

His lips are so soft and pillowy, I could kiss him forever. I moan into his mouth, and when his tongue starts to push against my lips, I open them so our tongues can glide all over each other. I want to climb him, but I can't, so I reach up and put my hands through his hair to try to bring him even closer to me. Tugging at his bottom lip with my teeth, I pull away, smirking at him.

"And you say you are less experienced. Fuck, babe, you're wicked... pure sin." I laugh as he tries to rearrange himself in his pants, and I get a glimpse of his huge bulge. Fuck me, my body is on fire, and my panties are soaked. *I need him.*

"Let's go."

He picks me up from the counter and I wrap my legs tightly around his waist. He carries me around the corner, then up the stairs to his room. My heart is beating so fast and I'm grinning widely at him. But I have a question playing havoc in my mind that I need an answer to before I can let this go any further. "Do you bring all the nurses back here?"

He frowns. "I have never brought a woman here before. You're my first."

The answer makes my heart sing and I cuddle in closer, sinking into his grip. I inhale his neck, getting a good sniff of his spicy, masculine scent. Knowing he hasn't brought anyone else here makes me feel good. I don't feel disgusting, or like I'm going to be just another notch on his bedpost. Once we get to his room, he sits on the end of his bed, still holding me so I'm straddling him. I can feel him through my clothes, and I rub up and down on him, which he rewards with a very low groan.

"See? Pure wicked. You're killing me."

I push his suit jacket from his shoulders, and he helps me shrug it off before flicking it across the room where it lands with a soft thump. My laugh ripples through the air. I feel cheeky with Mike, full of a new sense of confidence, but at that exact moment, something snaps in Mike and he stares at me with hungry eyes.

"Mike?" I whisper.

He stands up and drops me to my feet. Grabbing my top, he rips it up and over my head, then pushes my pants down over my hips. He stops, staring at me in my black cotton bra and matching panties.

His eyes are hooded and laced with desire. "So beautiful, so delectable... and all mine. Take my clothes off," he instructs.

My eyes sparkle and my pulse beats faster, vibrating in my chest, I cannot wait to see what's under his clothes. I have imagined him many times since I have seen him in scrubs and suit attire, and I already know he's broad and muscular. I start with his white shirt. I pull his shirt out of his slacks and unfasten all the buttons. I can feel him watching my hands move and I can hear his breathing slow.

Once they are all unbuttoned, I push my hands underneath the shirt and push it off his shoulders and down his arms. The shirt falls to the floor—fuck, he is perfect. I take in his lightly tanned skin with muscles everywhere, a six-pack with a deep *V* that's prominently leading to the real prize.

He breaks through my thoughts, saying what I was thinking of anyway. "Take the rest off." I don't seem to be doing it fast enough and he becomes impatient. "Now," he commands.

I nod and unbutton his blue slacks and undo the zipper, pushing them down his hips so they drop to the floor. He steps out of them and kicks them to the side, leaving him standing in Calvin Klein undies like a model.

I try to suppress a giggle and fail. "You're kidding, right?"

"What's so funny?" His tone is full of confusion and hurt.

"Of course, you're wearing Calvin Kleins. You look like you model for them." I shake my head, laughing.

He laughs too. "I take it that's a compliment?"

"Yes, it is. Mike, a big one." Smirking, I put my hands in his briefs and slide them down. My jaw slacks and I nearly faint at the size of him—that's got to be the biggest cock I have ever seen. *Fuck me.*

Realizing what I'm probably thinking, he strokes my cheek with his thumb and whispers, "I'll take care of you. It will still hurt until you get used to my size, but I'll make you feel good... I promise." His mouth curves into a smile as he puts his hands on my shoulders and gently pushes my bra straps down my arms. He then turns me around and unclips my bra, peeling it off and dropping it to the floor. Slowly, he starts kissing my neck, starting just below my ear and down to my shoulder. It's so soft that I find myself closing my eyes and leaning back against him. *This feels so good.*

The dusty kisses are so sexy.

"I want to see you," he murmurs in my ear. I turn around slowly and gaze into his eyes, which have gone straight to my creamy breasts that I know are a good handful each. A hiss leaves his lips. "Perfect, you're perfect."

I offer him a small, shy smile and he grips the edge of my black panties, taking them down over my hips and revealing my bare pussy. He takes a sharp breath and inhales my scent, which I can't help finding extremely erotic. He grabs my hips and throws me onto the bed. I let out a giggle as he prowls up the bed and opens my legs wide. I lie back down, trying to close my legs.

"Relax, babe, you're beautiful... perfect... I'll make you feel good," he coos in a soothing voice.

I take a few calming breaths, but my heart is still racing with anticipation and nerves. When I finally feel a long, slow lick on my pussy as he drags his tongue up to my clit, I scream in both shock and pleasure. Not knowing what to do with my hands, I drive them straight into his perfect hair. He keeps licking up and down before he concentrates on my nub, and I can feel the pressure building.

Seeking release and also trying to escape the intensity of it, I try to wiggle away, but he uses his arms and hands to trap my legs. After a few more strokes of his tongue and a tug of his teeth on my nub, I convulse, screaming his name over and over in a chant until I come hard against his mouth. My body relaxes onto the bed, but he is still licking me slowly. I loosen my grip on his hair—I was pulling it so hard during my climax that I'm surprised he didn't complain.

Once I'm down from my high, I hear Mike mumble, "Beautiful, sweet pussy." His words turn me on even more. I feel one of his arms move and he strokes his fingers at my entrance before he pushes one in. "So tight, oh so tight.

You're going to have to come again just so I can loosen you up enough for me to fuck you without hurting you."

He starts to pump his finger in and out, and it feels so good that I sink further into the bed. By the time he enters a second finger, I'm getting fire growing in my belly again. "Don't hold back," he grunts through his teeth. He leans up and sucks my nipples, lapping each one in time with the perfect strokes and pressure of his fingers, and after a few minutes I can feel my climax building, and my walls tightening.

"Mike! I can't take much more."

"It's okay. Come, babe."

Between sucking my nipples and his fingers deep inside, a minute later I'm screaming again. I shudder as I come down from the high, and when I finally open my eyes, his blue ones are glimmering back at me. He seems to be enjoying this just as much as I am. He crawls up over my body and kisses me. I'm weirdly turned on by the taste of my pleasure on his lips and tongue. He pulls back and starts to play with my tits, squeezing and playing with my nipples again, bringing me up again. Then I feel him at my entrance.

"Condom?"

"Are you on the pill?" I nod between kisses as he continues. "I'm clean, so we're good."

I don't think about anything else. I just nod again, and he lines himself up before he slides in, pausing and waiting for my body to adjust until, eventually, he is all the way in. I cry out and cling to his shoulders. He holds still, waiting for me to nod for him to start, before moving his hips back, pulling out so, so, slowly, and then sliding back inside. He does this over and over until I'm begging to come.

"Please, I need to come," I groan, my eyes closing in pleasure.

"Don't you dare come yet. We are going to come together. Hold it," he commands. He continues to pump a few more times. We both have a light sheen of sweat over our bodies, and I'm holding back with everything I have when I hear his order in my ear. "Come now."

I let go, coming so hard I see little spots in front of my eyes, and I feel his dick pump inside me over and over, until he is done and slowly backs away, pulling himself out.

Relaxing, I sigh contentedly, and he laughs before pulling me over him, so I'm draped across his body.

"How are you feeling?" he asks.

"Good, I have never come so many times in one night. This is a record."

My eyes are already closing, and just as I'm drifting off to sleep, I hear him say, "This is only the start."

CHAPTER 12

MIKE

I HEAR HER SOFT slow breaths and I realize she has fallen asleep on me. I'm in a state of bliss. She is a total dream, perfect body, smart, and courageous—she could totally ruin me. I stare at her for a while until a heaviness comes over me and I drift off too.

The next morning, I wake up to a warm body and I smile, remembering Alice slept here. She is still asleep, so I reach over to grab my phone and check the time and some emails. It's seven a.m. which is a sleep-in for me, as I usually hit the gym in the mornings. I lie here and reply to a few emails until I feel a flutter of movement on my chest and I know she is waking up.

"Good morning, beautiful."

"Mmm, good morning. What time is it?" Her voice is groggy.

"Half past seven," I say softly and put my phone down on the bedside table. I cuddle her to me. "Are you feeling sore?"

"Just a little, not bad though, considering." She giggles which makes me grin from ear to ear.

"Do you want to have a shower? Afterward, I will make you some coffee and breakfast." I kiss the top of her head.

"Yeah, that sounds wonderful, but I need you to give me a minute. This feels too good. I just want to stay like this for a bit longer."

I chuckle. "Okay, well, when you're ready, we will shower. I'd be happy to lie here with you all day, though."

Five minutes later, she raises her head and smiles up at me, and I lift my hand to touch her face, tracing my thumb along her bottom lip before dragging it down. Her eyes lock with mine and I can see the desire building behind them.

"Are you sure?" I ask.

She nods and hops up, holding her hand out for me to take. I grasp her hand and stand, guiding her into my bathroom where I turn one of the two showerheads on. I have two, but I don't want her using the other shower—I want to share, have her close to me, and wash her. Once the water is warm enough, I guide her under the spray. I pick up the bodywash and squirt a generous amount on my palm and gently massage her shoulders.

"This feels like heaven," Alice mumbles.

I smile as her body goes loose underneath my fingertips. Her moans turn me on again, and I don't think I'll ever get enough of her.

I keep massaging her for a while until the knots in both her shoulders are out. Then I get more bodywash and start rubbing her breasts and stomach from behind, before touching between her legs. She is wet with water and her arousal. I suck in a hard breath.

"Soaked," I say gruffly. I'm ready to go, but I need to be gentle, so I don't hurt her, especially as she is already a little sore.

She is moaning and writhing as I gently stroke her, my other hand touching her breast while she leans back against me. I ease a finger into her, and she moans louder. I slowly pump in and out of her and tug on her nipple with my fingers, and when I put a second finger in, she tightens around them.

"God, Mike. Ah, it feels so good. Don't stop," she pants.

Chuckling, I whisper, "Never. Come, babe. Give yourself to me."

I feel her clenching and she's riding my hand so hard and fast I know she must be close, so I turn her to face me. Picking her up, I push her against the shower wall and guide myself into her, slowly. I want to go hard, but I can't because she is already sore from last night, so with everything I have, I restrain my urges and take my time. I gently ease into her, letting her stretch around me. I grunt and groan, feeling the overwhelming tightness, and I have to hold myself back from coming too soon.

Once I am fully seated, I kiss her with a slightly open mouth and let her relax before moving torturously slowly—out and then back in, driving her mad in between kisses.

"Fuck me hard, Mike. Come on. Please... please." I pull out slowly, one more time, before filling her to the brim with one quick stroke. "Oh, mmm," she moans into me.

I fuck her hard against the shower wall until we are both about to blow, and I move my mouth to her ear and say, "Come." Then I bite her earlobe.

"Ahh, Mike!" She shivers in my arms.

We both come hard, and I hold her steady when I feel her go limp in my arms. Letting her recover for a minute, I lower her legs so she can stand, and I kiss her softly again.

"Wow, it just keeps getting better and better." Her voice is breathless, and her cheeks are pink.

"That's only the start. There's more if you keep begging me like that. But first, let me actually wash you."

She smiles at me slowly with hazy eyes before turning around. Grabbing the shampoo, I massage her scalp and wash her hair.

"I could almost fall asleep again. This feels amazing."

Laughing at her reaction, I tell her, "Not yet, Alice. You need to eat and drink first."

"Yeah, that's a very good idea."

I finish washing her hair before we get out and I head to my wardrobe to get dressed and come back with loungewear for Alice, who is smiling as she dries herself.

"Thanks."

"I'll start breakfast. Get dressed up here and I'll see you downstairs whenever you're ready." I kiss her lips and head downstairs to prepare some eggs, bacon, and muffins.

I put some music on the television quietly in the background and cook. The music is soft enough that I'm able to hear her footsteps coming down the stairs.

"How can I help you?" She wraps her arms around my waist, hugging me and looking around at the pans.

"No, I'm good. I have got it all under control. Thanks anyway. What did you want to drink?" I ask.

"I'll have water and a coffee, please."

I nod and step over to the fridge to retrieve a bottle of water and hand it to her.

She takes it from me. "Thanks." I plate up our food and hand her a plate before setting out to make our coffees.

I tilt my chin in the direction of the stool. "Now, eat that before I eat you." I say it, knowing it'll make her blush even more.

She smirks, walking over to the stools. She puts her plate down and drags one out from under the counter, hops up, and begins tucking into her breakfast. I finish making the coffees and sit down next to her to eat and drink.

When we finish our breakfast, I take the dishes to the dishwasher. After it's loaded, I reach for Alice's hand. Her fingers link through mine and I guide her to the living room.

"Come sit in the living room. I'll put some Netflix on."

"I really have to go soon. I have to get ready for work tomorrow."

"Yeah, I get that. The boss is a real hard-ass." I glance down at her with my lips turned up and she smiles in response.

"Just sit for ten minutes, and then I'll take you home," I plead.

"Okay."

I pick up the remote and turn the television on. She sits down next to me, and I grab her legs, draping them over the top of mine, and start stroking her soft calves. I feel so at ease with her like this. It seems so natural and far from the relationship I had with Amanda.

It's so much better.

Amanda never liked to sit and watch TV with me. And she definitely didn't like to be touched or held. Which all should've been red flags. But I'd hoped I was wrong about her cheating. Which of course I now know I wasn't.

"Are you ready?" I ask.

"Yeah, let's go."

I drive her home and park in the drive, but before I even have a chance to unbuckle my seat belt, she puts her hand on my chest. "Don't get out. It's fine. You don't need to be a gentleman like that. My roommates are probably waiting up or watching me through the curtains right now."

I chuckle. "Okay, and before you run inside, are you free Saturday night?"

She goes quiet and I'm about to withdraw the invite when she responds. "We work together, remember?"

"It's only a three-month contract. We will still act professional at work, but outside of the hospital we can be together. There is no policy in the hospital against relationships between colleagues, but I respect your choice." I grab her chin and lean in, kissing her lips softly.

She whimpers when I remove my lips from hers. "I want to take you out on a proper date. Just humor me. Please?" I kiss her again before she can respond, but this time, I use my tongue, coaxing her to relax. Alice groans, and I pull away, grinning. Her eyes are closed, and I watch as they slowly flutter open.

She sighs. "You can kiss, Mike. Like, *really* kiss."

"Thank you. You're quite a good kisser too... Now go! I'll talk to you tomorrow.

She shakes her head. "I'll think about it. No guarantees, so stop trying to distract me with your naughty mouth."

"Come here and kiss me once more," I say, wiggling my eyebrows and laughing.

She pecks me on the lips before diving out of the car, giggling to herself as she runs up to the front door, and then she turns around to wave at me. She looks like a goddess, and I am officially screwed.

I pick up a big bouquet of flowers on my way into work, hoping to make Alice feel better. I know sleeping with me is a risk and I want to thank her for an amazing time last night. I need to get to know her outside of the hospital setting. Having a formal date is something I never do. Well, not since Amanda, so it's kind of a big deal... one she doesn't know anything about. I want to tell her why I'm so casual these days, so she can understand me better.

My cell phone rings. I scoop it up from my desk. It's Alex. I accept the call and speak into the receiver. "Hey, what are you doing? This call is earlier than usual. What's up?"

"Hey, bro. Yeah, I'm driving to work. I just got called for an emergency. I just thought I would call and see if you're good for a game of golf this week?"

I double-check the planner Alice organized for me. "I'm actually off tomorrow if that suits you?" I ask.

"Perfect. I have the morning off too. I'll make sure no patients are booked from now until then."

My office door swings opens, and Alice quietly steps in. I instantly smile and recline back in my chair, watching her come toward me. I notice she is blushing and her eyes are glowing.

"I gotta go. I'll see you tomorrow." I don't bother waiting for him to reply before hanging up.

"Good morning." I stand and walk toward her.

"Morning, Doctor Taylor." She smirks.

I chuckle. "You only need to say that when others are around, babe. When it's just you and me, Mike is enough." I stare at her and wish right now I could grab her around her waist and pull her to me and kiss her. But I'm respecting her boundaries—even if it kills me. I smile. "I bought you something."

She frowns, and I chuckle at her expression. "Relax. It's nothing much, just a thank-you for last night."

"Mike, please," she groans. I turn around to grab the flowers, and I bring them to her. I see her eyes widen and become glassy. I slow my steps until I am standing in front of her.

I frown. "What's wrong? Is it too much?"

She shakes her head. "Nothing is wrong. It's just, you're the first man to have ever bought me flowers."

My eyes widen at her confession. "No."

She laughs. "Yes."

"Well, you better get used to being spoiled because when you're with me, this is normal."

Alice takes the bouquet from my hand and leans forward to smell them. She inhales deeply and then glances up with the biggest grin I have ever seen her wear. It's a look I want to see her wear regularly.

"Beautiful," she gushes.

"Just like you."

CHAPTER 13

MIKE

IT'S BEEN A FEW weeks since I have played golf, which is rare. I normally play with Alex every week. It's a slow-paced game that relaxes us and allows us to debrief about work, with the added bonus we are both extremely competitive.

I'm in my golf clothes and waiting alone in the lobby at the local club. I arrived here earlier than usual, but after a few minutes pass, I see Alex's car pull up. I watch him jump out and collect his clubs from the trunk and trek up the path to meet me.

A grin spreads across his face. "Hey, bro, hope you haven't been waiting for me long."

I hug him with my free arm before I answer. "No, it's fine, only been here for a few minutes and I've already checked us in."

He nods. "Sweet, let's go. I have to work this afternoon."

"What time are you starting?" I ask.

"I booked my first patient for three p.m."

"Plenty of time for me to whip your ass," I gloat.

We laugh and wander off to get the cart. Growing up, our parents weren't always around. Being doctors themselves, they gave us what they thought we needed... money. But we didn't want money; we wanted time with them. Growing up meant that Alex, Steph, and I became inseparable. We became each other's cheerleaders, and of course we teased the shit out of each other, but we have always had one another's backs through thick and thin. We try to have dinner as a family one Sunday every month. As our parents have gotten older, we tried to get them to be involved like a normal family... as much as we could get, that is.

I tee off and Alex chimes, "Nice shot."

Alex steps up to tee off now, and he hits it with his driver, slicing it off into the grass.

"Good hit. I hope you don't beat me again. I don't think I'll come out with you again if you obliterate me like you did last time." We laugh and mark our way to the cart to put our clubs away and drive off in the direction of our balls.

"What's the plan this weekend? Are we hitting Luxe?" Alex asks.

"Well, Saturday night I'm taking my new nurse colleague out to dinner."

His mouth hangs open. "Oh really? Who is she?" I can hear the shock in his voice, but I prefer to be honest with Steph and Alex, so I won't lie to him. Besides, he has met her, so I kind of need to tell him.

"Well, you actually danced with and kissed her months ago at Luxe. I was supposed to be hooking up with her after she went to the bathroom, but somehow, she ended up dancing with and kissing you."

"No fucking way. I don't remember that. So, I'm guessing I don't get a shot with her now? You're calling dibs and now I have to back off? Or is she still fair game and just a hook-up?" He parks the cart.

I jump out. "You're not touching her ever again. She is mine. No, she is more than a hook-up. I don't know exactly what we are yet. I'm trying to take it slow so I don't scare her."

Alex slides out of his seat and grabs his next club and I follow suit, pulling my seven iron out to hit my ball first.

"I hope you know I would never be like Liam."

My stomach knots when I hear Liam's name. "Oh, I know, and I'm sure if I had told you that I wanted her that night, you would have backed off." I line up to my ball, swing my club, and hit it, landing the ball directly on the green.

Alex scans the ground to find his ball. "This is the first person you've been serious about since Amanda, right? Over here!" He points to his ball and we both walk over in that direction.

Alex is right. I haven't had anyone get under my skin, not since Amanda over a year ago. No one has even come close to keeping me interested or making me chase. I have enjoyed different women for one or two nights and that's it. I never keep them around out of fear they will get too attached. Some of them hate me even after those two nights, but they get over it soon enough.

He lines up to hit his ball, and I stay quiet as he takes a swing. His ball lands near mine on the green. We walk back to the cart and jump in, continuing up to the green.

"Yeah, no one has caught my eye. However, she thinks I'm a massive player. I understand why, but I don't feel like that about her. She is different. I want to get to know her more, like, see and talk to her all the time. It's been a long time since I have felt this way."

"Have you explained to her what happened with your ex?" he asks.

"Not yet. Amanda came into the office, and it pissed Alice off for some reason. But I want to explain what happened, then she might understand why all the casual sex."

I don't feel bad for what I have done. I'm single and enjoy sex, crave companionship and intimacy. I never take them to dinner or hang out with them. It's purely platonic to fulfill a need, to release the tension, and to know I'm desired. I guess people would see that as me using them, but they are well aware that it's just sex between us, and they are more than happy for just that. On occasion, they want more. They think I'll change for them, but no one has made an impact on me, or made me want to change my mind. Amanda made me distrust women and their loyalty. I realize that it's unfair to other women, but it's hard to change how I feel. I feel broken and hope to find the right person who will make me whole again.

"Bring her to the Sunday family dinner. I'm sure she will love it. It might get you some brownie points from her and Mom." He laughs, wiggling his eyebrows at me.

"You know what? That's a great idea. I'll ask her. It will help her realize how serious I am about her. And Mom will go crazy."

"Would she ever? Anyway, enough shit talk. I need to focus, so I can kick your ass and then you can buy me a beer."

"In your dreams." I say, winking at him then get out of the cart and walk toward my ball. My mind is still thinking about how I called her mine. I wasn't joking. She's literally the woman of my dreams.

Chapter 14

Alice

Mike has been a good surprise. I'm really seeing a different side to him. He is respectful at work, understanding boundaries and keeping it professional. I hope it can stay this way for the entire three months. I have been on the ward for the past week and have only seen him from afar. Smiles are exchanged in passing, but all the women on this floor do it, so I don't stand out.

I need to go shopping for an outfit for Saturday night, so on my way home, I pass by his office. Opening the door, I peer in and see there is no one inside, so I grab a piece of paper and a pen to write down my number for him. I also tell him that I agree to Saturday night, and I ask him to let me know the time I need to be ready by.

I arrive home and I notice a text has come through. Not recognizing the number, I assume it has to be Mike, and a smile plays on my lips as I open the text.

Mike: *Be ready for five thirty p.m. sharp. I look forward to seeing you. Mike.*

I respond to his text, then walk inside to find Maddison and Tahlia folding laundry in the dining room. "Hey, girls." I drop my bag down on a dining chair and help them.

"You go take a shower, Alice. We can do this," Tahlia says.

"It's okay. It will get done faster if I help. Also, I wanted to tell you that Mike asked me on a date." I don't look at any of their faces; instead, I study the pants that I'm busy folding.

"No way!" Maddison whistles.

"Mm-hmm," I mumble back, unable to form words.

"I'm so happy for you," Tahlia says, and I glance up at her after I put the folded pants down. "Would you take me shopping tomorrow? I don't have anything nice to wear," I ask, rolling my lips.

"I would love to. Your car is at the shop getting fixed, so hopefully it will be done soon, Alice," Tahlia says.

"Oh, that's great." I sigh.

"Now, head off and shower as the laundry is sorted," Maddison orders.

The next day Tahlia agrees to help me find the perfect outfit, but Maddison needs to study so she stays home.

While we are driving, she asks, "Where is he taking you tonight?"

"I actually have no idea, which is why I'm struggling with what to wear. It's not like I have a lot of money to waste on an outfit, but I just want to feel good."

"Don't worry about that; we won't spend much. I'm sure we can find a bargain. I'm good at spotting them. If not, I can lend you some cash. I really don't mind."

"No, don't be silly. You're the queen of bargain hunting and I really appreciate you for taking me out to find something with me."

We arrive thirty minutes later at the shopping center and grab a space in the parking garage. Once we are inside, we each grab a coffee and browse around the stores. We have gone into about eight and found nothing so far. Entering the large department store, we notice a sale rack and walk straight for it. There are a few good dresses, so I take them to the changing room to try them on. They are all quite pretty, but one dress stands out. It's a sexy, short, black long-sleeved dress with some white print on it.

Tahlia whistles as I step out from behind the changing room curtain to show her. "Wow, you have to get that dress. He is going to love you in it. It's sexy."

I turn around in the mirror, tugging the dress down. "Don't you think it's too short? I'm worried it's too short, bordering on slutty instead of sexy."

She shakes her head violently. "No way, because of the long sleeves and high neck you can totally get away with it. Trust me. Keep your hair straight. With simple makeup, you can pair it with nude shoes. It will be perfect. It's the one, and it's on sale."

I can't disagree with that. "Yeah, that's true. Okay, done. Let's grab some lunch."

A few hours later a knock comes at the door and my heels click on the tiles as I walk to the front door. I have a shit-eating grin on my face. It's five twenty-five p.m., but to my disappointment, it's not Mike standing there.

"Hello, Miss Winters. My name is Sergio. I'm Mike's driver."

My brows rise. "Oh. Hi, Sergio. I'm Alice."

Sergio looks to be in his sixties, with short gray hair and he's wearing a black suit and tie. "Are you ready to go, Alice?"

"Yes, I am. I'll just run and grab my bag." I spin around and the girls are smiling at me. "Bye, girls." I wave at them.

"Bye," they chime in unison.

I follow Sergio outside and the cool air hitting my legs causes me to shiver. As I close the front door behind me, I notice a black limousine parked in the driveway—not what I was expecting. My mouth is open with my lips twisting up. I have never been in a limousine before, so this will be fun. Sergio opens the door for me to hop in and I take my time getting in, being careful to not flash Sergio or Mike my underwear. When I'm safely inside, I glance up and I feel my heart drop. Mike isn't here.

"Would you like a glass of champagne or wine, Alice?" Sergio's voice cuts through my thoughts.

He is looking at me from the door, waiting while I put my seat belt on. "Oh, yes, please. I'd love a glass of wine." He carefully reaches for a bottle of wine that's sitting in a bucket of ice built into the side of the limousine. He pours me a decent helping and hands it to me with a smile.

"Thank you." I take the wineglass and have a large sip. *Mmm, this is very good wine.*

"We will arrive at the destination in approximately thirty to thirty-five minutes, depending on the traffic. In case you need a refill, I'll pop the wine in this ice bucket here." He leans in and puts the bottle back.

"Okay, thank you."

He closes my door, and I ease back into the soft cream leather. The blue lights dim, and as music begins to play, I smile and sing to the lyrics.

CHAPTER 15

ALICE

THE LIMOUSINE STARTS TO slow before the movement completely stops, and leaning forward, I peer out the window, frowning when I see we are parked out in front of the Rialto Building. The door swings wide open and Mike is standing there on the footpath, holding his hand out for me. My breath hitches at the sight of him.

He is wearing a bone-colored suit with a white crisp shirt that is unbuttoned at the top. He has a five-o'clock shadow and his brown hair is styled to perfection. *He is Doctor Dreamy for sure.*

I unbuckle my seat belt with shaky hands and grasp his warm hand in mine and step out of the car. When I straighten up, Mike rakes his eyes over me, checking me out from head to toe before meeting my eyes again. The smoldering flame I see in his eyes sends a shiver that brings me pleasure.

He kisses me briefly before pulling away, smirking when I whimper in protest. "You look breathtaking tonight. Are you ready?"

"I thought we were having dinner first," I say, gazing up at the building.

He chuckles, and it's like he has been reading my thoughts because he has a stupidly handsome, lopsided grin on his face.

"We are, just up there." He gestures to the tower. He takes my hand and leads me inside, and I frown as I follow him in. *Where is he taking me?*

There is an elevator which takes us up to the top floor, and when we step out, I see a sign on the glass door ahead which says, *Vue de Monde*. It sounds fancy, and as we amble in, my jaw drops at the spectacular sight. It's a warmly lit restaurant at the very top of the tower with dark-gray walls, and unique gold art sculptures hung at various intervals, with rich black floors.

When we step inside, we are immediately greeted by a waitress. "Hello, how can I help you this evening?"

"I have a reservation for two, booked under Mike Taylor, for six p.m. tonight," he says smoothly.

The waitress smiles at him with her chest pushed out, and pays no attention to me, as if I'm nothing more than the handbag to some older rich guy. It irks me, but I don't let it show. She doesn't know me, so fuck her and her assumptions; she is clearly jealous.

"Yes, please, come this way. I'll take you to your table, and I'll be your waitress for tonight."

She guides us to the table in the back corner. Glass windows line the walls on one side—we have the best views of the city tonight. "Here's your table. Can I get you both a drink to start off with?"

I pull out Alice's chair and then take a seat opposite her. The waitress places the napkins on our laps and lights the candle in the middle of the table.

"Yes, please. We would like a bottle of your best Riesling," Mike says flatly, while smiling at me and giving her no attention at all. I feel myself blush. He makes me feel like I'm the only person in the world.

"Of course, I'll be right back." She hands each of us a menu, then spins and walks off.

Once we are alone, he smiles at me, and I smile back. He is infectious and charming.

"I have never heard of this place. It's grand. I feel famous or something," I tell him, laughing at the enormity of this place.

"It's the best restaurant in Chicago. I have been here once for work and have always wanted to come here to dine on my own time. I have just never met the right person, until now," he says, staring into my eyes, his words causing me to blush.

"You keep surprising me, Dr. Taylor. First, the flowers and now, dinner. What else is hiding up your sleeve, or will you pull a rabbit out of a hat?" I giggle, lightening the mood, although his eyes stay dark and hazy. If I had to guess, I'd say he is aroused. I pick up the menu to distract myself from just staring at him the whole night.

He laughs. "Definitely no rabbit or hat. Just a fun, enjoyable night, and this is just the beginning."

Would it be rude to just skip dinner and head back to his house right now?

I browse through the menu and there are just so many options, not to mention that half of the dishes have French names, so I have no idea what any of them are.

"Can you help me choose what I should get? It all sounds delicious."

He peers at me from above his menu. "We could share a few dishes and you can get a taste of everything, if that suits you?"

I fold the menu closed and drop it back on the table and nod. "That's a great idea. It saves me from trying to choose."

The waitress comes back with a bottle. "I have Mount Langi Ghiran Riesling." She picks up our glasses, pouring a taster into each, and she waits for our verdict.

Mike swirls it, then smells it before tasting. I take a small sip. "Perfect, yes." *Mmm, it's good. So smooth, not too sweet, not too dry.*

She pours a full glass for each of us and then looks between us. "Are you ready to order, or do you need some more time?"

"No, we are ready," Mike answers.

"Okay, what can I get you?" She smiles and pulls out a small iPad. *Fancy.*

"We would like to order the French onion soup with a cheese and onion brioche bun, the ratatouille, and the confit duck legs with braised lentils. For dessert, we will have the pear tarte tatin and the plateau de fromage. We will be sharing all of these dishes, thank you." He folds his menu and places it on top of mine.

Once the waitress has finished typing the order into the iPad, she grabs our menus from the table. "All great choices. We will bring them one at a time in a smooth transition. If at any stage you want a break, just let me know."

"Okay, thank you."

Once she walks out of earshot, he picks up his wine, and I mimic him when he holds his glass out and says, "I think we should cheers to you finally caving, and coming to the realization I'm not a complete dickhead."

I laugh. "I must have a screw loose. I think I need to get another doctor to check me out."

His brows draw together in a frown. "No other doctor will do such a thing."

"I'm just kidding. Geez, I'm playing with you," I scold, shaking my head at him. I raise my glass to toast. "Anyway, cheers to a great date tonight." Our glasses clink, then I bring the glass to my lips and I take a sip. Setting it down, I sit back, relaxing as I continue staring at him.

He leans in. "I want to know more about you, Alice."

"There isn't too much to tell. I am originally from Bendigo Park, which is where I was born and raised, before moving to the city for college, which you already know because it was on my application letter."

"I did. I knew you were smart from that application. What else?" he ponders aloud, smirking at me from across the table.

"I have a sister, Claire, who is younger than me and is studying teaching at college. Then there is my mom, Angie, who is working as a receptionist in Bendigo Park. We are a small family and remarkably close, so I try to head back to Bendigo Park as often as I can."

Thinking of my mom and sister almost kills me with how much I miss them. I wish they didn't live so far away. I love my roommates, but it's just not the same. My mouth becomes dry, so I reach for my drink and sip some more of the wine. Our first course arrives, and it looks delicious, but I can't help frowning at how small the portions are.

"And what about your dad?" He is looking at me with a blank expression.

I pick up my drink and drain the glass, not caring how classless it is. I need the confidence that the buzz of alcohol can give. I set the empty glass down, taking shallow breaths. Glancing up at Mike, I answer in a quiet voice. "He died."

Sympathy flashes across his face and he leans forward, grabbing my hand and holding it. "I'm so sorry, Alice."

I shrug in response. I gaze down at our joined fingers and rub my thumb over his soft, big hand. "It is what it is, I guess. He died five years ago in his sleep. The doctor said it was from a heart attack."

I keep my gaze down at my rubbing thumb, then take my hand away. "We should eat this before it gets cold."

It's quiet, and I can tell he is thinking about what he wants to say next. The sounds of our cutlery hitting the bowl are the only noise between us. We have just finished the soup and bun when the waitress brings the duck and ratatouille, then tops up our glasses.

"Is that why you wanted to get into nursing?" Mike asks curiously.

I glance up into his curious eyes, picking up my glass and taking a sip, before I nod, adding, "Yes, I was shattered, but beforehand I had no direction or idea of what I wanted to do, and when that happened, I realized I wanted to help others. It was a dream my dad and I had for me when I was young. So, I feel like I'm fulfilling that dream of his."

Remembering how lost I was as a teenager and how rebellious I was, if I had my time again, I would have enjoyed all those precious moments I had with my father, and not spent so much time out, or staying at my friends' houses every weekend. It's probably why I'm such a homebody now.

I bite my lip, then I confess, "I actually really wanted to work on the cardiac ward, but now I feel happy that my direction has changed—the work is incredible, and the staff are so encouraging, helpful, and fun to work with. I can't complain."

His eyes flick all over my face and a satisfied grin forms on his mouth.

My stomach growls, reminding me that the main dish is probably going cold. I take a portion and eat, now talking in between bites. "This is so good. Now I'm going to compare every other restaurant to this when I can't have it again."

"I'll take you whenever you want," he offers.

"Mike, don't be crazy. But in all seriousness, I think my father had something to do with me finding you. I know it sounds silly, but I just feel it." I bite my lip to shut myself up.

His brows shoot up in surprise. "What? I'm not crazy. I'd be happy to bring you here every week, and you're not silly. I wish I could have met him."

His eyes are sincere, and I feel at ease talking to Mike about my dad. *I miss him so much.* He will never get to walk me, or my sister, down the aisle, or meet his grandchildren, or watch us grow up to be women he would have been proud of. It's definitely a hard pill to swallow, and it makes me appreciate my time on this earth even more, because you never know when your time is going to be up.

"You're not taking me here every week. Really, that just solidifies what I thought," I chastise, shaking my head and laughing at him.

We finish the main courses and our bottle of Riesling. I feel light-headed, so I drink water with the desserts, which are mouth wateringly delicious.

I hear him take in a deep breath. "What about your exes? Why did you two break up?"

I twirl my fork in the last bit of the pear tarte tatin and peer up from under my lashes to meet his eyes. "I only had one short high school relationship, but we broke up when my dad died. I wasn't in love with him, so I ended it and focused on my studies instead. I haven't had anything serious since."

I remember how heartbroken Trevor was, but I didn't have time for him. I needed to be with my family. Besides, I think I was just comfortable with him, rather than passionately in love with him, because after we broke up, I never missed him. Looking back now, I realize how wrong that is.

"Nothing since then?" He perks an eyebrow up in question.

I shake my head vigorously. "No. I have had hook-ups here and there, but nothing serious."

We finish our desserts, then the waitress brings the bill.

When I go to grab my purse, Mike covers my hand with his and shakes his head. "Don't. I took you on a date, so I pay the bill. That's how it works."

I nod and sit back. "Okay."

We get up, thanking the waitress, and Mike grabs my hand before opening the door for me. Exiting the restaurant, we wait for the elevator to arrive.

He is standing close to me, still holding my hand, when he breaks the silence. "Thanks for coming. I had a wonderful time. I can't wait for part two. Did you have a nice night, babe?"

I smile. "Yes, Mike, it was a wonderful night, thank you. I have never been on a date like this ever."

The elevator doors open, and we enter, and Mike hits the ground floor button. "Where is part two?" I ask.

"My house." Mike's voice is gravelly, and he squeezes my hand firmly.

My breath starts to quicken, and the anticipation makes me feel as though there are butterflies in my stomach. "So, errr, there is something on my mind that I want to get clear about."

I feel the heat of his stare on my face. "Mmm, ask away."

The elevator reaches the parking lot and when the doors open, I trail beside him to his car. "At Luxe you were talking with a brunette, the same one in your office the other day. Who is she?" I ask.

Mike opens the car door for me, and I climb in, watching him through the windshield as he walks to the other side and slides in. Turning toward me, he sighs. "My ex, Amanda." He turns back around, starting the car. "Let's drive back to my house and finish this conversation there. There's clearly a lot more we need to discuss."

CHAPTER 16

ALICE

WE ARRIVE BACK AT Mike's house and when we are standing in his kitchen, he turns to me. "Would you like a glass of wine?" he asks.

I nod. "Yes, please."

He pours a glass of wine for each of us. I take a seat on a stool at the kitchen counter.

"Your house is spectacular. I have never seen anything this grand in my life. This is a dream house." I scan the modern interior, half expecting to wake up and realize Mike and this entire evening has all been a dream.

Laughing at me, he tells me, "I do love my house. It was designed by me for me. But enough about my house. I have something else planned now, and it will be a great place to finish the conversation we started at dinner. Bring your wine and follow me outside."

"Sure." My hands begin to tremble, so I clutch the glass with both hands to hide it. Sliding off the stool, I walk around to follow him.

He opens the sliding door and closes it behind us. I step out from the paved alfresco area and stop, completely speechless. There in front of my eyes is a grand outdoor projector screen, with fluffy cushions on a rug in front of it, and tables laden with snacks. There are roses and candles everywhere, all lit up, and it's breathtaking. My eyes widen and my lips part in sheer surprise. I pull one of my trembling hands to my neck and start rubbing the back of it, unsure of what to say.

This is even better than the dinner. It's so... me.

Realizing I haven't said a word in several minutes, I quickly clear my throat. "This is stunning."

His beautiful big smile that reaches his eyes is back, and he grabs my hand. "Come on, let's take a seat."

He ushers me over to the rug and my hand tightens in his when a gust of a cool breeze whips my legs and I shiver involuntary.

"Let's grab you some of my clothes so you're more comfortable." He is still holding my hand, but with the other he's gesturing toward my dress. "Even though I love that dress, and how sexy you look in it, I want you to enjoy the movie."

I blush at the way he stares at me with his eyebrow raised, wearing a sexy as sin smirk. I feel my body starting to heat and a throb between my legs. I shuffle side to side to try and rub the ache.

"You are killing me here. I'm trying to go slow." His eyes darken to a deeper shade of blue. "Let's go get you changed."

I follow him up the stairs and into his wardrobe to switch my dress for a cozy pair of fleece gray jogger pants and a hoodie. The hoodie smells of him. His sexy spicy scent is all over it, and I pull the collar of the sweater up and deeply inhale. *Mmm, so good.*

We head back outside and take a seat on the rug. He pats the area in front of him, smiling. "Come here."

I shuffle over until I'm sitting between his legs, leaning my back against his hard body. He wraps his arms around my middle in a tight, warm hug. He pulls a blanket out from next to him, whipping it into the air so it drops over our legs. I twist my head to peer at him. He smiles and leans down and kisses my lips in a too brief kiss.

I slowly blink my eyes open, staring at his heated gaze. "Why me? You could have anyone you want. I'm nothing special."

He moves his head to look away before returning his eyes to mine. "There is a connection I feel toward you. I haven't felt this way with any other woman. It confuses and annoys the hell out of me because you make it so difficult," he teases.

I laugh up at him. "Well, I... How do I say this? Just don't fuck me around. I can't keep denying I have feelings toward you. But I still don't understand why you are single. No marriage or kids, at your age... Should I be worrying why you're not settling down?"

His laugh vibrates against my back. "You make me sound like a dinosaur, or like I'm some antique."

I can't help laughing aloud. He is funny, which surprises me. He keeps surprising me. I keep thinking the bubble will burst any moment. *And I'll be the one left hurt and trying to piece myself back together.*

"I have had one serious girlfriend, which you know about... I thought she was the one, but I was young and dumb and got completely blindsided." He tears his gaze off mine and up to the stars, like remembering all this is hard. I rub his leg to offer comfort and let him know that I'm listening, and I care.

My brows furrow. "Why, what happened?" I ask.

"She fucked me over. She cheated on me with my best friend, Liam. It went on for years behind my back. So, since I ended it just over a year ago, I feel it's easier to not get attached to anyone. That way I don't have to worry about trusting and getting hurt again. It's even hard to trust new friends. I stick to a really small circle of people and my family."

I gasp and cover my mouth with my palm at his confession. "That's awful. I'm sorry. That's so shitty of Amanda and Liam. I'm gathering you aren't friends with him anymore?" I softly question, watching him.

He is still looking away when he draws up one leg and presses his hand against his cheek.

I can feel his deep inhale through my back. "Fuck no. I couldn't be more hurt if he ran me over with his car... but the real kicker here is she screwed around on him too, so karma really is a bitch." He smiles wickedly as he stares down at me and then pecks my lips.

"Why did I see her with you at the nightclub and then again in your office?" I ask.

He sighs loudly, shaking his head. "She wants me back and is always begging me for forgiveness. But I don't want her at all. She doesn't get the hint no matter what I say or do. I just try to ignore her, hoping she will go away."

I nod against him and the tension in his body lets me know he is ready to move the conversation away from his ex. I want to know more, but I don't want to push him right now.

"Moving on from them. What about your family? Tell me about them." I have finished the wine and when he notices, he takes my glass to refill it.

"What movie would you like to watch?"

"I don't know. I'm happy talking for now, but maybe we could listen to some music or something."

"I can put some music on while we talk." Untangling himself from me, he gets up, and when the cool air hits my back, I wrap the blanket more tightly around me.

He puts the music on quietly, and he settles back behind me, wrapping me tight. He kisses my temple, and his breath tickles me when he leans to talk into my ear. "Where were we?" Goosebumps cover my skin at the sensation.

"What about your family? You were going to tell me about them."

He lies back more, settling me down with him. "Right, well, I am the oldest. I have a brother, Alexander, and a sister called Stephanie. Alex is a neurologist and Steph is a dermatologist, and my parents, Margaret and Paul, are both general practitioners at their own clinic."

My eyebrows rise in amazement. "You're kidding,"

"Talking of family, I do a small dinner at my parents' once a month. It's this Sunday. Since we've just established this isn't casual, I would love it if you would come with me."

My back stiffens and my body goes rigid, trying to process what he is asking. It all feels sudden, but I'm the one who said I don't want casual, so he is offering more than that. I'm starting to get a headache from the high and low emotions, and the wine.

"Before you answer, I just have one last bit of information to tell you. I don't know if you're aware of..." I attempt to lift my body up so I can turn around and look at him, but he won't let me. My heart rate picks back up as I wait for him to finish. "You know the guy you kissed at Luxe? That was Alex, my brother."

I jump up too quickly for him to reach out and grab me as I spin around to face him. *Fuck.*

"Mike." I reach out and touch his face. "I'm so sorry. I had no idea. I would never have done that if I'd known. I saw you talking to Amanda, and I was jealous, so I let him dance with me, then kiss me. But I pushed him away." Shaking my head, I continue. "God, I feel awful. What an idiot I was." I drop my chin, avoiding his eyes.

He puts his finger under my chin, lifting my face to his so my gaze is focused on his. "We didn't know each other then. And we weren't a couple. I just wanted to tell you because, obviously, Alex will be there at dinner, and I don't want it to be awkward for any of us. However, I am surprised you haven't seen him at work."

"I was so drunk that night, and I didn't feel anything toward him." I already want to forget this conversation. I rub my forehead, trying to figure out what to do next.

He leans forward and presses the most tender kiss to my lips. He tries to pull back, but I groan and grab his face, holding him in position with both of my hands. My earlier thoughts go out the window when my arousal hits.

I decide to distract us both from the past and climb up onto his lap, straddling him. I feel his dick growing hard with appreciation, which makes my sex achy with desire. I rub myself up and along and then down on him. We both groan at the sensations caused by the friction. I shove my hands through his hair and pull his head back slightly to gain better access to him, and when he opens his mouth with a groan, I take the opportunity to stick my tongue inside, kissing him deeper. His body responds in an instant and he places one hand on my face and the other on my back, guiding me. He takes control from me, and I eagerly follow his direction.

After a minute, he rolls me over and he is on top, kissing me deeply. My head is on the pillow and my body is on the rug. He pulls away from the kiss and I whimper at the loss of his lips. My body is blazing and searching for relief. He pushes the sweater up and laps at my nipple before moving to the other one to show it the same attention.

I am writhing in desire underneath him. "Please," I'm begging now, and I don't care how pathetic I sound. I want him so badly. He has wound me up so tightly.

He hovers over me and kisses my neck. I feel him smile, enjoying the needy pain I'm in. He pecks my lips, whispering, "Soon."

"Unfair." I sulk, and his chest vibrates against me when he chuckles.

He doesn't quicken his pace. If anything, he drags it out even more, which is infuriating.

"You're so fucking beautiful Alice," he grunts as he removes my pants, leaving my panties on, even though they are soaked through.

"You're so ready for me. So, fucking wet. God, do you know how much I want you right now?"

I close my eyes, lying there unable to answer him, and wait for him to remove my panties, when a hard bite on my clit through the material makes me scream. "Ahhh."

"The smell of you is so fucking intoxicating," he says in a low voice that causes me to shudder. I'm so close to coming just from that. My eyes spring open and I look down to see Mike staring up at me. His eyes are so dark and intense it sends a shiver down my spine. "I'm so hard right now. I can't wait to have you."

He moves forward and I watch him, unable to tear my eyes away from him. He leans into my sex, and I feel his nose brush my clit through my panties as he slowly inhales. "Fucking delicious."

I'd normally feel so uncomfortable with that, but Mike makes me feel alive and sexy. He does what he wants, and I watch from under heavily hooded eyes. Goosebumps erupt all over my skin but not from the cold. It's from anticipation as to what Mike will do next.

He moves up to my hips and uses his teeth to tug down my underwear until they're all the way off.

He then leans back and uses his fingers to spread my lips wide and licks. Hearing him groan and moan while licking me sends my body into a state of near pain. Searching for release, I try to grind my sex on his face, but Mike pulls back.

"Not yet baby," he rasps.

I whimper and moan at the loss, but he doesn't leave me waiting long.

The next thing I feel are his fingers entering me and I scream. "Ahhh."

I'm so close to coming now.

I ride his fingers until he stops and pulls back. As I slowly open my eyes, I see him push his pants down and he frees his huge cock. Wrapping his hand around it, he guides it to my opening and enters me in one motion, stilling when he has filled me to the brim. "You feel so good," he says hoarsely.

"Mike," I whimper.

He leaves me feeling full and stretched, and because of his size it's bordering on painful. Even after a few moments when I thought by now, I would have adjusted to his size, it still aches. He waits until my walls relax and then starts to move, his pace torturously slow.

"Mike..." I plead again. "Harder please."

"I'm not going to last if you keep begging like that," he grunts.

I wrap my legs around his waist to push my heels into his back. It doesn't encourage him to move any faster, and instead he continues at this torturous pace. He leans forward to kiss me, and as he speeds up, I feel myself climbing higher. "Yes!" I choke in a ragged breath.

My eyes are shut tight and when the words, "That's it baby. Come now," leave his lips, I instantly unravel and come hard, my body shaking violently, sending him over the edge with me. He collapses next to me, and we both lie there panting heavily and trying to catch our breath.

Once my breathing has returned to normal, I lean up on my elbow and draping my other hand across his stomach, I stare at him. "Thank you, I have always wanted to have sex under the stars."

He lifts his head up and smiling, he pecks my lips. "Are you ready for your movie now?" he asks.

I laugh. "Mmm, yes, please."

He turns off the music and presses play on the movie and comes back to sit with me, positioning himself so he can cuddle me from behind. He doesn't say a word, just holds me throughout the whole movie. Nobody has ever held me like this before.

When the movie is over, I turn in his arms and peer up at him. "I think I should go. It's getting late, Mike."

"Stay here tonight?" he suggests.

"I don't think so, Mike. It's all so much so fast. Even meeting your parents so soon, it's a lot to take in." I sigh.

"We met months ago. It's what I want and how I feel that's important, not the society norm. I don't see my family all that often. It's a casual dinner and I don't want to hide you," he replies.

"I don't know." I bite my lip, the alcohol and tiredness fogging my thoughts.

He smirks down at me and brushes his lips on mine, leaving the softest of kisses on me, in between murmurs. "Is that a 'yes'? Say you will stay and also come tomorrow, please."

"What if they don't like me?" I ask.

His brow lifts. "Is that what you're worried about?"

I nod back without a word.

He stares into my eyes. "They will love you."

His lips recapture mine, way more demanding this time. I pull back and whisper across his lips. "I'll stay...but I can't go to family dinner. It's too soon. Next month, sure."

CHAPTER 17

ALICE

A MONTH LATER

I am getting ready to head to Mike's family dinner and have thrown all my clothes over the bed. I keep holding different outfits up against me in front of the mirror to see if they will work, but I can't decide. I plonk myself on the bed, confused and upset. *What should I wear to impress his parents?*

I have never met a guy's parents before, so I pace my room, scanning all my clothes. *I hate that I can't afford anything nice. I should cancel. I'm going to feel so out of place.* They all have money and are doctors, and then there will be me, dressed in my local discount outfit, and just an intern nurse. I pick up my phone from my bedside table, scroll to find his number, and hit dial.

He answers on the first ring. "Hey, babe, what are you doing?" His voice is sexy and sultry, *and ugh.* I crumble at the sound and just want to go back into his arms.

"I don't know what to wear tonight. Do I really have to go? I don't want to." I know I sound whiny, but I want to make a good impression, and I don't think I can.

"You will look amazing in anything. It's just a casual dinner, so don't dress up. It's nothing exciting."

I huff. "Trust you to say that. You're not the one meeting my family."

He laughs at me. "Babe, just pick something to wear and wear it. You would look hot in a brown paper bag. I can't wait to peel whatever you put on, off you later," he growls, his tone getting deeper.

"Oh, really? Well, how about we just skip the dinner and go straight to that?" I'm already feeling better. He knows just what to say to get my mind to relax.

"Yes, really, now find something to wear and I will pick you up soon. And you're not getting out of it."

"Fine, okay. I'll see you soon," I huff. Hanging up, I toss my phone down on my bed. I look around and decide on a pair of jeans, because I can dress them up with a nice top.

Tahlia pops her head in. "Someone needs a hand. It looks like a bomb went off in here." She gestures at the mess all over the room.

"Yes, please. I have only chosen these jeans, but now I need to decide on shoes and a top."

Tahlia walks into my room and sifts through my things, picking up different tops, and then finally says, "Here, pair this singlet and this blazer with the jeans, and then some wedges. I think you will look classic and have the perfect 'meet the family outfit.'"

"You're a lifesaver."

"I'll be in the kitchen. Come find me when you have it all on." She walks back out of my room.

I get dressed and look in the mirror, assessing my outfit. It looks good, but it's just missing a belt. I pop a belt on and check in the mirror again. I smile at my reflection. *I love it.* I feel sexy and classy, but also casual. I wander out and into the kitchen, and when Tahlia turns around, she smiles widely.

"See? Perfect! In another life, I'll be a stylist."

"You should, you're so good. Now I'll go do my hair and put a little bit of makeup on. I want to appear older. I don't want his mom to know how young I really am."

"You're overthinking it. Age doesn't matter anymore. You can't help who you like or love." She winks knowingly.

Oh God, did she just say that? I haven't said anything to him yet about loving him. *How can she pick it up so easily? Does that mean he knows too? And how does he feel?* I shake my head because I don't have time to think about the answers to these questions. I finish blow-drying my hair, and when I turn off the hair dryer, I know Mike's here because I can hear his smooth, deep voice.

I grab my purse from my bed before heading out to the kitchen. My palms are starting to sweat, and my pulse is rapidly beating inside my chest. I'm giddy seeing him again, but I need to calm down. Taking a deep breath, I walk out to meet him.

I reach the living room where Mike is reclined in the gray L-shaped couch, watching the television. "Hi," I say.

His head snaps up to face me and he rakes his eyes down my body. "I don't know what you were so worried about. You're perfect."

I feel the heat in my chest rise to my cheeks. "You'd say that no matter what I'm wearing." I roll my eyes.

I can see Tahlia smiling in the background. *Great, I have an audience.* I peer down at my toes, embarrassment creeping over me.

"But you are. I'm very lucky." I hear his footsteps as he walks over to me. He lifts my chin up with his finger so his eyes can stare into mine. When he kisses my lips, it lasts a bit longer than a peck but is not long enough to be a proper kiss either. I sigh.

He frowns. "Don't you want to pack a bag?"

"I have work tomorrow, remember?"

His hands drop to my shoulders, and he starts rubbing them. "So?" he questions. "You can stay the night and I will drive us both to work."

"I don't know if that's a great idea. I need to actually sleep before work." I feel warmth spreading over me as I admit this.

"And that's my cue to leave. See you, lovebirds. Have a good night." Tahlia heads off to her room, leaving us alone.

"Pack a bag." The sultry, sexy voice I can't seem to refuse is back. He slides his hands from my shoulders onto my hips.

I sigh. "I'll be right back."

I walk into my room and grab a bag and begin to pack. I zip up my bag and carry it out.

Mike takes the bag from me and asks, "Got everything?" I nod. "Let's go."

He walks me out, his hand firmly on my lower back, sending chills down my spine. *When will the fireworks in my body stop?* They only seem to be getting worse.

On the drive over, I feel tension in the back of my eyes. I have given myself a headache with the overthinking. *I'm hoping they'll like me.* Mike is holding my hand in the car and I stare down at our entwined fingers, lost in thought.

Mike is so different from the person I believed he was. He is so thoughtful and caring. There is no sign of the egotistical player that I heard he was and also assumed about him. Yes, he is successful, but he works hard for what he has and that shouldn't be frowned upon. He's allowed to be proud of his accomplishments.

We arrive at the edge of a gated area and wait to be buzzed in. Mike drives through the set of gates, following a long driveway up to his parents' house. It's a white, two-story building, surrounded by a beautiful garden, with stunning flowers everywhere. *Seriously, does anyone in this family have a shit house*? I'm now completely mortified he came to the rental I live in. I'm sure he must have felt like he was visiting a third-world country, not his girlfriend's house. *I just want to curl up and die, right now.*

"You have been quiet for a while, babe. Are you okay?" he questions, leaning over with concern etched on his face.

In my head I count to ten to calm my heart rate down.

"Yeah, I guess. I'm just really nervous. I'm probably very different to the kind of woman they would expect you to be with."

He frowns. "I don't care what they say. It's what I want and feel that matters."

While I appreciate the response, it hasn't eased my thoughts. *Where is the 'they will love you' line? Yep, I'm officially dead.*

"Come on, let's get this show on the road, so I can take you back home and have my way with you." His eyes are shimmering with promise, but my heart rate is peaking, and I have a slight sweat beginning to form on my back.

I laugh, trying to sound like I'm not every bit as nervous as I really feel. "Keep it in your pants, hot Doc."

I start unbuckling my seat belt before opening the door. He races around to help me out of his sports car. Marty is a pain to get in and out of, no matter how expensive or nice he looks.

We walk up to the house holding hands, and though I'm sure he can also feel mine starting to get clammy, he doesn't say anything. I'm one step behind him, trying to use him to shield myself.

Before he can turn the handle, the door flies open and his parents are standing there, beaming at us both. "Good evening, and welcome, Alice."

"Hello, um, thanks for having me." I smile up at them, thankful my voice doesn't wobble.

Mike pulls me into the house, and I shake my hands with his parents, who introduce themselves even though Mike told me their names already.

"My name is Paul, and this is my wife, Margaret. Please come inside. We have heard so much about you."

I squeeze Mike's hand. I hear him chuckle.

Paul and Margaret look to be in their late sixties, slim, and both have short gray hair, but Margaret's is just above her shoulders.

Mike kisses his mom on her cheek and shakes his dad's hand. "Hi, Mom. Hi, Dad."

We follow Paul and Margaret through the entryway and farther into the house. The color scheme and décor are light and breezy, with wooden timber floors, and all their cabinetry is white and has glossy finishes. I glance around, wondering if this is the house Mike and his family grew up in. It seems so cold, and everything looks so new that it doesn't have the usual homey feeling.

We stand in the kitchen and Mike speaks. "Are we the first ones here?"

"Yeah, you are, Steph and Alex should be here any minute, though."

As if right on cue, I hear the door open and then close with a heavy bang. Alex appears, wearing a shit-eating grin.

I feel Mike stand a little taller next to me. My breathing starts to quicken, so I once again count to ten to calm down.

"Hey, Mom." Alex walks straight over to give his mom a cuddle and kiss, and then he walks to his dad, shaking his hand before giving him a loving slap on the back.

I smile at their exchange. It reminds me of my own dad and how I would love to have one of his hugs right now.

I can clearly see that Alex has a different relationship with his parents than Mike does. Mike seems to have a wall up and I'm slightly surprised by that because Mike hasn't mentioned he has any issues with his parents. *I'll have to ask him about it later*. Alex wanders over to Mike and me. I stiffen and feel my chest tighten, suddenly feeling awkward.

Alex kisses me on my cheek. "Hey, Alice."

"Hi, Alex," I squeak.

He then shakes Mike's hand, "Hey, bro."

He's acting like nothing happened between us, and I can sense how uncomfortable Mike is. The air around us is thick with tension.

Mike breaks it the moment he answers his brother. "Hi, Alex."

Margaret steps in and asks everyone what they would like to drink.

"A beer would be great," Alex says.

"I'll have the same. Babe, do you want anything?" Mike asks, glancing at me.

I feel like I want to drink a bottle of wine, but I figure that would be inappropriate.

"Just a glass of water for now, please. Do you want a hand, Margaret?" I offer.

She shakes her head. "Oh no, dear, you relax. You're our guest tonight." Smiling at me, she then strolls off to get the boys their beers and a glass of water for me.

I hear the opening and closing of cupboards and then the fridge. She sounds so busy in the kitchen while we are all talking, and I feel bad she won't let me help.

"Okay, come outside and have some nibbles while we wait for Steph and Chris—they shouldn't be too much longer," she orders.

Mike leads me outside by my hand, and as we walk out the door, he leans in toward me. His breath touches my ear, and he whispers softly so no one else can hear, "Are you okay?"

He's so sweet. He can probably tell that I'm still feeling on edge about Alex being here.

Nodding, I squeeze his hand to confirm, and softly whisper, "Yes."

When we step outside there is an outdoor table holding a spectacular platter piled high with a range of deli meats, fruit, sweets, crackers, and dips. They are all elegantly laid out in a seamless pattern.

"Wow, Margaret, did you do all this?" I point to the platter. Stepping over to the table, I grab a plate and start selecting a mixture of different things to eat—it all looks so good and delicious.

"Yes, dear. Now that I'm retired, I have plenty of time to work on things I love, like cooking. I took a semester at college studying cooking." She grabs herself a plate and fills it up.

I move back to stand next to Mike but continue talking to her. "That's impressive. So, how did you meet Paul?" Mike stiffens beside me, and I frown.

"We met in college when we were studying for our MDs." She peeks over at Paul, who smiles and nods at her. "I retired last year, but Paul still works a few days a week."

"Do you miss being a GP, Margaret? Or are you happy you retired?"

I wonder how I would feel about giving up the career I love, and thinking about it, I'm sure it would be so hard to do. I have loved every minute—that might be partly due to Mike—I'm excited to go to work every day, and I love every second I am doing it. The adrenaline, the fast pace, and knowing I'm going to be helping people is such an honor.

"I did. At the start it was extremely hard to go from working to retiring suddenly. It was an extremely hard adjustment. I was moping about it at first, if I'm honest. I was wondering how I was going to fill my days, but then I started joining different classes and clubs. Then my feelings started to change and keeping my brain active and myself busy has worked wonders. I have tried lots of different hobbies, but now I'm in a weekly book club, a golf club, and I'm about to start a course in baking."

My smile grows at her confession. "That's great, and if it makes you happy, then that's wonderful. I don't know how I would feel if I had to give up nursing right now." Talking about it brings a slicing pain through my chest.

A thoughtful smile curves her mouth. "Oh, yes. Mike mentioned you're in your graduate year of nursing at the same hospital. Are you enjoying it?"

I laugh and glance at Mike, who is watching me while he eats some food. *How can he eat that amount of food and still have no body fat under those clothes? It's so unfair.*

Facing Margaret, I feel myself flush, embarrassed I was just thinking of her son in that way.

"Yes, I am. It's been exciting. It's a wonderful hospital. Did you know I work with Mike?" I ask.

I can feel his arm snake around my back. He holds me against him by my waist. He really does enjoy talking about this.

Margaret smiles up at Mike and then back at me, her eyes bright with pleasure. "No, I didn't, but I'm surprised Mike agreed to have a nurse to teach."

Mike and I crack up laughing, knowing very well he didn't want me there, but had no choice. We keep that between us.

Behind us, I can hear someone calling, "Hello? Hello, where are you guys?"

Margaret excuses herself and I see a woman with brown hair coming into view with a taller blond male behind her, and I guess this must be Steph. She is greeted by her mom before coming and greeting all of us. She walks out the door, and she is breathtaking, with sky-blue eyes that are framed by big, black lashes. I glance at her stomach to the obvious bump. *Mike didn't mention she was pregnant.*

She heads toward Mike and me, wearing the biggest grin. She wraps her dainty arms around Mike, giving him a hug. "I haven't seen you for weeks, busy boy. I've missed you."

She slips back out of the embrace, her hands cradling the bump, and he smiles brightly back at her. I can see that there's a strong bond between them, causing my own lips to turn up into an easy smile.

"Yes, Steph, it's been a while," he says softly, chuckling at her. I warm at their loving exchange.

She playfully hits his arm. "Too busy to call your sister, I get it." She turns her attention to me. My eyes widen when she leans over to hug me. "And you must be Alice." I reach my hand up and stroke her upper back and she begins to laugh, rubbing her bump as she pulls back. "Sorry about that. I forget it's in the way sometimes."

I grimace and elbow Mike in the ribs. "Mike never mentioned you were expecting. Congratulations. How far along are you?"

He throws his hand over the spot where I elbowed him, wincing. I roll my eyes at his playful dramatics. "Ouch, and I didn't mean to forget, sorry."

I purse my lips at the thought of my own family before responding. "So, you should be."

Steph beams and her eyes watch our exchange with a grin. "I'm twenty-eight weeks along."

The blond guy she arrived with comes up and holds out his hand. "My name is Chris. I'm Steph's husband. It's lovely to meet you."

I smile and put my hand in his for a quick shake and then take it away. "Congratulations, Chris, not long left. I didn't see any other children, so am I right in guessing this one is your first?" I ask.

"Yes, definitely the first, maybe even the last." She rubs her belly, chuckling.

"You will change your mind," Margaret says from behind Steph. "You forget about the bad parts of being pregnant, and then you will have more. The food is ready, so can we all bring our drinks and head inside to the dining room? Steph, I'll grab you a glass of water. You go sit down."

Steph winks at me, then leans into my ear and whispers, "The best part of being pregnant is how your family and husband do everything for you."

I laugh, shaking my head. "Thanks for the tip, I guess?"

I go to step inside, but Mike captures my hand, spins me around to face him, and kisses me. I gasp into his mouth and then melt into his arms as I return the sweet kiss.

He pulls his lips away an inch. My eyes flutter open and I stare straight into his blue eyes. "Are you feeling better now you have met them all? Can I get you a proper drink now?" he asks, smirking.

I chuckle. "Yes, much better, thank you." I smack his chest and I have this urge to kiss him again, so I tug on his top, drawing him closer to me, and close the distance between our lips.

I hear a deep groan from behind me. "Get a room," I hear Alex say, poking fun at us as he heads inside.

Mike removes his lips from mine with a hiss and just shakes his head. "Come on, let's get you some wine and have dinner. The quicker we eat here, the quicker I can eat you for dessert."

My mouth falls open with a gasp, and I playfully punch him in the arm. "Shhh, I'm meeting your family. Don't be dirty here. It's gross," I warn before turning on my heel and moving inside.

"Babe, no one can hear. Settle down." He pinches my bum to get me to hurry inside, and I squeal.

"Stop it and behave!" I scold, but I'm smirking as I say it, because I actually love it when Mike has his hands on me.

Mike raises his hands up in surrender like he didn't do anything wrong.

We get our wine and walk into the dining room to join everyone else. The dining table is long, and Paul is sitting at one end, while Margaret is at the other. Mike guides me to sit down next to Margaret. I frown but take the seat he offers. I have spoken with Margaret a lot and have hardly said more than two words to his dad. It almost seems like he doesn't want to talk to his dad.

Dinner is laid out all down the middle of the large table.

"Alice, dear, Mike didn't say if you are allergic to anything, or if you have any special dietary requirements, so I hope you don't mind what I have cooked for dinner."

"No, no allergies. I definitely don't have a special diet, and I can't wait to taste everything," I reply.

She bows her head and places a palm to her heart. "So different from Amanda," she mumbles under her breath.

CHAPTER 18

MIKE

I GLARE AT MOM from across the table. *Shut up, please.* I'm willing her to glance at me so I can mime for her to zip it because I don't want a discussion about exes at dinner. I want Alice to enjoy herself, not hear about my ex.

But of course, Mom is too busy fussing with the food on the table, so she continues. "She was always on a different diet every time she came for dinner. She wouldn't just eat what I cooked. She was way too high-maintenance." She shakes her head.

I cannot believe it. Everyone is quiet until Alex starts talking to my dad, and I say quietly, "Mom, please, not now." I can't help the stern tone that comes out. I don't like talking to Mom like that, but she needs to drop this topic.

"Sorry." She winces, retaking her seat once she finishes grabbing her food.

Just as I sink into my seat and start eating, Steph decides to drop a bomb. "So, Alice, would you be interested in having children in the next few years? Obviously, you know Mike is thirty-eight, so he needs to settle down soon." *Fuck.* She winks at me, but I glare back, clenching my jaw.

I lean forward and say in a hushed voice, "Enough, Steph. I know you're coming from a kind place, but to be honest, it's none of your business," I snap.

Alice grabs my arm, pulling me back so she can see Steph. "Mike, it's fine, seriously."

She's smiling warmly at me, trying to calm me down, but my heart is racing a million miles a minute. *How can she be okay with answering these questions?* She's only just met them, and they are already asking very forward and personal questions. Hell, *I* haven't even asked her about marriage or kids.

"To answer your question, Steph, I haven't thought much about it. But thinking about it right now, my answer is no. Probably not in the next ten years," Alice responds confidently.

I'd stopped listening until then. I hear cutlery hitting the plate with a clatter. *Excuse me, what did I just hear her say?* I feel like I've been kicked in the stomach. *Ten years.* I must not have heard correctly. How could she not want kids in the next ten years? I know she's a lot younger than I am, but I'll be forty-eight by then. I can provide for her. I have a good job, a car, a house, money, and stability. She would have a comfortable life, and hell, so would our kids. *But it's not fair to her to have her put her dreams aside so maybe she would be better suited to someone her age.*

Fuck, I just want to get out of here and go home. I'm shattered. How did I read her so wrong? I realize it was my cutlery that has been dropped, so I pick them up and continue to eat. I'm not angry, I'm gutted. I know we've not been together for very long, but I thought Alice could possibly be my future. But then again, I once thought the same thing about Amanda.

We finish the dinner and help pack up.

I turn to Alice, waiting for her to finish her conversation with Mom before I ask, "Are you ready to head off, Alice? We have work tomorrow and I'm a little tired."

We say our goodbyes to everyone and walk back to the car. My mind has been trying to figure out how to talk to her about this, and I keep coming up empty.

CHAPTER 19

ALICE

SOMETHING IS OFF WITH Mike.

Walking to the car, hand in hand, I ask, "You seem awfully quiet. Are you okay?"

He opens my door for me to get inside and I stare up into his eyes as he answers, "Yes, I'm good, just a little tired."

I see a different emotion in his eyes, one I haven't seen before. I don't understand it, and my eyebrows furrow in thought. He closes my door, walks around the front of the car, then jumps into the driver's side and drives off.

When we arrive at his house, I follow him as he marches straight upstairs to his room, carrying my overnight bag in his hand. He dumps the bag on the bed and quickly turns to me, grabbing my head roughly between his two hands and bringing me to his lips. Passionately, he tugs my lip, nipping it hard. Something is definitely off with him, but I'm going to turn it around and make him forget whatever is bothering him.

I kiss him back hard, sucking on his tongue and pushing him away slightly so I can remove the shirt he is wearing. *My God, he is magnificent.* I kiss his pecs and run my hands softly over his torso, feeling his soft chest hair beneath my fingers.

Feeling daring, I sink to my knees in front of him and gaze directly into his eyes. I watch as they widen.

"Babe, what are you doing?" he asks.

I grin up at him when I hear my nickname come from his lips. "I want to taste you." I lick my lips, looking directly up at him.

"Fuck," he grunts, closing his eyes. "You're trying to kill me." He thrusts his hand through his hair.

I smirk and return to what I intend to do. I unbutton his pants and tug the zipper down, before removing his pants and briefs altogether, freeing his cock. I can't show my nerves. I want to enjoy this as much as I hope he will, and I'm sure he will make me stop if he finds out I haven't done this before, insisting on me taking small steps. I want him to give me everything.

He steps out of his clothes and kicks them to the side. He strokes my hair and face, while staring at me with such desire that it sends a shiver running all over my body. He is magnificent and far too good for me. I've no idea what he sees in me.

I need to stop thinking.

I grab his cock at the base and lick the head before putting it slightly in my mouth. Sucking the tip gently, I then pull it out and lick him slowly from the head to the base, and back up to the tip. Noticing a bit of precum coating his skin, I lick it off and moan. Glancing up, I see Mike's eyes burning with fire. Wrapping my hair around his fists, he closes his eyes and pushes into my mouth in such a hard thrust I almost choke. I barely manage to catch my breath, but I concentrate on what I'm doing and do my best to ignore the reflex telling me to gag.

He groans, "Fuck, babe." I suck and move him in and out, while sliding my hand up and down in rhythm with my mouth. "You're so good," he chokes out.

This is the encouragement I need to be daring, so I grab his balls and caress them between my fingers. I'm so turned on right now, but I can't think about myself, no matter how aroused I am or how badly I want to put my fingers in my panties and bring myself to climax. I know I'm soaked through.

"I'm going to come in your mouth if you don't stop now," he warns.

I smile around him and move faster until I feel his balls tighten and his hands grip my hair more firmly while he fucks my face until I can taste his salty cum on my tongue and feel it shooting down my throat. When his cock stops pulsing, I gently remove my mouth and look up at him, smirking. *How is he still hard?* His cheeks are flushed, and a light sheen of sweat is covering his body. He removes both of his hands from my hair and helps me up. Welcoming the assistance, I struggle to stand on numb and trembling legs, before I ask nervously, "Was that okay?"

"It was more than okay. Fuck, it was amazing. Now, strip naked and get on all fours on my bed in the next two minutes because I'm going to fuck you so hard."

I giggle and strip as quickly as possible and head over to the bed. My heart is beating faster in my chest and I'm sure I felt my arousal trickle down my thigh. He is insane, and he has no idea how incredible he is. I tremble with anticipation when he stalks over to me.

"Good girl," he growls from behind me.

I feel him at my entrance, and I can't wait, so I edge back. In one thrust, he fills me to the max and I scream. I'm so full, and though there is pain, it quickly turns to pleasure as soon as my walls adjust to his size. Then he starts drawing in and out painfully slow.

"Faster," I moan.

He doesn't change his rhythm, so I try to move with him. This only makes him chuckle, and grabbing hold of my hips, he says, "Trust me to make you feel good."

I nod and try to take slow breaths and just push through the building pleasure. I'm shaking and I can't take much more of this. I don't know if I can hold myself back much longer. The build-up is agonizing, but finally he starts pumping into me faster and harder, and already I'm so close.

"Don't stop, pleeease!" He reaches around to touch my clit and I come so hard I feel dizzy.

"You feel incredible," he grunts behind me.

My body quivers as I come down from my orgasm.

"Fuck. Alice," he rasps out as he reaches his own climax deep inside of me. Afterwards, I want to flop onto the bed but he catches me. Holding me and pulling me flush against him while I regain my energy.

When he catches his breath, he gentle lowers me to the bed and kisses my cheek. "Babe, we better get to bed. We have to be up early in the morning." He steps away from me, and walks off to the bathroom. I hear the water from the shower hitting the tiles and I slowly get up, grabbing my bag to find my pajamas. I walk in only to find him already stepping out.

"Don't want to join me?" I question.

Smirking at me while he dries himself with a towel, he responds, "Next time. Right now, I'm beat and I'm ready to pass out."

"Okay, I won't be long."

I step under the hot spray. *This really is the best shower.* I quickly shower, dry off, and climb into his bed. He is facing away from me... *So strange.* I really don't get it. If he is upset with me, I don't understand why. Shaking off my thoughts, I settle in, and it's so comfortable lying next to him that I drift off in minutes.

In the morning I wake to Mike's arm draped over me, and he's cuddling me from behind. I'm so warm and comfortable that when I hear the alarm go off, I groan. *Not fair.* He stirs and rolls over, turning off the alarm before returning to his previous position.

"Good morning," he says huskily in his sleepy voice. I smile, enjoying the warmth of his body and how cozy I feel.

"We better get moving. Otherwise, we will be late for work." He rolls me so I'm on my back and I'm gazing up at him, and then he kisses me before slipping out of bed and walking to the bathroom. I lie there for another minute before getting up and grabbing my bag to find my work clothes.

Once Mike is done in the bathroom, he makes his way down the stairs, calling out as he goes, "I'll start breakfast!"

"Okay," I yell as I walk into the bathroom.

Once I'm ready, I go downstairs to join him in the kitchen. Walking in, I see him cooking at the stove. *Why is it that every time I see him in a suit, I just want to peel it off him?* He is a handsome sight in his navy suit and light-blue shirt, and I would love nothing more than to strip him and have a repeat of last night, but we have no time for that this morning.

"Can I help you?" I ask.

"No, I'm almost done here, and then I will make us coffee." He continues to stir the eggs on the stove.

"I'm happy to learn how to use the coffee machine if you want to teach me when you're done with the food." I feel a flutter in my stomach, the same sickly feeling I had last night. Something is still off with Mike.

"Sure." He dishes up eggs, bacon, and toast, and it smells and looks amazing. *I can't believe he cooked.*

"You didn't have to go to all this trouble. Really, I would have been happy with cereal or buttered toast," I say slowly.

He quickly pecks my lips. "I don't mind. I told you, I love cooking. Now, let me show you how to work the machine."

He shows me how to make coffee on his huge stainless-steel machine, and then we sit down next to each other on the stools and eat our breakfast. *Mmm, this food is cooked to perfection.* We sit in silence as we eat, which is a bit strange for us, but I try not to overthink it. Once we finish, we pop the dishes in his dishwasher—it feels very domesticated doing chores with him.

"Are you ready to go, Alice?" he questions. He scoops up his car keys and wallet.

"Yes, I'll just grab my bag."

We hold hands in the car, and I momentarily forget Mike's strange mood. Once we arrive, he leans over and kisses me. This kiss is hungry, and it feels almost like he is savoring it, trying to memorize it, and I can't shake this weird feeling I keep getting. *Is it because I slept with him? Now that he has conquered me, will I just be another nurse he fucks and leaves?* I try to shake it off, but it's so hard when he keeps giving me such mixed signals. Once we break apart, I smile at him and he smiles back before giving me another soft peck.

"Let's go," he says, and then he exits the car, making his way around it to open my door. Always, such a gentleman.

We enter the elevator and Mike goes rigid next to me... *Why is he acting so strange?*

Chapter 20

Mike

I had another amazing night with Alice, a blow job for the record book, and sex that was better than the first few times we did it, even though I didn't think that was possible. Then to wake up spooning her—it felt so right. It's a shame we aren't fit for each other. I know I won't get her to change her mind on kids and settling down, and it's not fair to her for me to try. I can't even believe I really want this, but Steph is right. My age has a time limit and I do want to be a father one day, but I can't trap her, so I must let her go... even if it crushes me to watch her move on with another man.

I know I have been quiet last night and this morning, and Alice has noticed my behavior, but I can't help it with the thoughts that are running through my head. *This situation is fucked.*

When I don't think my day can get any worse, Amanda is standing there, staring between Alice and me and smiling knowingly. *Fuck. Why does she have to be here?* The elevator feels like it's moving awfully slow today, but when people exit on the ground floor, I almost run out. I will need another coffee to help me survive the day.

"Hey, Mike. Wait up!" Amanda calls. *Fuuuck!*

I clench my jaw and I turn around to face her. "Yes?" I spit.

Alice is standing outside the elevator, watching me with a confused expression. I nod in the direction of upstairs. She nods her understanding, leaning over to press the button to go up. She doesn't need to see my ex and me talking right now when we already have issues to discuss. I watch the doors close before I drop my gaze to Amanda.

"What do you want?" I ask, and Amanda smirks, which only angers me further.

"Who's that?" She jerks her head in the direction of the elevator.

"None of your business. My life is no longer your concern." I'm fuming; my body is shaking, and my hands are balled into fists.

"I need to talk to you." *Her continued smirking is really pissing me off.*

The muscles in my jaw quiver and I snap. "You know what? Fuck off, Amanda. I don't have time for your shit."

I storm off, forgetting about the coffee, and I take the stairs leading to my floor. I want to burn off some frustration. *Women are fucked.* It's so much easier when feelings aren't involved, and I can just sleep around for fun.

I march into my office, and slamming my door behind me, I practically throw myself into my chair, ready to begin work, which will be a welcome distraction. Alice is on the ward today, so when a knock comes, I growl in frustration. *I swear it had better not be Amanda.*

I snap, "What?" I'm sitting at my desk turning my computer on, and when I glance up and notice that it's Kate, I immediately feel guilty. "Sorry, I'm having a really shitty day." I grimace.

Smiling kindly at me, she walks toward me, holding out papers for me. "That's okay, Dr. Taylor. Here, this is the document you need to fill in about Alice."

I take the papers from her outstretched hands. "Thanks."

Her eyebrows rise a fraction. "Do you need anything? Coffee or water? You look awfully pale today."

Kate has been working with me for ten years, so she is able to tell when something is off and throwing me into a mood.

A deep sigh leaves my lips. "No, thanks. I just have a lot on my mind. I should just get started for the day."

"Let me know if you change your mind." She turns on her heel and strides out of my office, closing the door softly behind her.

I log in and take a breath, leaning back in my chair to close my eyes for a second.

What do I want to do with my life in the next few years? Could I give up marriage and kids for Alice? I don't expect it right now, but maybe in a couple of years—a compromise.

My phone rings on my desk. I pick up the receiver to find that I'm being called to an emergency surgery. As I rush to get there, I hesitate. I should probably call Alice to witness the surgery, but I decide I need the space more right now. I know a part of our agreement was to keep work and our relationship separate, but I need some time to think.

Being in the surgery gives me the adrenaline rush of an emergency situation—I love and crave this feeling. I have such a strong sense of purpose and power in doing this, and that gives me a happiness I can't describe. Arriving to my office late, I realize I still have so much work to catch up on, but I am finding that the space is helping calm me down. I send off a text to Alice.

Mike: *Alice, I have been in surgery with an emergency. I still have heaps to do. Do you think you could find a lift home? I don't want you waiting around all day for me to finish.*

Alice: *I'm happy to wait.*

Mike: *No babe. Go home and I'll call you later.*

CHAPTER 21

ALICE

I FINISH MY SHIFT on the ward and grab my bag from my locker. I grab my phone and see a text from Mike. I scrunch my face up. I haven't heard from him today, and I have no idea where he went, so when I open the text and read it, I sigh loudly at the message, but then I quickly get angry. Why didn't he offer to take me with him into the emergency surgery? He knows I'm here to learn and that I have studied well in order to prove myself. Why will he not allow me to follow when I have worked my ass off to get where I am?

I can't think about him right now and why he is doing this. I need to find a way home soon. I pick up my phone and scroll through my contacts until I find Maddison's name. I decide to walk down to the cafeteria and grab a coffee and stand to the side to wait while I text Maddison. I don't want to call in case she is out or studying.

Alice: *Hey, Mads, sorry to do this, but are you busy?*

Maddison: *No, what's up?*

Alice: *I just finished work and I need a lift home. Mike can't take me home today, change of plans.*

Maddison: *Sure, I'll come now.*

Alice: *Thanks, Mads.*

I grab my coffee and move back to stand to the side when a dark shadow appears over my phone. I wince, and when I peek up, I see that it's Mike's ex, Amanda. *What do you want?* I glare up into her eyes and roll them. I have no interest in her or what she has to say. I'm mad at Mike anyway, so I don't need her drama on top of it.

She clears her throat. "Hi there. It's Alice, right?"

I stare blankly at her, and then I shrug. "I guess."

I'm trying to be subtle about how uninterested I am about speaking with you. She doesn't seem to get the memo. Either that, or she doesn't care. I watch her closely as I put my phone in my bag and take a sip of my coffee, never breaking eye contact. I refuse to appear weak.

"I'm Amanda. Mike's ex." Her smile and voice are almost sickly sweet.

I have been staring for a while when I realize I haven't said a word. "Yes, I'm aware of that. How can I help you?" I reply boldly, hoping she doesn't realize how much she has rattled me.

"I just noticed he was with you this morning, looking very cozy together, and I wanted to warn you that he is going to leave you as soon as he gets what he wants—if he hasn't already," she says.

Now that it's just me and her, I'm able to get a good look at her. We are so different, polar opposites. She is so alluring—a real doll—while I'm average. I put on a front to make myself look tougher, wearing it like armor. Her looks make me feel insecure—and I hate it.

"He can't and won't commit to any woman, and no matter what you think you can offer, you're just wasting your time." She is talking to me like she is my friend, by pretending she is offering me some great advice, when all she is doing is showing me how desperate she is.

She can hardly talk. Not when she left him for his best friend. I think it speaks volume of how "nice" a person she is. The half hour I have left to wait for Maddison can't end quickly enough. I desperately want to get the fuck away from her and this hospital. *What a nightmare.*

I feel a soft muscular arm drape over my shoulders and a large hard male body moves to stand flush with my side. One of my arms is crossed into the bend of the other, holding my coffee and protecting myself. I instantly freeze, until I turn and see Alex standing beside me, stony-faced and staring at Amanda. I feel relieved knowing it's him, and I stand taller even as I soften slightly. His expression is hard, and he's vibrating with anger. Clearly Alex is not a fan of her either, but Amanda doesn't seem fazed by him in the slightest. It feels like there is ice in my blood.

"Amanda, what are you doing?" he barks.

"Nothing, Alex. I'm just talking to my friend, Alice, here." She flutters her eyelashes, saying it like we actually *are* friends. *Ugh.*

"Liar. Alice wouldn't be friends with you. You need to stay the fuck away from Mike and Alice. If I find you bothering either of them again, I will hunt you down and make your life hell. Trying to scare Alice won't bring you closer to Mike. He doesn't want you—get it through that thick skull. You fucked his best friend behind his back. *You* did that—not him. So, fuck right off and move on. Mike deserves to be happy, and you are the last person who could give him that."

"He is such a player, Alex! Come on! He will be so bored with Alice. Look at her. What can she offer?" she scoffs.

I bite my lip. I mentally count to ten, trying to calm my speeding heart rate down.

"You're just a nasty, spiteful bitch!" he shouts.

Amanda just throws her head back and laughs, a wicked throaty laugh that sends goosebumps rising all over me, and I decide I can't stand anymore of this.

I clear my throat, and yell, "Mike and I are none of your business!"

Without waiting for a reply, I turn and glance at Alex, who drops his arm from my shoulders. "Thanks, Alex."

He nods and his lip quirks up on one side before hugging me. I'm on the brink of crying so I step back out of the hug and walk off, standing tall with my head held high. I refuse to stay there for another second. I walk outside and suck in fresh cleansing breaths and look around for

Maddison's car, sipping my now stone-cold coffee. *Fucking great.*

I throw the coffee in the bin and wait for the shock to wear off and for my body to stop shaking. My brain keeps rehashing her words over and over.

My eyes swell with tears, but I refuse to let them fall, because once I open the dam, I don't think I will be able to stop them. I refuse to do this at work in case anyone I know notices me. I have just had to deal with his crazy ex—once again! Alex was kind and supportive, but he's not the person I wanted or needed.

I needed the comfort of Mike's arms blanketing me, and him telling me I have nothing to worry about. Instead, he has been off and distant toward me without talking to me or telling me what's wrong. I spot Maddison's car and relief instantly floods through me. I take a deep breath, quickly walk up, open the passenger door, and jump in, collapsing into the seat.

"Thanks, Mads. Sorry to spring this on you." It feels like I'm talking with a really dry mouth, making me sound off.

"All good. So, are you going to tell me what happened?" Concern etches itself on her face when she gets a look at me.

"Oh my God, Maddy, where the fuck do I start?" My voice is shaky.

I close my eyes, giving myself a pep talk to not cry over him, telling myself he isn't worth the tears. I hit my head against the headrest, frustrated, before blinking my eyes open.

"It's okay. Just tell me everything right from the start. You know I've got you." She smiles and pulls out into the traffic and heads in the direction of home.

Her words set me off and I feel the hot tears spring to my eyes in a second. Then they fall and continue falling for what feels like a really long time. I cover my face with my hands and just cry into them until I have no tears left. I feel Maddy rubbing my thigh, trying to offer me comfort at the same time as driving.

As I cry, I can hear her soft angelic voice coo, "It's okay, I've got you. Let it all out and then tell me what's going on."

After another few minutes, I slowly stop shaking, and as the tears finally ease, I drop my hands from my face and wipe away the remaining droplets with my hands. I'm sure that my face is a snotty mess.

"Sorry, Mads. I have been holding that in for a while. Now, to fill you in. You know how I went to the family dinner last night?"

Her brows rise. "Yeeeah."

"That wasn't a problem. He has such a wonderful family. I got to meet his parents, his sister, Steph—who is pregnant—her husband, Chris, and his brother, Alex. Dinner was lovely. His mom cooked, and they were all really kind and welcoming—it was sweet, actually. Something weird that I did notice though, was that Mike and his dad seem to have some kind of tension between them." I frown.

"Really? I wonder why?"

"I don't know what's going on there, but they didn't talk to each other much and Mike avoided him as much as possible. It's super weird and I don't know if everyone knew something but me. They all seemed to love me, but near the end of dinner Mike was super quiet." I replay the night in my mind as I tell Maddison the story. "He wasn't rude, just... off. Then when we got to his house, he was quiet and distant. It was like he'd started pulling away from me. This probably sounds weird, but I just feel it."

Her brows crease. "Hmm, that does sound strange, and you can't recall any conversations at dinner that could have caused his mood to shift?" she questions as she tries to help me figure it out.

I think about it, but I really can't recall any odd topics or responses from Mike. The only odd gesture was between Mike and his dad, but that had nothing to do with Mike being off with me.

I shake my head. "No, Mads, it was such a nice dinner." I feel like I'm losing my mind over it. I keep thinking about it over and over in my head.

"And to continue, we get to his house and have the most amazing sex. I then shower and after I get out, I notice he is on his side of the bed, facing away from me."

"What?" Maddison gasps. "No cuddles or kisses? Just... nothing?"

"Uh-huh. I was so tired that I actually passed out pretty quickly, and when I woke up, he was spooning me." I smile at the memory.

"Aww," she coos at me, placing her hand over her heart.

I laugh. "It was nice, yes, but then he got up and was quiet again. Don't get me wrong, he wasn't rude, but he was different. You get me? Or am I totally confusing you now?"

"No, I'm following. Continue," she encourages.

"Today, I got a text from him saying he is staying back at work, something about an emergency surgery and paperwork, and can I grab a lift with someone because he doesn't want me waiting for him. I'm supposed to be going to these surgeries with him, so I don't know why he didn't ask me."

"Okay. The quiet is fine, some guys can be like that, but the fact he has been quiet and distant, and then just sends you a text to get a lift home with someone else. That's just fucking rude. Why didn't he come visit you on your floor or call you?" She is annoyed for me. I can see her jaw ticking. I'm relieved she understands. I don't feel quite so crazy for worrying about this.

"Oh, it gets better." I start laughing and she turns to look at me, raising her eyebrow.

"Oh, God, that doesn't sound good." She winces. "What happened? Come on, hit me with it."

"I decided to grab a coffee and wait in the café for you, when his ex-girlfriend, Amanda decided to come up to me and start warning me about Mike. She was saying some shit about how once he gets what he wants, he is going to leave me if he hasn't already, and that he can't commit to any woman."

"Whoa, no fucking way!" she blurts.

"Yeah, and she was even nice enough to tell me how much of a player he is, and how he will be bored with me 'because what can I offer?'" I wince because that comment cut deep.

Maddy hits the steering wheel. "What do you mean 'what can you offer?' Fuck, you are such a beautiful and intelligent person. He is so lucky to have you! I wish I'd been there to give her a piece of my mind."

"It's okay. Mike's brother, Alex, came up and defended me. He told her to fuck off."

I'm laughing, but in all seriousness, talking about it with Maddison brings the shakes back on. "This is why I didn't want a relationship. They always leave, or they aren't happy with just one woman." I start to get emotional again. My eyes don't have any tears left. Otherwise, I would be crying again.

"Don't give up. They aren't all like that."

Fuck guys. They always let me down and always leave me. And when I love them, they hurt me. The feelings that come over me hurt my heart, and it's a feeling I have had once before, and I never ever wanted to feel it again. I guess I should be happy I never told him I loved him. *I love him.*

Maddison pulls up the drive at home. "Take a shower. It will help you feel better. While you clean up, I will order some takeout and ice cream. We can relax and watch Netflix. Sound good?"

I'm not that hungry, but I don't want to sit alone thinking in bed, so I nod. "Yeah, thanks."

By the time I've showered and dried off, Tahlia is home, and dinner is here.

Maddy hands me a pizza box. "Come, let's sit, eat, and binge-watch *Friends*. By the way, while you were showering, I told T about what happened to save you from retelling it. I hope you don't mind."

I half smile up at her. "Thanks, I definitely don't mind."

Tahlia looks at me with sad eyes and says, "Boys suck."

I chuckle. "That's putting it nicely. Let's just enjoy our night, no more boy talk."

CHAPTER 22

MIKE

THE NEXT DAY, I'M in my office filling in a variety of patient-related paperwork. Alice has the day off, and I'm doing my best to distract myself. I don't want to stop to think about what I saw when I went downstairs to get a coffee yesterday...*Alice and Alex embracing.*

I have to finish all this paperwork that's sitting piled up in front of me and is also scattered all over my desk. Once this is done, I will go home and have a drink.

I really wanted to talk to Alice about each of our future desires, because it's been playing heavily on my mind. I worry we are on two different paths, but after seeing her and Alex yesterday, I won't bother. I'm doubtful that I could ever completely trust her.

I have a few pages left when I hear a knock on my office door. It swings open, and my head snaps up. My breath hitches in my throat. Standing there is Alex, wearing his usual smirk, and I instantly tense in my chair. He clicks the door shut and my jaw is tight as I watch him stroll on in as if nothing is wrong.

He drags the chair out that Alice normally sits in and collapses down, reclining back with a sigh and making himself comfortable.

"Hey, bro, you're still doing paperwork? You slacker." He chuckles.

My jaw ticks, and I glance at him with dark and assessing eyes. His smug smile is pissing me off. I don't answer him. Instead, I lower my gaze and return to my notes from this morning's surgery.

"How's your shift been today? Any interesting cases?"

"Actually, pretty shit," I mumble.

I peer up at him while my brain runs through the memory of this morning's surgery—another emergency, another car accident, and another death. I suck in sharply, thinking over the emotional roller coaster of the last twenty-four hours. Having him here is fucking with my head. I need space to calm down and think.

"What do you want, Alex? I'm busy," I ask impatiently, gesturing to the papers in between us. I just want him to spit it out and leave me alone.

He exhales a breath. "I know things are getting serious with Alice..." He pauses, waiting for me to reply.

"Yes?" My eyebrows crease, and my gaze meets his.

"I just wanted to mention something." I'm staring down my nose at Alex. His face has a conflicted expression which is sending my body temperature rising. *Mmm, I really don't like where this is going.* I cannot believe what I'm hearing.

"I know. I saw it with my own eyes," I snap before he can speak. I'm furious. I rise from my chair, blood surging to my ears, and I have no more words to say. I lean over the side of the desk, gripping the edges of it, adrenaline pumping my veins. I hear his steps, then he touches my shoulder. That sets me off, and without warning, I shove him.

"Jesus, Mike. What the fuck? He stumbles back with a frown.

"I don't trust you haven't done anything more with Alice. You want her. I have seen it with my own eyes!" I yell.

I turn around and swipe my hand hard across the desk, sending all the papers and objects on top of it flying to the floor. "Fuuuck!" I'm so angry, I'm shaking violently. I don't wait for him to say anything or try to stop me. I turn, grab my phone and briefcase, and then take long strides out the door without a second glance, leaving Alex in my office.

All women are cheaters and there is no such thing as "bro code." This is exactly why I didn't want to fall in love again. My heart is disintegrating. I get inside my car, slam the door shut, and sit in the cool interior, trying to calm down. Once my breathing has evened out again and my hands have stopped shaking, I drive home.

When I get through the door, I toss my keys on the counter and kick my shoes off. I then head to the liquor cabinet and pull out a bottle of scotch and a glass, taking both into the living room. I put some football on and drink the rest of the night away. After a few glasses of scotch, I decide to call Alice. She answers straightaway.

"Mike, we need to talk. You have been strange. Why didn't you let me know about the surgery? You should have called—"

I can hear the anger in her tone. I don't bother answering her questions.

"I need a break." I don't wait for her response. I pull the phone away from my ear and hang up. I turn my phone off after that, so I don't have to deal with anyone. I close my eyes and lie down, passing out from the tired, sad, drunk state that I have found myself in.

Chapter 23

Alice

I SLUMP DOWN IN defeat, dropping the phone beside me as I hang my head in my hands, and a stream of tears begins to fall. I try to blink them away, but there is no stopping them. My heart constricts so tight, it feels like it's being ripped out from my chest, leaving a burning hole behind. Maddy mutters under her breath, and I hear her feet patter as she goes to pick up my phone.

"No, please don't. He asked for a break," I choke out.

I really don't want them to go to battle for me. He isn't worth it. *Fuck.* How am I supposed to work with him? I need the money and we both signed the contract. *I have no way out.*

"Fuck. The asshole must have switched his phone off." I frown at hearing Maddison.

"I'm so sorry." I feel Tahlia sit next to me. She hugs me, cooing and stroking my hair.

"Cocksucker," Maddison mumbles.

I laugh at her choice of words. I feel shattered like a glass that's been dropped off a counter and has disintegrated into a million pieces. *That was my heart.* Losing my dad five years ago was tough, and it took forever to let anyone else in, but Mike weaseled his way into my heart, only to suddenly not want me and leave. I feel the urge to be sick and I push Tahlia off me. Getting up, I run from the living room into the bathroom. I cuddle the bowl and empty my insides over and over until all I can do is dry heave.

I can hear the girls in the distance, but all I can make out is a fuzzy noise over my pain. I stay like that for a while until Tahlia and Maddison pull me up and tuck me into bed. I lie down and stare at the picture in the frame that's beside my bed. The picture is of my family—my mom, dad, Claire, and me, all smiling happily. I don't sleep for what feels like hours, but I must have drifted off at some point because my phone buzzing wakes me up the next day. I reach out to my nightstand and look at it.

Three missed calls from my manager, Kate.

Five missed calls from Blake.

Three missed texts from Blake.

I open the text messages first.

Blake: *Where are you? Kate called me. You had me down as an emergency contact. She's asking if I know where you are.*

Blake: *Are you okay, Alice? Did something happen?*

Blake: *If you don't call me back ASAP, I will hunt you down, bitch.*

That message makes me smile, but I'm not ready to deal with anyone right now. I try to swallow but my throat is dry and gross. I get up to grab a bottle of water from the fridge. I walk out into the living room where Maddison and Tahlia are watching television. They quickly sit up when they hear me. They must have been waiting for hours.

"Can I get you something, Alice?" Tahlia says softly as she walks over to the kitchen counter.

I shake my head. I can't talk until I drink something. I open the fridge, grab a bottle of water, and chug it down.

"Are you okay?" Tahlia asks.

When I finish the bottle of water, I pop the empty bottle in the bin and turn to them. "No, thanks, girls." I half smile and wince at the pain in my throat and at how scratchy my voice is. "No, but I guess I will be or should I say, have to be." I glance up sadly at Tahlia.

The girls' eyes hold a mix of sadness and helplessness, which brings tears to my eyes. But I refuse to let them fall. I walk to the kettle and flick it on to make tea, then I grab a cup, turn around, and lift it up to silently ask if they would like one. They both nod, so I grab two extra mugs and grab the tea bags and make us all tea. I clutch the hot cup and carry it to the couch when I remember work and Blake.

"Ugh, girls, could you do me a favor?" *I sound really rough.* "Could you call Blake and tell him what happened? I can't bear to talk or to work, so I know he can do it for me. Tell him I won't be in today."

The girls look at each other before looking back at me. "He called us already and we told him. I'm sure he will tell Kate you're sick, but I will call and make sure he does," Tahlia says, walking off to call Blake.

I expect he'll come around at some point when he is off work, but at least he can tell Kate I'll be off, and then I can just sit and be miserable for the day. I don't want to face the hospital. The thought of working with Mike nearly makes me sick again. I need to get my head and heart sorted before heading back there. I need to get my power back, but that day is not today.

For the rest of the day, we watch back-to-back episodes of *Friends* and drink lots of tea. I haven't got much of an appetite, so I only nibble on some cookies. The girls have taken today off from their studies and work to hang out with me. I appreciate the support even if they aren't going through it themselves. Just having them here makes me feel less alone.

The doorbell rings. *I didn't realize the girls ordered takeout. I wonder what they ordered.* Blake is walking toward me and seeing his face makes me instantly start to cry again.

"Oh, honey, don't cry. Please. I'll start crying and that's no good for anyone. It's not a good look. I have the ugliest cry."

I smile on one side. It's half-assed, but I am trying. I stand up and hug him. The fact that he came here to check on me means so much to me. After a little bit, I feel more settled, and I take a deep breath and step back, giving him a strained smile.

"Thanks for coming here tonight. I appreciate it, but you didn't have to. You must be tired from work."

"Of course, I had to come! For you not to turn up at work and then to ask for a day off, everyone is worried. Plus, what are friends for?" He rubs my back.

Oh God. My mouth opens. *I didn't even think of that.* "What will I tell them?" Frowning, I look at Blake for answers.

"I just told them you were really sick. Kate was really worried. But I said you will be fine for tomorrow. You will be okay by then, won't you?"

"I don't know what to think or feel at the moment. I'm still in shock, and also confused. Why did he end it?" Looking down, I let a breath out. "What did I do?"

"Honey, you did nothing wrong. Don't say that." I didn't realize I said it out loud. I thought it was just in my head. Blake is hugging me now and rubbing his hands up and down my back. I sigh because it feels so nice.

"It's just how I feel. I'm going to shower quickly, and then I need to eat." I push away from Blake. I need to freshen up. I feel disgusting and I want to put on fresh sleepwear.

"We will organize dinner while you shower, and it will be done for when you are out. How does that sound?" Tahlia asks.

"Perfect. Thanks, T."

I leave them to sort out dinner, then go into the bathroom to shower. I just want to be alone for half an hour. Turning it on to hot, I stand under the scalding water and wail. The burn on my back is giving me the feeling that I crave, and I slide down the shower wall and cry into my legs, feeling safe that the water will drown out the sound so I won't have any of them worried and rushing in here.

I sit and cry until the water runs cold, and then I stand up and rinse. Jumping out, I look at myself in the mirror and wince when I see that I look like death. My face is ghostly white, both of my eyes are red and bloodshot, and the skin around them is puffy.

I walk into my room in a bathrobe. I open my wardrobe and see his clothes that I wore home after our first date folded on the shelf, staring back at me. I shiver with vivid recollection and quickly rip open the sleepwear drawer, taking a set out and slamming the door closed, not ready to face anything that reminds me of him yet.

Not feeling hungry now, I walk out and announce, "I'm so tired, guys. I'm going to jump in bed. Thanks for coming over, Blake. You really didn't have to. Thank you." I hug each of them individually.

"Anytime, hon. I'll call you tomorrow. Have a good sleep. I'm sure you will feel better after that."

I smile faintly, then look at Tahlia and Maddison. "Night, girls." I wave at them all and turn to my room.

"Night," they both say back.

I check my phone before sliding under the covers—no new texts or messages. He hasn't bothered to check on me. *Great.*

CHAPTER 24

MIKE

I WAKE UP TO the worst migraine. *How much did I drink last night?* My head is thumping so hard it feels like it's about to explode. I try to sit up, but I feel like I want to vomit, so I just roll over and throw my arm over my eyes. My stomach starts to growl, and I strain to remember when I last ate. I don't even remember eating dinner last night. Come to think of it—*I didn't*—I last ate a sandwich for lunch from the café.

I need to get up and find some food or order something greasy to kill this hangover, but I'm still so tired, and I end up falling asleep for another hour.

I push myself up off the couch and enter the walk-in pantry and grab some bread to toast. I use my phone to order some takeaway to be delivered. I'm thinking of a greasy cheesy burger and fries with a large Coke, so I order McDonalds and eat the toast until the fast food arrives. My head still hurts, so I grab some painkillers from the medicine cabinet. I take them and settle onto the couch to watch some football while I dive into my food.

Turning on my phone, I notice missed calls from Alex, my mom, and one from Alice. Not in the mood to deal with anyone today, I put my phone away and spend the remainder of the day watching TV and sleeping.

The next day, I get up and hit the gym to sweat out the disgusting feeling of the shit drink and food I consumed yesterday. My mind is a mess. I keep getting flashes of Amanda, my dad, and then lastly, Alice and Alex. All of this is pissing me right off. Thinking of them while running on the treadmill pushes me to turn up the speed. For ten minutes, I run faster and faster until I'm dripping with sweat.

By the time I finish, I'm heaving and trying to catch my breath. My chest burns as I suck in each stinging breath. I pushed myself to the point of pain, but it's helping soothe my anger. When I finally compose myself, I move over to the weights section and work out for another hour. The frustration has helped me lift a lot more weight than I normally would, and my muscles are throbbing from the exertion.

Even though the blood is pounding in my ears, it doesn't stop my mind from replaying all the moments we've shared together. Including the dinner date. The way her eyes brightened in awe, and the gorgeous smile she wore all night. Fuck!

Why am I thinking of her and our happy times?

I was so sure she was different, but of course I was wrong. I leave the gym, and as I get to my car, my phone lights up. Looking down to see who's calling, I groan. *Alex.* I decline the call and carry on with my day. I'm not in the mood for his shit or his shitty excuses.

I scroll through my contacts and see one of the casual women I used to call and hit dial, but I can't bring myself to go through with it, so I hang up after the first ring. When she calls back, I don't answer it. *I have never been this messed up over a woman before.* I drive home with the plan to get through some more work, to take my mind off everything and get ahead.

CHAPTER 25

ALICE

I'M BACK AT WORK today, and my heart is still crushed. I hate that I'm going to run into and have to work with Mike. Actually, I'm dreading it, because I know I look like a mess. I have hardly eaten because I have had no appetite. My stomach hasn't been feeling right, and I just want to sleep or throw up.

When I arrive at work, I go straight to Kate's office. I knock on the door and wait.

"Come in," she calls.

I open the door and I let out the breath I was holding, relieved to see that Mike isn't in here. I smile at Kate to ease the tension that's clearly written on her face. She stays seated at her desk. I wander into the office, clicking the door shut behind me.

I swallow. "Good morning, Kate. I'm so sorry about yesterday. I was so sick I couldn't get out of bed. I must have eaten something bad," I lie as I drag a chair out and sit down.

She shakes her head. "No, don't be sorry, Alice. I was really worried. It's not like you to not be at work or at least call me. I'm just glad you're okay." Her expression and voice are full of concern.

"I'm better now and I'm sure I'll be back to normal soon." My tone is apologetic as I answer.

"Mike has a conference to attend, so he won't be in this week. Please, can you hang out in there today and organize his paperwork? For some reason, when you're not around it's a disaster."

I smile. I uncurl my fists that I didn't realize I had coiled up so tight.

"Oh, Kate, thank you. Are you sure? I don't want anyone angry or thinking that I'm getting special treatment. I'm sure I'm fine to work on the ward if that would be more helpful."

She frowns. "No, Alice, you need to ease back in and if you feel like you need to leave early, please let me know."

I smile gratefully. "Thanks, I will. I'll be in Mike's office if you need me."

"Call me if you need anything," she says seriously, eyeing me sideways.

I chuckle. "Yes, Kate, I am fine—really."

I stand up and walk out her door, straight into Alex, who is about to knock on Mike's door.

"Morning, Alice." Alex grins as if everything is fine. *Doesn't he know his brother dumped me?*

I squint and look more closely at Alex's face. He has a concerned expression. "Are you okay?" Not letting him get a word in, I continue, "You look rough."

He laughs, but then stops, his tone becoming serious. "I'm fine, and I don't want to discuss it."

I whisper harshly, "Alex. Tell me, *now.*"

He sighs, sensing he won't win this battle. "Mike and I had a little disagreement, but it's fine. It was a misunderstanding." He tries to walk off, but I grab his wrist, stopping him.

"What? Are you serious?" My mouth is slack with shock, and my brows crease in confusion.

"Alice, I'm not having this discussion with you. Is Mike in today?" He nods in the direction of the door.

"No, Kate said he is at a conference for a week."

He sighs. "Well, I'm off then. I'm just trying to catch him."

"What does that mean? Alex, what is going on?" I plead.

"I honestly don't know. That's what I am trying to find out," he huffs.

"I'd better start work." I push open the door, but before I go through, I watch Alex walk off toward the elevator.

What the hell, Mike? What the fuck is going on?

The moment I walk through the office, I get smacked in the face by his scent, and my eyes prick and begin to fill with tears.

I refuse to let him affect my work. I *need* this job. I *need* the money. He will not ruin this for me. I'm strong and I can get through this.

I get to work reorganizing the office and sorting the paperwork. The papers are just skewed all over the desk again. I look over at the bookcase and remember I haven't brought his Tabner's book back, so I make a mental note to be sure I do that.

The week actually goes by pretty quickly, and I'm still so relieved he hasn't been here. I feel the stronger and more powerful Alice slowly returning. Time has gotten away from me, and I should have been out front ages ago. I hurriedly put away a patient's file, then grab my bag and head out. As I scamper toward the elevator, I see Mike ahead of me, and I realize he hasn't noticed me because he is talking to a group of doctors. I quickly dart behind a wall, panting as adrenaline runs through my veins. I watch them until they pass, and as they do, I check Mike out from behind.

Mike is in a stunning designer pale-blue suit and pink shirt. *Who knew pink and pale blue could look so good together?* Obviously, Mike does, because the suit is perfectly tailored to his physique. I notice the group are all engaged in whatever he is saying. They look mesmerized, and I remember feeling the same way, getting lost in his intelligent and charming personality. He has an aura about him that screams power and success. It sucks you in.

Once I realize I'm alone again, I quickly walk to the elevator and press the *Close Doors* button. While keeping an eye on the direction they went in, I watch carefully in case they come back. I'm relieved when they don't and the doors finally shut. Alone in the elevator, I manage to breathe for the first time since seeing him again.

The day was so full on that I'm wrecked when I eventually get home. I had a great day, but now I'm mentally and physically exhausted.

I'm going to grab some fresh clothes to put on after I take a shower when I see his clothes in my wardrobe again. I pick up the sweatshirt and bring it up to my nose and inhale deeply. It still smells like him. Closing my eyes, I remember the night I wore them. It was the best night we had together. Mike was in his most raw and honest state. *Where did we go wrong? Ugh, I miss him so much.*

I put the loungewear and Tabner's book near my bag and write a note for Mike. I will leave these in his office tomorrow when I put the book back. I need to move on.

No matter how much it hurts.

Chapter 26

Mike

CONFERENCES ARE DRAINING AS hell. Although, there was a positive that came out of having one this week—it gave me another day's break from seeing Alice. There was no way I would be ready to deal with her so soon. I needed time to think. The conference consisted of the usual kissing the hospital board's ass, along with giving tours and talking to the funding committee members. In total, I'm forced to spend a twelve-hour day talking, not one of my passions. I say what I have to when asked, but I prefer to be with my patients and save lives. *Isn't that the goal of becoming a surgeon?*

When Kate pulled me aside last week and informed me that Alice was off sick with an unknown illness. I had to hold myself back from asking her too many questions. Her plan is to ease Alice back into work with shorter days, meaning definitely no committee meetings. The hospital board and committee left beaming with pride and offering to donate more money, which is always the goal. Equipment and research are what every hospital needs. The primary need for every hospital is money.

When Kate first told me, I felt a twinge of guilt and then I remembered that she doesn't want the same future and I can't trust her. Considering Alice's passion and drive for nursing, it really surprised me she took a day off.

Walking through the corridors, I feel a rise in adrenaline as I get closer to my office.

I slowly open my office door and sigh in relief. I'm here first. Noticing immediately that everything is back in order, just the way Alice does it. I carefully scan the office and take note of how clean the dark wooden desk looks. Now I can see the polished surface—no more papers strewn everywhere. I love the feeling of having a clean space. I just don't seem to know how to keep it like this.

I'm walking around my desk to sit down in my chair when my phone rings in my pocket. I pull it out and glance down, noticing Mom's name flashing across the phone screen. I can't avoid her forever and it's not her fault one of her sons is a dick. Answering before it goes to voicemail again and before Alice gets here. Running my hand through my hair, I take a deep breath and accept the call.

"Mom."

"Mike, where have you been? I have been trying to reach you all week, and you haven't been answering your phone. I have been really worried about you. I'm too old for this type of stress." She is talking fast, making it hard to follow. I take a seat and turn my computer on while listening to her.

I feel a pang of guilt in my gut. *I hate worrying Mom with my problems.* "Mom, I'm fine. I'm just really busy at work. I didn't mean to worry you. Really, calm down, please."

"Are you sure?"

"Mom, everything is fine. I promise." I sigh.

I hear the door click and look up from my desk to watch as the door opens slowly. I feel my body stiffen, awaiting Alice to enter. I have my phone against my ear and my other hand is gripping my armchair in a death grip. My heart is beating so hard and fast in my chest, I feel like I'm back on the damn treadmill. *Why does she have to have this effect on me?*

My eyes track her as she carefully enters my office, and when I notice she is holding a large bag, I frown. *What's in there?* She strolls to the desk quietly and I watch her place it on the floor, just next to the desk. She then opens the bag. I can hear the rustling of it, and I see her retrieve a book, which I notice is the Tabner's I lent to her. She hasn't looked in my direction yet—or at me at all.

My mom is still talking in my ear, and I make sure to respond with a "Hmm" here and there, so she still thinks I am listening, but my eyes don't leave Alice. She returns the borrowed book to the shelf, sliding it into the gap.

I snap my eyes away before she realizes that I'm checking her out. I go back to the phone call, attempting to concentrate on my mother.

"Well, I'll bring some dinner over when you're finished at work. Is there anything in particular you feel like for dinner?" she asks.

"No, anything will be great. Okay, I'll see you later."

"Okay, son. I love you."

"I love you too," I say and hang up. The corner of my lip lifts as I gaze down at my computer. I have really missed my mom. I hate that I've been ignoring her phone calls, but I've been snapping at everyone lately, and I don't want to do the same to her. She doesn't deserve to be on the receiving end of my asshole behavior.

The clearing of a throat pulls my attention from the computer. I glance up in the direction of the noise and I'm taken aback. Stilled into shock, her face is pale, her beautiful blue eyes are now sunk deep into the sockets and there is a dark shadow under both of her swollen eyes. *What happened to my Alice?* It's like the life has been sucked out of her—or maybe she really was sick. She is still beautiful, but she has lost the sparkle in her eyes. I guess I should be glad she is hurting—but truthfully, I'm not. It's splintering my heart. You can't flick the switch off how you feel, like you would a light switch. Time heals all wounds, even the deepest of cuts.

"You look different."

"Err, thanks, I guess," she mutters under her breath.

I want to ask if she should really be here, but then that would mean more conversation with her, and right now, I'm not interested in it. I can tell she is awaiting direction, so I quickly look at our calendar and emails—bingo—we have an interstate trip planned next week and I don't know if she is aware.

"Next week we have another interstate trip, so we need to prepare for that this week. I'm speaking at the event as a guest speaker, so it's important to be prepared."

"Makes sense. How can I help?"

"I'll type out some notes now, and then can you make a PowerPoint presentation?"

"Yes, I can." Her pleasing attitude is not convincing. I miss the smart-ass Alice. *Where has my feisty woman gone?*

She pulls out the chair in front of my desk and sits down opposite me, then reaches for the mail and starts sorting through it. I look away because I want to say something, but I don't know what. *What's wrong with me? Why my brother? Why can't we want the same things in the future?* But nothing leaves my lips. I pinch them together to prevent anything coming out that isn't work related, and I turn my focus back to the task at hand. Getting the notes done to give her something to do means there's less chance of a conversation happening between us.

I wish in this instance that I had a window, because it's feeling hot and stuffy in here with her and I'm craving fresh air. The more I'm around her, the more I remember our good times. I run my fingers through my hair and type away. Time slips away, and it's not until I hear Alice speak that I stop.

"Thanks for today, Doctor Taylor."

I glance up from my papers and I grunt back, "Thanks." I put my head back down, but I glance up at the bag Alice has placed on my desk.

"This is yours. Thanks for letting me borrow them."

My brows crease, and I stand up and gaze down at her. Alice's eyes are sad, but there is still a lingering heat in them. I see fire and desire—the air turns thick with it, and my chest is desperate for air. But I cannot peel my eyes away. She is everything that I want, but I just can't. I need a little time. Even staring at her and knowing she would love nothing more than for me to spread her on this desk and fuck her hard, can't change how I feel. *Having a heart sucks. I wish I were the tin man.*

Alice walks out, and I open the bag. Peering inside, I see my sweats and a card. I grab the card, open it, and read.

Mike,

I'm returning the clothes I borrowed.

Alice X

Looking at the gray loungewear, I'm reminded of our first date. I get flashbacks of how she came to my house dressed in the tightest and sexiest dress I have ever seen. The memory makes me smile because she thought it was just going to be dinner, but the way her face lit up when she got to see the second part was priceless. That night was the most effort I have ever put into a date, and she is the first woman to ever step foot into my new house. The sex under the stars still features nightly in my dreams—*she wore this loungewear much better than me.*

I scrunch the card in my hand and go home.

After having a quick shower, I get dressed and I'm just about to make my way downstairs when I hear my front door open.

"Hello, Mike," she yells.

"Hey, Mom. Come on in." I walk up to meet her and hug her. Her scent, which makes me think of home, surrounds me with the mix of floral and spice that makes my heart feel light. "Did you want a drink? I was just going to make myself a coffee."

"Yes, love, a coffee would be great. I'll make it. I'm sure you had a busy day."

She tries to walk past me, but I hold out my hand. "Mom, please, I'm a big boy. I can make us one. You're not my slave and you know I appreciate your help with my house, but I'm not incompetent." I smile down at her before turning and stepping to the coffee machine.

My mom is my world. I value the time I get with her now. We missed out on lots of family time, spending more time at our friends' houses and eating with their families, just to get the normal family dinners. Our parents worked long hours—we had chefs and nannies, but it's not the same. I think she feels guilty and keeps trying to make up for it now. But I'm over it. *I get it.* She wants to provide for us in case my dad was ever to leave the family.

"So, love, did you want to talk about the real reason you've been avoiding me and the family?"

I turn around to face her, hurt filling my eyes. "Great, so Alex has gone running to you?"

"No. But he had no choice but to talk to me. You're avoiding everyone. I was worried." Her arms are crossed in front of her, and her eyebrow is raised in question.

"He deserved it," I huff.

"No, Mike, you're wrong. He didn't, and if you would listen to him, you would know that. You're so damn stubborn."

I turn back around and try to concentrate on the task of making coffee, then steady my shaking hands by putting the coffee pods in the machine and some milk into the frother. Anger is rising in my body and it's not her fault, so I don't want to take it out on her. I place a cup of coffee in front of her while meeting her eyes.

"What?" I ask, exhausted.

"He isn't your father." She spits the words out with such venom, they are aimed to sting—it works. I wince.

I take a breath. "He danced with and kissed Alice, Mom. And then I caught them in the cafeteria together."

"Yes, I'm well aware of that, but not when you and Alice were together. He isn't like Liam or your father. Don't treat him like them. That is totally unfair. I don't know about the café, but I know he isn't interested in Alice. He has been talking to someone else."

My eyes widen at her confession. *Who is Alex talking to?* I falter, taking a step back.

She continues without waiting for me to respond. "I'm sorry you had to witness your father cheating on me with his secretary, but it's not a reason not to trust or forgive people. I'm over it and we have worked hard to get where we are. We had you kids to think about, and we worked hard on our relationship together. I am happy."

I swallow hard. I haven't even taken a sip of my coffee yet, but I need to. I need to moisten my tight, constricted throat. I remember that day like it was yesterday. I had come to my parents' clinic to discuss my rotation selections. My parents owned the clinic, so we all had a key. I didn't call. I just turned up and walked in. I walked into the vision of their young redheaded receptionist and my father in a passionate embrace—half-dressed, with her lipstick on his lips. I was so stunned I dropped the keys I was holding when I walked in. I remember looking straight into her eyes, and the shock on her face is etched in my memory. Her emerald eyes were scared and wild as she fumbled, trying to scramble out of his arms. I remember saying the vilest things to them, but I had never been so disgusted.

My dad was fumbling with his clothes when I approached him. With fire burning in my eyes, I snarled, "You will go home and tell Mom your side before she hears mine. I'm out of here. I can't stand the sight of you." I walked off, straight back outside, and got into my car.

I haven't spoken more than a few words to him since that day. My mom wants us to go to therapy, but I just have no desire to spend any energy on him. My time is valuable, and I won't waste a minute of it with him.

I know he told my mom that night because she called me the next day to say they were going to therapy and to not say a word of this to anyone, including Alex and Steph. Honestly, I wouldn't want to tell them because it would be like reliving it again and I have no desire to. I was so hurt for my mom. She worked hard at the clinic and also at home whenever she could, and I will never understand why she stayed with him. Obviously, the receptionist was replaced, and no one has spoken about it until today.

I sip my coffee, deep in thought.

Her voice breaks me from the memory. "I told Alex to come here so we can discuss it over dinner. Please, Mike, listen to him... for me. He has no feelings for Alice. You have it all wrong. You and Alice are so perfect for each other. Everyone can see it. You love her, son."

"Don't be ridiculous, Mom,"

She chuckles. "If you didn't love Alice, this wouldn't matter to you. You wouldn't be heartbroken, moping around, and upset at your brother. You have been with so many women..." I eye her carefully. *How does she know?* I never introduce my casual flings because I don't bring them here. "And no one has come this close to you, not even Amanda. Alice is a sweet soul, kind, and with the biggest heart. I know she loves you too." She winks at me with a smirk on her face.

I shake my head. "I doubt that, Mom. She gave me my stuff back. Plus, I've treated her horribly, so she probably never wants to see me again." I shake my head.

"Not always, son. We women don't like to have reminders lying around and bringing up memories of happier times. You need to talk to her. There's something worth fixing there." She is smiling and drinking her coffee. The doorbell rings and Mom glances up from her cup. "Answer that, it's your brother."

I nod, put the coffee on the counter, and walk toward the door to let him in.

Alex is standing on the doorstep in jeans and a long-sleeve khaki top, a cautious expression on his face. "Hey, bro."

I pull the door open wider to allow him through with a smirk. "Hi, come in."

He chuckles as he walks into my house, and I close the front door behind him.

Following him into the kitchen.

"Thanks, I'm assuming Mom is here and has already spoken to you? That's why you're laughing and not shoving me some more." He has stopped walking to turn around and face me and is now looking at me with a question in his eyes.

"She sure is. The queen of meddling and fixing things is here. I think she is going to cook us up a big dinner. Did you want to come and watch the game with me?"

"Sure."

"Do you want a drink?"

"Yes, please. A beer would be great."

Mom isn't here, so she must be in my laundry room. I grab a beer for Alex, pick up my coffee, and lead him into the living room.

I clear my throat. "I'm sorry for shoving you. I just, ugh, fuck, the Amanda shit has screwed with me, and I don't really trust anyone."

He looks up, nods, and takes a sip from the bottle. "I get that, but I danced with and kissed Alice once at the club. We spoke about that. She isn't interested in me and I'm not into her—she wants you, man." He winks.

I frown. "But I came down to the cafeteria at work and I saw you had your arm around her all cozy. And then you came into my office the very next day and I lost my shit."

"You mean the day Amanda was baiting Alice?"

I sit up. "What, no, what are you talking about? What did she do to Alice?" My lips thin with irritation.

His brows crease. "Didn't you see her standing in front of us?"

"No, I didn't see her there at all! I wouldn't have pushed you if I did. What did she fucking say?"

"Just telling Alice that you will get bored, you will leave her, and you know... just a bunch of shit to make you sound like a player. So, I put my arm around her to say, 'I got you, sister.' Amanda can be intimidating, and you of all people know that. Anyway, I told her to fuck off." His face splits into a shit-eating grin.

I take a deep breath. "She hasn't done anything to deserve any mistrust. My head is just so fucked up."

"You two are meant to be. You will work it out." He smiles.

I nod, leaning back into the couch, and continue to watch the football game in silence. Mom prepares us all dinner, and we sit around my dining table eating and talking together until they leave. *Now, I'm alone again.*

Getting changed upstairs, I find that my mom has put the clothes Alice returned on an empty shelf in my wardrobe. Laughing out loud to no one in particular, I shake my head. She really does behave like I'm still a boy, and when I walk over to the bed, I notice she has opened the note Alice wrote to me, leaving it on my bedside table.

Taking a deep breath, I prepare to relax for the night. I make a mental note to book a therapist appointment and talk to Amanda. Then I can work on getting Alice back, and the best way to start that is by having a good time on our trip.

Chapter 27

Alice

I can't bear the thought of going away with Mike next week when I am struggling being around him as it is. My emotions are all over the place. I am trying to eat more to regain some of the weight I lost, especially after noticing the horror on Mike's face at the sight of me. *Like I haven't looked in the mirror and seen it already.* I know I need to sort myself out, so before I leave today, I need to talk to Rachel and Kate.

Spotting Rachel on the ward, I walk up to her and clear my throat to get her attention. "Excuse me, Rachel, could I talk to you for a moment?"

A frown flashes across her face before the fake smile is quickly plastered on. "Of course. What's up?" She is glancing nervously around to make sure no one can see us having this conversation. *It's like she is embarrassed to be seen with me.* Shoving that thought aside, I say what I need to say.

"Would you take my spot next week to go on a trip with Doctor Taylor? Something came up and I can no longer go," I lie.

"Um, duh, of course. That would be amazing. Thanks!" she squeals.

I internally roll my eyes. "Could you just not mention it to him until you're already at the airport? I'd like to keep it as a surprise. I'm sure he will be thrilled to have you there." I give her the biggest, fakest grin and hand over the documents she'll need. *Take that, Mike.*

I swallow the bile that tries to rise up my throat. I hate lying, but I need to look after myself. *I cannot do this trip, no way!* Him being around all the time would suffocate me. I *need* more time and space. Instead of going on the interstate trip with Mike, Blake has plans to take me on a fun day outing. I have no idea where he's planning to go, but I look forward to the surprise. If anyone is going to be able to get me out of my funk, it's Blake.

The last stop before heading home for the day is Kate's office. I hand her my request form for a much-needed week off so I can visit Mom and Claire.

CHAPTER 28

MIKE

A WEEK LATER, I dial the number for a psychologist I have found. She is highly recommended and is constantly being raved about, and her waiting list shows how good her reputation is. Lucky for me, someone canceled this week. The next person I plan on destroying is Amanda. *If you fuck with what's mine, you will be burned.*

I've already rang my lawyer and demand that she arrange a restraining order against her for me and Alice. I don't want her near either of us again. She is harming my future. As I finish filling in the papers, there is a knock. *Who could that be?*

I'm not expecting anyone at the moment, but I see a shadow appearing and realize it's Alice. Her brows are creased. "Sorry, Doctor Taylor, I, err, know you're probably not expecting me. I got a weird call and an email this morning about some restraining order against Amanda. I didn't organize that. Did you have something to do with it?"

I huff from my chair, my nostrils flaring with pressure, and I stand up to walk around the desk. "Yes, Amanda is not to be trusted. She is harmful to you and me. I will not tolerate her behavior. I will keep us safe." I feel my eyes narrow in anger at her, remembering my little trip.

"While we are on the topic of crazy people. Alice, why the fuck did you send that moron? You should have been there!" I ask.

She looks at me, puzzled, but I can see the wheels turning in her head. But no words leave her mouth. I watch her lips open and close repeatedly, which just makes me twitch. "Alice. Please. I'm talking to you. Answer me, please!" I bellow with frustration, raking both hands through my hair as I pace in front of her.

"I'm sorry. I can't be around you, Mike. It's just too hard for me." Alice is standing there watching me through her big blue eyes.

With the air crackling between us, you wouldn't be able to hear a pin drop in my office, just both of us breathing in the stuffy air. I'm tired of constantly fighting my feelings. I have tried burying them. *Fuck it.* Crossing my office to stand in front of Alice, I grab her face and drag her to me.

Then I kiss her with everything I have. Her lush, pillowy lips follow mine, matching my rhythm. My heart is beating frantically in my chest, and my cock is straining in my pants. *I want her and I fucking need her right now.*

I walk her backward a few steps until she hits my desk. I reach out without breaking our lips and swipe everything onto the floor and lean into her, forcing her to lie on my desk. This has been my fucking dream, having my way on my desk with Alice. *Oh, I have missed her.* I take her top off and she stills. Her eyes pop open and she pushes against my chest, forcing me back.

She shakes her head violently. "No, Mike, I can't do this."

I stumble back, my jaw slack with shock. *Did I do something wrong?* I don't get a word out before she turns and storms out of my office. It's like my brain couldn't register what was happening to get the words out of my mouth.

"Fuck!" I shout to no one as I finish clearing my floor and placing everything back on my desk. Another knock comes and I get up and rush to the door, hoping it's Alice and she has changed her mind. But as the door opens, my smile drops and my back turns to stone. *Amanda.* "Did you not get the message? I can have you arrested just for being here," I spit.

"Please, Mike, why are you doing this? We should be together. I can forgive you for playing around. We both made mistakes. Please, drop the restraining order."

All the hairs on my body are on end and my eyes are blaring my anger directly toward her as I bite out, "You have got to be kidding. Are you fucking high right now?"

"Don't be ridiculous, Mike." She rolls her eyes and puts her hand on her hip.

"You fucked Liam... for *years* behind my back. Don't tell me you forgot that? He was my best friend. I can never forget or forgive either of you. Get the fuck out before I call security!"

My breathing has picked up and I'm so wound up with frustration. *What can't she understand about this?* "I'm leaving, and if you come near Alice or me again, I will call the fucking police."

I open my office door and storm toward the elevator. My back has a layer of sweat coating it from all the tension. The elevator is empty, and I sag against the wall, closing my eyes. *This day can't get any worse.*

CHAPTER 29

MIKE

I HAVEN'T BEEN SLEEPING well for the last few nights. Just thinking about opening up to a complete stranger about my life, to my fears and thoughts—it scares the fuck out of me. I'm always on the go and I never think about looking after myself, especially my mental health. But losing Alice has definitely changed my mind, and I know I need to sort my head out if I want to win her back and have a healthy relationship. I'm done being angry with life. *I can do it—I can talk to a stranger about my feelings. The quicker you get there, the quicker it's done.*

Standing outside the building, my hands start to sweat but I tuck them into my suit pants to keep myself from fidgeting. I walk up to the receptionist and peer around, wondering why it's unusually quiet in here.

I clear my throat and speak softly. "Hi, um, I'm Mike Taylor and I have a five-p.m. appointment with Dr. Keating." I'm leaning over toward her side of the desk so only she can hear me speak, because there are other people waiting in the room and I don't want them hearing my name. I keep turning around and checking to make sure no one I know is here. *Is it too late to run?*

The receptionist glances up from her computer and talks so loudly I inwardly grimace at the volume. "Good evening, Mike. Do you have an insurance card and a referral letter from your local doctor?"

I frown at her, puzzled, and the sweat is now moving toward my forehead. *What is she talking about?* I lean forward again. "No, when I booked the appointment, they never mentioned anything about bringing a referral, but I do have my insurance card." I grab my wallet out of my pocket and hand the card over to her.

She stops typing and takes the card from me, bringing it toward her computer and filling my details in. "No, not everyone does, but just so you know, if you get a doctor referral, you can get a small discount."

I lean back, understanding now. She isn't going to know that money isn't an issue for me. She finishes typing in my details, hands back my card, and I pop it back into my wallet. "Okay, Mike, please take a seat in our waiting room. The doctor shouldn't be long." She points toward the seats where other patients are seated and waiting. *How late is the doctor running?*

"Thank you." I smile and then turn around, scanning the room for a spot to sit. I locate an empty chair in the corner and take a seat. Keeping my head down, I take my phone out and start scrolling through my emails. My leg is bouncing up and down nervously. *How much longer?*

From my left I hear a soft, older woman's voice call out, "Mike Taylor?"

I glance up and notice she is looking around at the few people who are sitting, so I stand and put my hand up to let her know I'm here instead of answering.

As I walk toward her, she notices me approaching and says warmly, "Follow me this way."

We make our way around the receptionist desk. I feel my heart beating fast in my chest, and my palms are starting to sweat again. I feel like I am running a marathon. *What am I doing?* I try to take slow, deep breaths to calm myself down while I follow her into what must be her office. *You can do this. Think of Alice.*

We enter a softly lit room, with a large brown desk that has a chair behind it. In the middle of the room is a cream sofa with a recliner chair beside it. It surprises me that it's not sterile and cold like I had envisioned.

Ushering me to the couch, I let her direct me. "Sorry to keep you waiting. My name is Doctor Anne Keating. Please, take a seat and we will get started."

The couch is soft and comfortable to sit on and I sink into it. I glance up and notice she has walked to her desk to grab a pen and paper. She then steps over to the recliner across from me. Anne looks to be in her mid-fifties, with short, wavy gray hair. She's wearing tortoise shell-patterned glasses and an emerald-green blouse. I feel my back straighten and my body tighten at the sight of the pen and paper in her hand.

She smiles. "Don't worry, Mike. The pen and paper are only for certain notes, like names. Until I get to know the people in your life, I'll need a reference." I drop my shoulders again and relax a little. *Makes sense.* "What brings you here today?"

Looking directly into her eyes, I laugh awkwardly. "Where do I start?" *Help me.*

Anne offers me a kind smile. "How about this—have you seen someone before?"

Shaking my head, I answer, "No, never."

"Well, if there is nothing urgent that needs addressing, then I would love to start with your childhood." She gets her pen and paper ready, and I take a deep breath, then lean back into the couch. *Where do I start?*

I gaze out her window instead of at her and begin speaking. "My family consists of my mom, Margaret, and my dad, Paul. I also have a younger brother and sister, Alex and Steph."

"You are the oldest?" she asks.

"Yes, that's correct."

"Hmm." She writes this down. "How was your relationship with each of your parents?"

"My family are all doctors, including me." I feel embarrassed to say it, but she will understand when I continue, and I know I need to be open to work on myself.

She pops a brow. "Everyone?"

"Yes, my parents are local doctors, and they have their own clinic, although my mom is now retired. My brother is a neurosurgeon, and then my sister is a dermatologist."

"And what are you?"

I laugh. "Oh yeah, I'm an orthopedic surgeon." I'm glad she doesn't seem to have recognized my name. Either that or she is pretending not to know. Regardless, I'm happy she is being quiet about it. She is sitting silently, waiting for me to continue. *Where was I?* "When we were growing up, my parents were always working. My mom was attentive when she was home, but it wasn't the same as having traditional parents."

She is taking notes, but she pauses to ask, "And your dad?"

I take an audible breath and gaze down at my clasped hands before meeting her eyes again. "We were close. He was someone I admired growing up. Yes, he worked a lot of hours, but he would play with us kids when he could."

"What did you mean by traditional parents?"

"We had nannies growing up because my parents weren't always there, and my friends didn't have that. They had parents who took them to school, did homework with them, and had dinner together. Not us. We only had our parents for an hour before bed."

"And how did that make you feel?"

Gazing out the window, I'm unable to face her and I don't answer straightaway, thinking back to how I felt. "I remember at the time being sad and jealous of my friends." I shrug.

"Have you ever told your parents you felt that way?"

I don't ever recall telling my parents anything. I've always been too afraid to upset them. "No."

"How was your relationship with Alex and Steph?"

I grin because I have great memories of times we spent together. "Wonderful."

"Talking about them makes you happy. I can tell by your smile. Your face lit up."

I feel a warm flush spread across my cheeks. "We were so close growing up. We used to play pranks on the poor nannies, and we actually chased a few away over the years." I laugh.

"If you could make any positive changes in your life, what would you make happen?"

This stumps me for a minute, and I frown. *I need to think of the best way to word this.* "I want to be able to trust people in my life wholeheartedly, and improve my relationship with my father." Saying it out loud feels surprisingly good.

"I can help you with both of those, but just so you know, the rebuilding of trust takes time, patience, and work, just as it does to establish it in the first place. What do you feel is the issue with your father?"

"I caught him cheating on my mom. I still feel very angry toward him and also confused as to how and why he would do that to her, and us."

"Have you ever asked him why he did it?"

"No, I can't." *There is no excuse.*

"It is important to talk to him. I know you might feel uncomfortable, but if you find out the reason why and get your feelings out to him, you can then work on your relationship. But you both require dignity and respect in order to rebuild trust. I want you to start working on a few things before our next session. One of those being that you need to start saying what you mean and meaning what you say. You need to stop saying things that you won't follow through on—even the minor things—and give him the benefit of the doubt even just a little bit. This will be hard and you will want to put up walls, which you can at the start, but here and there you should try to let them down."

"But how do I have a conversation without shouting or attacking him? I go from zero to one hundred in a second with him in front of me."

"This entails maturity, to be perfectly frank. You need to give him the opportunity to talk, and you need to work on methods which will allow you to talk about difficult feelings in a way that is helpful and respectful. I want you to let yourself be vulnerable, starting small."

My mouth tightens into a thin line. *How do I do that with someone I can't stand? This is going to be hard and will push me beyond my comfort zone—but maybe that's her goal.*

Anne smiles and leans forward in her chair. "I can see you are shocked, but please listen closely. Trust is built when the other person has the opportunity to let us down or hurt us, but they do not allow it to happen. Take small, gradual steps to rebuild the trust between you. How about going to a sports game or play tennis? Maybe find something you can do that is outside, but will also give you the time to talk. Can you think of anything that you two could do together?"

It doesn't take me long to respond because we both like to do it, but it's currently at different times. *I've been avoiding going when I know he'll be there.* "I guess we could play a game of golf."

"Great idea, and that's all the time we have today. I am sure you have a lot to think about. Thank you for coming. I sincerely hope I didn't scare you off and that you come back." I smile and stand. She follows suit, and once she has put the pen and paper on her desk, I hold my hand out to shake hers. She steps over and puts her soft hand into mine.

"Thank you, Dr. Keating, for your time. I will work on having a conversation with my father and hearing him out. Thank you again. I will be back soon."

I have a splitting headache from all the information I have processed. On the way to my car, I take out my phone, and before I can lose my nerve, I take a deep breath and I quickly type out a message.

> **Mike:** *Can you meet me for a 9-hole game of golf tomorrow at eleven a.m.? I'm ready to talk. Mike*

I press send before I change my mind and decide to delete it. The dots start bouncing around straightaway as he types a response. *I can't believe I'm really doing this. Can I forgive him?*

> **Dad:** *Yes, that would be lovely. Thank you, Mike. I'll see you tomorrow. Love, Dad*

Throwing my phone into the console of the car, I turn on my music and pull out onto the street.

CHAPTER 30

MIKE

WAKING UP EARLY THE next morning, I feel slightly nervous about the day ahead, so I get up and make my way down to the hospital to check on a patient whose health has been declining since their surgery on Thursday. I have been receiving phone calls about the patient all night regarding their low blood pressure and high heart rate. Before meeting Dad, I need to visit the patient, so I won't get phone calls during our time together.

I put my active wear on in case I have time to head to the gym for a quick workout, too. I need to burn some of these nerves off with activity. I don't want to be frustrated when talking to him. I need this to work, to then help me with Alice.

I pull into my parking spot and ride the elevator up to the ward. I chat with the charge nurse to discuss their concerns. After reviewing the patient's chart and assessing their condition, I decide not to take the patient back to the

OR but watch and review instead, as well as creating an appropriate treatment plan.

The nurses are happy, so I take off in order to grab a coffee from the cafeteria before meeting Dad. I come out of the main elevator and glance up, spotting Alice who is ordering something from the barista. I warm at the mere sight of her, my lips twitching with the words I want to say. *What do I say first?* My legs refuse to move, but I force myself to snap out of it and go join the queue.

There are only a few people between Alice and me, and she hasn't noticed me yet, so I use the opportunity to stare and take her in. She has her work uniform on, and I get flashes of memories of her perfectly tight body—she had the softest skin I have ever touched beneath my fingertips. I still crave her.

Looking at her now, all I want to do is walk over and kiss the shit out of her. *Would she let me?* Her hair is tied up in an untidy ponytail and her bangs are all messy over her face. She has no makeup on, but her lips are still pink and pouty, which makes my dick tingle at the thought of wrapping her hair in my hands and yanking it hard while kissing her. She hasn't looked up, but I know behind her bangs is a magnificent pair of vibrant blue eyes. I want to take her back to my office and finish what I started with her on my desk the other day. I shiver with hopeful anticipation.

The barista looks up and winks when he catches my eye. I know all the employees well. I order daily and pay my bill in advance. It makes my life so easy—I added Alice to my bill when we started dating. Even though she knows I pay for her, she hasn't taken advantage of or gone crazy with it, and this is why she is different. I was expecting her to message me about it, but she didn't. I haven't heard from her at all.

After she orders, she moves to stand in the waiting area for her coffee, and my eyes follow her every move. As she walks past where I'm standing and I catch a whiff of her vanilla scent, it causes my pulse rate to rapidly increase.

I hear the barista calling out in the distance, which breaks me from my trance. I glance over, catching him smirking and shaking his head side to side. *Busted*.

I quickly walk up to the counter and sheepishly place my order. "The usual, please."

He nods and I take off in the direction Alice went. She is on her phone, gazing down at it with a blank expression on her face.

I stand directly in front of her, comb my hair back with my hand, then put it in my pocket before I whisper, "Alice."

She jerks her head up. Her beautiful eyes immediately meet mine and widen with shock and recognition. She doesn't say anything as she takes a small step back, which makes my casual smile transform into a big shit-eating grin.

"I miss you, babe. I made a mistake and I want you back."

CHAPTER 31

ALICE

I WAS ROSTERED FOR an early morning shift, and it's a Saturday, so I'm already dead tired. I have been here since six thirty a.m. and I decided to grab a coffee on my break and take a walk to perk me up. I'm still waiting for my order and am passing the time by scrolling aimlessly through Facebook and Instagram. When I hear *his* voice just in front of me, my body goes rigid, and I slip into a state of shock.

I glance up to see a familiar set of dreamy ocean-blue eyes. I am so shocked that no words can form in my brain, and I have to take a small step back while I try to steady myself. The man is overwhelming me all over again. Every one of my senses is heightened in his proximity.

I was not expecting to see him here on a Saturday. Raking my eyes over his body from head to toe, I note that he is wearing workout clothes, sneakers, and a shit-eating grin. *Fuck.* He is sexy, which he knows damn well.

I snap back to reality when the words he's saying register. "I miss you, babe. I made a mistake and I want you back."

That frustrates me so I snap, "I'm not your 'babe.' Do *not* call me that and especially not while you are here. Also, why have you been paying for my bills at the cafeteria? You do realize I can afford it myself, right? Besides, you are the one who broke up with me, so you shouldn't even be doing this!" I'm glaring at him and I stand a little taller. *I'm not taking your shit, you beautiful bastard.*

His smile widens an inch, which annoys me further.

"Yes, I understand. But I want to look after you." He is standing there all cool, calm, and collected, while my body temperature is rising and I'm trying to not explode in public. I take some breaths to help me stay in control.

"Why? I'm not yours to look after, not anymore," I snap, giving him a pleading look. *Why is he is doing this?* "I don't need your help. I earn my own money from having my own career." *I don't need your money.*

Being this close to him means I can smell his scent—so spicy and masculine. Meeting him all those months ago to now working so closely alongside him has given him the power to destroy me and literally bring me to my knees.

"I'll repeat, I miss you, and I care," he whispers, barely loud enough for me to hear. His expression and tone are firm. It's as if he's annoyed at me for not knowing this.

My head is spinning because he is repeating the exact same sweet things he spoke not too long ago. *I can't bear this. I need space.* The barista calls out my order, and relief immediately floods me. *Space, finally! I need air.* I turn my head to see where the barista has put my drink, and I storm off to get it. Unfortunately for me, it's not only my order that's ready, because as I pick up my cup, the barista is putting more orders down.

I can feel Mike right beside me, his body and his size overwhelming me. His hand softly brushes the back of mine, which makes the hairs on my body stand up. I snatch my cup up—too quickly—and spill my coffee on the counter. Sighing, I grab a handful of napkins to clean up the mess.

"Are you okay?" Mike questions.

I turn to see Mike waiting for me, holding his coffee. *Why are you still here?* "Yes, I'm fine. I need to get upstairs; my break is over," I bark and walk off in the direction of the main elevator.

"Alice! Wait! You only just ordered." His stern tone makes me stop in my tracks. *What now?* I fight the urge to turn around. *I hate how he has the power over me with his voice, but I can't seem to ignore it.* His hard and serious expression makes me soften slightly. I sip what's left of my drink and wait for him to start talking. "I need to explain to you why I broke things off. I have my reasons and I want the opportunity to tell you. Please?" The vulnerability in his tone breaks my resolve, shattering something deep in my core. I'm so unsure of what the right thing to do is, but right now, I don't want to hear it.

"I can't, Mike." Before I decide to give him the opportunity to say anything more, I walk off toward the elevator, quickly calling out over my shoulder, "Bye, Mike."

CHAPTER 32

MIKE

How am I going to get her to listen to me? She took off so fast and I don't have the time to chase her right now. I have to meet up with Dad soon. I walk off with my coffee toward the elevator and drink it on my way down to my car.

Driving to the gym, I feel pumped, and the energy starts kicking into action in my veins. I get the best sprints in, and by the time I'm done, I have a sheen of sweat dusting over my skin and trickling down the middle of my chest, making my shirt cling to me. I hit the showers at the gym, get my golf clothes on, then jump in my car and roar down the freeway to the golf resort.

I haven't been to the golf resort with my father in years and I don't know how good he is now. Growing up, he was the one to teach Alex and me how to play and how to do it well. We even competed in a few local competitions, but we didn't want to make careers out of it, although we do enjoy playing for fun and beating each other. Now that I'm here with Dad, it brings back memories of how patient he was when he taught us, and how we did have some good times together.

I spot his four-wheel drive in the parking lot, and I roll up next to it. He isn't in it, so I get out and peer around to see if anyone else I know is here. It's all clear, so I retrieve my clubs out of the trunk. My car isn't the most practical for putting clubs in, but I'm not getting a shit car just to put clubs in. My Aston is my pride and joy and I worked fucking hard for it. It's sexy, powerful, and fast, just like me. If I were a car, this would be it. *Except for Alice nicknaming it Marty... That's not a sexy name.* But I warm at the thought of her, reminding me why I'm here.

I press the lock and drag my all-black Vessel golf bag behind me. Just like my car, my golf bag and clubs are top of the line. I always get questions from fellow golfers admiring my bag while I'm playing.

I reach the entrance to the golf club. Now my palm is sweating, making it hard to keep a good grip on my bag as I slowly walk up to the desk and check in. On my way over, I spot my dad and instantly stiffen. I begin grinding my teeth. *No going back now.* Dad beams and waves like an idiot. I roll my eyes and a dark laugh leaves my lips.

Dad walks over, quickly dragging his bag behind him, and pausing in front of me, he holds his hand out for me to shake. "Hi, son."

I glance down at his hand. *It's now or never.* I take a deep breath and raise my hand slowly, then shake his outstretched hand. He yanks on my hand, tugging me forward, giving me no chance to escape as he pulls me in for a hug and slaps my back.

"Thank you for today," he says into my ear. I jerk back, trying to put distance between us. He releases me and lets me stand back. "You won't regret this."

"I hope not," I murmur under my breath, so he can't hear my negativity.

"Have you checked in yet?" I ask, staring directly into his eyes. They are the exact same color as mine. There is no mistaking him for anyone other than my father.

Shaking his head, he replies sheepishly, "No, I thought I'd make sure you turned up first. I didn't want to pay only to be stood up."

"Trust me, I thought about it," I say coldly.

I have to keep my guard up. I need to hear his reasons before we even think about going back to being father and son.

"Let's check in." I tilt my head in the direction of the clerk.

We walk side by side over to the large white desk that has wood paneling on the walls behind it. I smile at the woman who is professionally dressed in her navy suit.

"Good morning, I have a booking for two at nine a.m. under Taylor."

"Good morning, gentlemen. I'll sign you both in. Is there anything you need for your game today?"

"Just a set of cart keys, please."

"Of course." She walks to grab a set of keys and two bottles of water, smiling warmly at me as she hands them over. "Here you go. Hope you two have a nice game. Let us know if we can get you anything else."

"Okay, thank you."

The golf resort was designed by skilled architects to be luxurious, with a modern twist. The building features interior walls of exposed brick, glass views in every direction, and a white render complete with a white peak, indoor and outdoor dining, and they have rooms for overnight stays. This is *not* your basic golf course.

We step out through a double set of glass doors and silently walk over to our assigned cart and put our bags in the back. My heart is beating fast; my nerves are kicking in, and I'm waiting for the serious part of the day to finally arrive. It is pure torture waiting for him to bring up a conversation. To give my brain something to do, I jump into the driver's side. *Take control.* We park near the first green, head around to our bags to get our clubs and balls and get ready to tee off.

Pulling out my driver and golf ball, my dad follows suit, and I wander over to the green with him on trembling knees.

My dad whistles appreciatively. "Nice clubs, Mike. Are they TaylorMade?" he asks, trying to get a better look. I freeze when he is standing close again.

"Yeah, M5, 9 degrees. It's so smooth and light."

He is trying to make conversation, which I appreciate. It's melting one of the icicles that I have built around my heart. I'm overthinking how to bring up the conversation we need to have, and I'm waiting for the right moment. After we hit our first balls, I'm going to bite the bullet, or I will end up playing the worst round of golf in my whole life. I need to get my nerves under control. I hit the ball, and it sails perfectly into the spot I wanted it to go. *Thank God.*

Dad's turn is next, and he also has a good first hit. As we wander slowly back to the cart, my feet feel so heavy that it's like I'm walking in concrete, and my forehead is starting to perspire. Clearing my throat, I prepare to speak.

"I want to talk to you about the past. That's why I asked you to come meet me today."

"I figured."

I gaze out onto the course and not at him, but I feel the weight of his stare as we come to a stop beside the cart. I have to give him credit because he isn't bowing out; he is looking directly at me and talking.

"Why?" Three letters, but so powerful... and it's the one word I have wanted to utter but been too scared to actually hear the answers to in case the pain splits me in half. I turn to face him because I want to watch him as he answers.

He inhales deeply through his nose; his nostrils suck in before flaring out with his exhale. "To put it simply, we were both emotionally withdrawn from our relationship."
What?

"What do you mean?" My brows crease. I fold my arms across my chest.

"I was feeling neglected, and she fell out of love with me." His eyes look pained, and his head droops. My eyes widen in horror. *What the fuck?* Before I have a chance to process the statement, he continues. "It's not an excuse. I feel awful, and it never should have happened. It was just once."

Rolling my eyes, I scoff aloud. "Yeah, they all say that."

"I'll admit, son, we flirted a lot to begin with. It started out just nice, but then she began paying me even more attention and I fell for it. It's not an excuse, but I am just telling you what happened."

Not having the words to say to that, I drop my arms and I turn around. Heading to the cart, I jump in as he slowly follows. *I need some space for a second.* I sit there holding the steering wheel, gripping it like a vise. My head is thumping out the start of a headache. He hops in next to me quietly, waiting for a reaction, no doubt fearing I'll fly off the handle or not talk anymore. But I need to get Alice back and begin trusting her. I can't keep going around in circles and the therapist strongly suggested that talking to him will help. I need to figure this out. *I can do this.*

"I still don't get why you would do it when you have us kids." I close my eyes, hoping that when I snap them open again, I'll understand his logic.

"I didn't plan it. I love you kids and your mother. Over time, we'd both worked too hard and neglected each other. She fell out of love with me, and then I cheated on her. We both hurt each other, just differently."

"Why did she forgive you? How could she?" I open my eyes and turn to face him.

"When it happened, we fought a lot. I hurt your mother and I hurt my kids, mainly you. For that I am truly, deeply sorry. I can never erase that. After a few weeks, we were talking things over and realized we had both made mistakes in the relationship and we needed outside help. We couldn't keep fighting and we deserved to try to make it work for our marriage and you kids." I nod, so he knows I'm listening. My lips are rammed shut like a vise. No words can come out of me, so nodding is all I can offer.

"One night we decided marriage counseling was the best thing to try. We went regularly for years and to this day we still go at least once a year."

"What? Really?" I splutter, my eyes widening as my mouth slackens. *When?*

"Anne helps your mother and I work through our life changes and helps keep our marriage happy. If needed, we visit her individually if she feels we need to work on something alone."

My breath quickens. "Sorry, who did you just say?" *No, it can't be, can it?*

Laughing softly, he apologizes. "Sorry, we call her by her first name. We have known her a while, but her name is Doctor Anne Keating." *No fucking way!*

I'm speechless, staring at him and waiting for an "I'm joking" speech. But it never comes. Of all the people I could go to see, I made an appointment with the exact same doctor my parents use. *No wonder she wanted me to talk to him. This makes sense now.*

My headache is getting worse with every minute that passes, and I want to finish this conversation for the day. "Let's finish the game. I need to get out of here."

Two hours later, I win by the skin of my teeth. I'm so lucky to scrape that win, because my dad is actually *very* good at golf. I had a lot of fun, surprisingly.

On our walk back to hand the keys to reception, I say, "Thanks for today. I have a lot to think about. I just need time to process."

I should say more, but I just don't know exactly what I want to say to him or how. I have some answers and it has me thinking. I just need to work out how to move forward with him.

"I understand, son." He gently slaps my back and squeezes my shoulder.

At first it feels awkward, and I tense up. This whole touching thing is new, and I'm not sure I feel comfortable enough with him yet. He drops his hand and I instantly relax. I head to the car, wheeling my bag, lost in my thoughts.

He shouts and waves before jumping in his own car. "Bye, and thanks again for a great day."

I wave and hop into my car without saying a word.

I wish I could pick up the phone and call Alice to ask her what she thinks. She would know the right things to say. But now that I have worked on rebuilding trust with my father, it's time to turn my attention to Alice. I climb into my car and drive straight over to Alice's house. I need to talk to her, to try again. *I'm not waiting another minute. I want her back.*

I park out front and notice her car isn't there, but I walk up her driveway to the house anyway. I know she'll have finished work for the day, and I can always wait for her to come back if she is out at the shops. Taking the steps to the front door, I knock... I hear nothing. I frown and look through the windows, but I can't see anything because the curtains are all closed. I know the girls are home because Maddison's and Tahlia's cars are in the driveway, so I knock again. Five minutes later, I'm beginning to get impatient, so I hit the window this time. *It's afternoon; why are they still asleep?*

After a minute, I hear footsteps and movement coming from inside. I take a step back, run my fingers through my hair, and then put my hands back in my pockets. The door creaks open a smidge and Tahlia peeks around the door. She looks rough. I tense. *Have they all been out clubbing?*

"Good afternoon, Tahlia. Did I wake you?" I ask.

"Hi... ugh, yes." Tahlia's voice is raspy, like she has been smoking all night. She grimaces when she tries to swallow.

"Sorry, but I want to see Alice." I pull my hands out of my pockets and cross my arms over my chest.

Tahlia grabs her head, groaning. "Shhh, my head hurts. Don't yell. She isn't here."

I am not speaking very loud. I chuckle. "Nice hangover. Where is she then? Or when will she be back?" I question.

"Ugh, well, she went to her mom's house for a week."

"What? Why?" I ask softly, dropping my arms instantly as I take a step forward.

"Umm, well..."

"Spit it out," I say firmly, frustrated and annoyed. I like Tahlia. She's a great friend to Alice, but I need her to tell me where Alice is and why she left.

"She needed space, so she booked leave from work. Didn't you know?" Her brows crease at me.

Why didn't Kate tell me? Fuck! "I need the address, Tahlia."

She opens the door wider, surrendering. "Come in. I'll find the address and write it down. I shouldn't be doing this. She will kill me when she next sees me, but I know you two need to talk. She is miserable without you."

I step into the house, closing the door behind me. I follow Tahlia down the hall and into the kitchen, where she pulls open a drawer and looks through the handful of papers. I stand, leaning my hip against the counter, tugging my hair nervously. *I hope she finds it.* The thought of Alice being miserable pulls at my own aching heart. *I need to fix the mess I've created.*

"Ahh, here it is." She pulls out a little address book, puts it on the counter, and begins flipping through it. Waiting for her to find it feels like it's taking hours, but after a few minutes she finds it and looks around.

"I'll type it in Google Maps. Don't worry about writing it down."

She nods, her shoulders relax, then she shows me the address so I can type it in.

After I type it in my phone and put it in my pocket, I glance up at Tahlia. "She drove alone, in Lady?" I question.

Rolling her eyes, she giggles. "Yeah, she drives those roads all the time. Calm down, caveman."

"Her car is a bucket of shit."

"Agreed, and I have tried to tell her that many times."

"I need to find her."

I walk back to the door and once I reach for the handle, I turn to Tahlia, who is following closely behind me, and I say sheepishly, "Thanks, Tahlia. I know you didn't have to help me... but I do appreciate it."

"Anytime. I hope you two can figure it out." She offers me a half smile.

I turn around, open the door, and head back to my car. I pause at my driver's side door and glance up at the house, where Tahlia waves before going back inside. I set up Google Maps and start the journey to Alice's mom's house. The entire way there, I think about what I am going to say to Alice to win her back.

CHAPTER 33

ALICE

I FINALLY ARRIVE AT Mom's and Claire's. They are already waiting for me on the front step. I can see them waving with matching big grins on their faces. *My family is my life.* I texted them when I left home, so they knew when to expect me.

I hop out of the car and walk straight up into my mom's warm arms. I sigh, relieved and happy. *It's so good to be home. I have missed them so much.* "It's been too long," I say into Mom's shoulder.

She rubs my back while we hug, which sends warm shivers over my body. My family are cuddlers. I remember when growing up, we'd watch movies on the couch, and Mom or Dad would lightly tickle my back, making me fall asleep. *It was so warm and relaxing.* Watching movies in the living room were our treasured family moments. Since Dad died, I've tried to keep them going when I'm here, so we remember the good times. Even if it's hard and sad, we all manage to smile and enjoy the time together. At least with us all being girls, we can watch romance movies with no moaning and groaning.

Pulling back from our warm embrace, I'm wearing the biggest smile on my face. *My heart feels full and content.* "Hi, Mom."

"Hi, sweetheart." She pats my hair.

"Let me grab my bag. Then we can go inside and catch up."

Claire has beaten me to it. She has my bag in her hand before I've even turned around. "I got it." She winks, and I move over to hug her.

"Hey, Claire-bear."

"Hey, Ally."

Claire is a spitting image of our dad. She is younger than me with hourglass curves, our dad's olive skin, rich black hair which flows down her back, and our vibrant blue eyes. She is stunning, and I used to be so envious, but as I have gotten older, I became proud. She isn't just a beauty; she is smart too. She is studying teaching at the college in Bendigo Park because she doesn't want to leave Mom alone. And I'm so grateful to her for that. I can't bear the thought of Mom being alone, but I can't move until I have a few good years of experience in the busy city and spent time exploring the different types of nursing and patients.

Mom's little cottage house is a classically designed house, and I love it. It has a white picket fence. In the garden there is beautiful, thick green grass, and lining the house are white roses and hedges. It's not the biggest house, but it is a large block of land compared to some of the city homes.

I follow Mom and Claire inside, and Claire pops my bag into my old room. It hasn't been touched since I left except to clean. Mom lets us change what we want when it suits us—she wants us to feel at home when we come back, which I'm always grateful for. She keeps the house modern without losing the cottage feel, with its stunning hardwood floors and white country-style kitchen. I walk to my room to put the rest of my stuff down and head back out to the kitchen.

"Tea, dear?" Mom asks, flicking the kettle on.

"Mmm, yes, please." I need tea and something to eat after being on the road. I open the pantry to help Mom get the tea bags and make the tea.

Claire is busy clearing the table. "I'm so happy you're back, Ally. I have missed you. I'm sure you have so much to fill us in about. It's been ages."

I laugh, beaming at how enthusiastic she is. "Yes, don't worry, I will." I put the cups on the table and Mom brings out a plate of food that she has prepared. My stomach grumbles, reminding me I have hardly eaten today. "This looks great, Mom, thank you. You didn't have to go to all this trouble."

"It's nothing much. Take a seat."

We take our spots at the table. None of us ever sit in Dad's seat. It is always left empty. If anyone comes over, they sit in it. But we as a family always leave it empty for him. It feels like he is with us.

"Okay, okay. Hmm, where to start? So, as you two know, I got the position on the fracture and emergency ward, which has been amazing. Seriously, it's so fascinating and I'm learning so much. I'm still finding my feet, but it's been great."

They coo and drink their tea. I grab some cookies to eat because I'm feeling sick from not eating.

"Any boys?" I sip my tea at the wrong moment because as soon as Mom says it, I cough and spit tea everywhere. She grabs a napkin and starts cleaning it up. "Are you okay, Alice?" she asks, rubbing my back while I try to calm my burning chest.

After a few coughs and trying to clear my throat, I nod, unwilling to talk yet, and take a nice sip of my tea. "Yeah, sorry, it just went down the wrong way."

I don't dare tell her about the Mike situation because I'm not interested in hearing any more opinions. I hear my phone beep in my bag, but I don't get up to check it. The most important people know where I am, and I am here with the others. Whoever is texting can wait. *I need to change this subject.*

"The team on my ward is amazing, and Kate is just the nicest boss I have ever had. She is so caring and approachable. I love going to work. Oh, but there is also this bitch at work. She is a total nightmare."

"Isn't that where the famous doctor... what's his name? Oh, I can't think right now... it will come to me. Just give me a minute." Claire starts tapping the table with her fingernail, bouncing in her seat, willing the name to come to her. *Don't remember his name, please.*

"Oh! That's it! Doctor Mike Taylor!" she shouts, happy that she finally remembered.

My eyes bug out of their sockets. *Shit. How does she know?* "Never heard of him. Are you sure he is from my hospital?"

"No, I'm sure. He is insanely hot, Alice. How have you not seen him around?" *Great, it keeps getting better and better.*

"Err, maybe I have seen him, and he is alright I guess." I shrug.

"Are you kidding?" She drops her head back, exacerbated.

"He isn't famous. He isn't a celebrity." I roll my eyes at her.

"Ohhh, yes, he is! Let me show you."

"You girls." Mom giggles and gets up from the table. "I'll grab us some water."

Claire pulls her phone out of her pocket and is scrolling through it with a look of extreme concentration on her face. *I can't seem to run away from him. He is everywhere.* I thought by coming here I'd be safe from hearing about him.

"Here it is. I knew it was him." She stands up and strolls over to me, putting her phone in front of my face.

I stare directly at the photo of Mike, who is staring motionlessly back at me in a delicious navy suit. *Damn it, why is he fucking hot? If only Claire knew how well I know him, and how much hotter he is beneath the suit.*

"He is hot, isn't he? But look at his work. He has so many awards. He was voted the best in the world for orthopedic surgeons."

"Can I read it?" I take the phone out of her hands to read the article. Claire is standing directly behind me as Mom places glasses of water on the table. "Thanks, Mom." I take a big sip, hoping the icy water will cool my now burning-hot body down, as Claire heads back to her chair.

"Of course... I can't believe you didn't already know this." She digs into the food Mom prepared as I read the article in front of me. I'm already halfway through and I'm floored. *He is amazing, like seriously fucking ridiculously smart. I never knew this scale of intelligence. But this is more than smart, this is Einstein level smart. Holy shit.*

"Wow," I mutter under my breath, still reading.

The doorbell rings, breaking me from the spell. Mom looks puzzled. "Who is that?" She checks her watch and heads to the door, clearly not expecting anything or anyone.

I take another mouthful of water.

"Good afternoon, are you Ms. Winters?"

I know that voice. His tone is so seductive, and it's running through my body. Even from afar, it has such a strong effect on me. *What in the world is he doing here and how did he get this address?*

"Hello, yes, that is me. How may I help you?" I can hear the smile in my mom's voice. *He is a charming son of a bitch. Great.*

"I'm a friend of your daughter, Alice, and I was told that she is here. Also, these are for you." Smooth talk to persuade Mom to let him in. *Please don't invite him in. Please.*

"Oh, my favorite flowers, thank you. Alice is here, so why don't you come in? We just sat down for a late bite to eat. Come join us."

My entire body tenses, waiting... I can hear his footsteps coming inside, the front door closing, and then Mom's steps following Mike's. It feels like everything is moving in slow motion when really, it's been only a minute. I quickly close the browser on Claire's phone because I don't need him thinking I'm some kind of stalker.

I know he is standing behind me because I can feel the heat and energy coming from him, and my body is buzzing from him being so close. *Damn traitorous body, get a grip.* I'm looking at Claire, who glances up.

"Whoa, no way." She is laughing and smiling as she darts her eyes between Mike and me until she finally stops on mine and her eyes widen. She points at her phone. "Liar! You do know him," she accuses in a mocking tone. *Fuck my life.*

I can feel my cheeks heating, and right this second, I want the ground to swallow me up.

"Did I miss something?" Mike questions, and Claire drags her eyes up to meet his. I can see her eyes shimmering at him in delight.

"I was showing my sister the news article about your awards that she clearly does know about." She looks back down at me with an arch in her brow.

"I know him, and I didn't know about that." I push out the phone toward her.

Mike chuckles. It's the sexiest sound and I feel it right down in my bones. "The awards were only recent. Anyway, I'm Mike. It's nice to meet you." His hand and arm shoot past my left shoulder and Claire sticks out her hand to grip his.

"I'm Claire, Alice's younger sister, and yes, I know who you are," she says, grinning wider.

Mom speaks up then. "Come, Mike. Please take a seat. Did you want a tea or coffee?"

"Please, Ms. Winters, I would love a black coffee." He makes his way over to Dad's chair and pops himself in it.

I glance over at Mom whose cheeks are now slightly pink. *Oh God, it's getting worse the longer he stays.*

"Please call me Angie," she says, shaking her head before turning toward me. "Don't be so rude, Alice," she accuses, while grabbing a vase to put the flowers in.

"I haven't done anything, and I haven't said a word," I huff back.

"It's okay. I should have warned you I was coming." He is sitting directly across from me at the round table. He is beaming at me cheekily, and then he winks. A shiver runs through me.

I need to talk to him alone, but at that moment, Mom brings his coffee over. "Thank you, Angie."

She smiles at him in return. *Mom loves him already... great.* I bet she wouldn't if she knew how much of a player he was or how much he hurt me.

While he sips his coffee, I take him in. He has on a white V-neck t-shirt that is perfectly fitted to his toned body. His arms are tanned, defined, and his long fingers wrap around the coffee cup. *I want him to hold me and wrap his fingers around me.* His hair is roughly styled which makes me think he has probably been running his hands through it all the way here. When I bring my eyes down to his lips, I can almost feel it in my sex as his tongue darts out to swipe along the bottom one. I dart my eyes to his, which are mocking me with a devious twinkle. *Gosh, why does he have to look so hot?*

I stand up quickly. I feel uncomfortable, and I need a minute to regroup. "I'm going to grab my shoes, so when you're done with that coffee, can we go out back and talk?" I walk off toward my bedroom without waiting for him to respond.

I get into my room and grab my handbag so I can get my phone and text the girls. I notice a few missed calls from Tahlia and also a text.

> **Tahlia:** *Mike came looking for you this morning. I told him your mom's address. I am so sorry. Please talk to him. You guys need to work things out. Tahlia*

Fuck. I am going to kill her when I next speak to her. I don't have time to call her, and I don't need anybody overhearing it, especially not Mike. I throw my phone back in my bag, grab my shoes, and put them on before making my way back to the kitchen. Mike has finished his coffee and is helping Mom and Claire pack up as they ask him work questions. He notices me enter straightaway and smiles darkly at me. The pull we have when we are in the same room is strong, and I can't help but smirk back.

He looks perfect in my mom's house.

"Are you ready?"

"Yes." He puts the towel down to follow me.

"Mom, we are going out back to talk."

"Okay, dear."

I move to the sliding doors, opening it for us. I step out and hold the door open, and once he steps into the garden after me, I shut the door behind him. I saunter past him and guide him up to the old swinging chair that was my father's favorite place in the garden. He used to tell me made-up stories whenever we sat here alone. I climb up onto the metal frame, and Mike sits next to me. With our thighs touching, heat surges between us, flowing through my body, and a throb begins in my sex.

CHAPTER 34

MIKE

I FOLLOW HER OUTSIDE toward a seated metal swing, which looks very old. It overlooks a manicured family garden, which has a mixture of vegetables and flowers—it's magnificent.

Walking behind Alice means I get to check her ass out in her jeans. *Better than the navy uniform she wears at work.* Her hips swing side to side and I just want to squeeze and spank her ass, but it's not appropriate right now. She takes a seat on the swing, and I sit intentionally right beside her, so our bodies are touching. I have this *need* to be as close to her as possible... always. This connection is new and unexpected.

I thrust my hand through my hair and turn my head to gaze at her while I speak. "Alice, I'm here to try to talk to you. I realize you don't want to talk at work, and I completely understand. It's inappropriate and it also won't be a quick conversation... I went to your house to have this conversation with you, but you weren't there. Tahlia told me you were here—well, I should say I forced her to tell me where you were." I smirk.

She laughs and mumbles under her breath, "I bet."

Her laugh sends a spark of joy through my heart, but I pretend not to hear her words, and I continue to talk. I need to get everything out in the open if I'm going to win her back. "Firstly, I want to apologize to you. I'm sorry I pushed you away and asked for a break without talking to you. I regret that so much." I touch her thigh with my fingers and her eyes dart to mine, darkening with desire. "I think if you were to give me a second chance, to be able to trust me, and hopefully date me again, then I need to be more honest about everything."

We are swinging slowly, and I'm staring at Alice, trying to gauge her emotions, but she has turned her face away and is looking out at the garden. I follow her gaze and take a big deep breath in. "My dad cheated on my mom, and then Amanda cheated on me. I decided to see a counselor and get help working through my trust issues."

Under my palm, I feel her thigh twitch. *What's that about?* I gently stroke her thigh with my thumb in a soothing rhythm. "Let me get it all out and get everything off my chest. Otherwise, I won't be able to tell you everything I really want and need you to know."

I swallow. "I argued with Alex for having his arm around you in the cafeteria. He told me later that you guys were talking to Amanda, but I didn't see her there. I only saw you and Alex. After him dancing and trying to kiss you in the nightclub and then that—I naturally thought you two were playing around behind my back. It was like Amanda and Liam all over again."

Alice gasps, but she doesn't move or say a word, and I continue to stroke her thigh, even though I can feel her tense muscles under my palm.

"I was so hurt and angry that my brother could do that to me, but I didn't hear him out when he came to my office to talk to me about what Amanda had said to you. I heard Alex, and saw his arm and body draped over you from afar and lost my shit. Mom came over and talked some sense into me about how I'm wrong about Alex. She even invited him over so we could talk," I pause to catch a breath looking up at the blue sky before I continue. "Obviously, I'm now well aware of the truth. You and he danced and kissed before we were officially even together, and the arm was to protect you from Amanda and her disgusting accusations—hence the restraining order. I get that now. I'm sorry that I doubted you. After talking to Mom, I realized I needed help. I can't do it alone and it's not fair to you to be with someone who won't trust you due to their own issues. I want to trust you, but I just needed to talk to a professional to see how I can begin to do that." Birds begin chirping loudly around us and I wait until they quieten to finish.

"So, I booked an appointment with the doctor and when I went there, she told me I really needed to hear my dad out to move forward. I needed to talk to him first and then work on our relationship. The therapist was great. I found her helpful. I obviously need more than one session, but it's a start. I met with my dad this morning to play a game of golf, and I got to ask him the biggest question I have been holding on to—why, and how could he do that to Mom and us? I heard him out and discovered that Mom had emotionally checked out of the relationship, so it wasn't just black and white. I can see that now. Now, get this, I also found out the doctor I went and had the session with... is also my parents' therapist."

"No way!" Alice gasps, turning her shocked face toward me. I'm sure I looked like she does now when I found out.

"Weird, right? Considering I never told a soul, I just looked her up and booked in. She was great, very professional and warm. I definitely need to book more sessions, because I haven't touched on the subject of Amanda and Liam. I want to be able to move on from the hurt, not carry the baggage around any longer. The last part that was playing on my mind was the fact you said you didn't want kids in the next ten years. I didn't want to hold you back. I know you want to have your career. And your passion is one of the things I am attracted to. I just realized in that moment that I want children with you... But I will just have to compromise because I would rather have you in my life than out of it. My life is so much better with you in it. You are so light, warm, and kind. You bring the best out of me." I don't speak for a while. I just listen to her steady breaths.

Alice speaks in a broken voice. "That's a lot to take in, Mike."

I slightly turn my body toward her, and I grab her hands in mine—they are so large in comparison; hers are so small and pale. I'm gazing down at them as I speak. "Alice, I'm sorry. I should have trusted you, talked to you, and let you explain. Instead, I broke things off and went cold without a conversation. I just shut down and don't let anybody in past my walls." Shaking my head, I think frantically, *I hope I don't screw this up.* "Fuck, I screwed up the best thing that's ever happened to me. I'm sorry." I glance up and Alice turns her blue eyes to me. They are rimmed with unshed tears. "I love you so much." I say every word slowly and clearly, meaning every damn one of them and hoping it will be enough. I see a tear leak out onto her cheek and slide into the corner of her mouth. I take one hand out of our joined ones and use my thumb to wipe it away. "Please don't cry, babe; it kills me that I've hurt you this deeply." I pull her into my arms and hug her soft frame, inhaling that rich, sweet vanilla scent that I love, and relief hits me. I sag when I feel her hands rise up and she hugs me back.

After a while, she pulls out of our warm embrace. I want to give her space, so she can come to me when she is ready. Wiping her cheeks free of tears with my thumbs, she glances back at me with her dazzling eyes.

"Thank you for the apology. I appreciate it. You hurt me when you left me without any explanation. I have missed you so much, but I can't just go back to where we were." The confliction on her face kills me.

I nod. "I understand. I just want another chance to maybe start over. That's if you want to?"

She glances away back into the garden. I can tell she is thinking, but I wish I knew what to do to help her change her mind.

CHAPTER 35

ALICE

HE HAS TOLD ME so much that I don't know how to begin processing any of it. Being here with him makes me miss him more, even in his space. *I need to use my head, not just my heart.* Looking at my dad's garden and swinging in his beloved swing, I wish I had a sign to help me—but then again, *Mike chasing me, being here in my dad's space, apologizing... That is saying something, isn't it?* Apologizing and truly meaning it from the heart, takes a lot. I stare out into the garden, then down at our joined hands for an answer.

"I need some more time," I whisper. My heart squeezes inside my chest and I feel fresh warm tears slide along my cheeks. "I'm sorry."

"Don't be sorry. I'm the one who fucked up." I hear a sigh leave his mouth. It would be so easy for me to forgive him, but I just need to make sure I make the right decision.

"What time do you need to drive back?" I ask, trying to break the tension.

"I'm off this weekend, but I best get back. I'm watching the football game tomorrow with my friends."

A twist of guilt hits my stomach that he drove all this way and has to drive back home again. "Oh, sounds fun."

I stand up from the swing and he does too. I lead him back into the house where Mom is messing around in the kitchen, clearly pretending to clean, but obviously watching us.

Claire is on the couch watching television.

"Hey, Claire, do you mind pausing that and coming to the table for a second, please? Mike is leaving."

Claire pauses the show, and turning to face us, the biggest and cheesiest grin immediately lights up her whole face, but when she sees my face, she frowns. I glance over my shoulder, noticing that Mom is already standing at the table, but her face is a little more reserved, clearly wondering what is going on. *I know this is the right decision. I need a little bit of time to think away from him.*

"Thanks for inviting me in. It was lovely to meet you both." He hugs my mom and Claire and kisses them both on the cheek.

I lead him down the hall and out the front door, then I walk with him to the car without saying a word.

As we arrive at his car, he turns to face me. "You have a wonderful, supportive family, and I wish I could have met your dad."

"Me too. You would have loved him and got along so well."

"I bet."

"Text me when you get home," I say, gazing into his sad eyes. I feel his hand press into my hair and arch my face up. My heart accelerates. Our lips inches apart, I can feel his breath tickle my lips, and I blink and slam my lips shut to prevent words escaping.

I reluctantly pull out of his grip and take a step back. Our eyes locked, his hand drops, and he rips open his car door. I watch his frame climb into the car and reverse out of the drive and drive away. I stand there alone, taking a few deep breaths before I enter Mom's house. When I get inside, they are sitting at the table, all eyes on me. I sit back down in my chair. I feel myself flush red from the chest up. I hate awkward conversations or conversations involving me.

I clear my throat. "So..." I keep my eyes on Mom when I talk, and she watches me back with curiosity etched on her face. "Err, so, obviously, I need to tell you about Mike."

They wait patiently for me to begin.

"I met Mike at work, and we have kind of been dating." I wince and glance across at Mom, whose mouth is turned up in the corner.

"That's wonderful news. I'm happy for you. He seems like a gentleman. The way he looks at you, you're clearly special to him."

If only she knew.

Before I can say anything, a slap comes from beside me. "Ouch! Claire, what was that for?" I yell.

"I knew it! Why didn't you say something sooner?" she demands, raising her eyebrows at me.

"I didn't want to say anything until I was sure it was serious."

"Yes, I understand. Well, hopefully next time he can stay longer." Her statement is really a question, but I don't want to talk about this any longer.

My stomach grumbles. "I'll order us some pizzas for dinner and let's watch a movie." I get up from the table and grab the takeout menus.

Claire chooses a movie, then the pizzas arrive and we eat while watching without another word. I hear my phone chime. I check it. It's a text from Mike.

Mike: *I just arrived home. I miss you. Again,*
I am sorry.

I don't answer. I just enjoy hanging out with my family. Once the movie is over, we get up, and Mom kisses my cheek, then turns to Claire and kisses her too. "Goodnight, everyone."

Claire strolls off to her room too, waving. "I'm stuffed too. Good night."

"Good night, Claire," I say before crawling into my bed after an emotional day. As soon as I get into bed and lay down, I think about Mike's words. He told me he loved me and discussed openly about having kids. We've fought so hard that I need to take a moment to let all his words settle. Since we've met it's been such a rush. There's no doubt I love him I think I started falling the moment we met.

On Monday, I wake to the smell of bacon and coffee, and opening my eyes, I smile when I remember where I am. I get up, feeling tired, but I'm happy because I am back home. I grab my t-shirt and jeans and move to the bathroom to clean up. I wander into the kitchen where Mom is at the stove turning bacon, and I peek around but cannot see Claire.

"Good morning." My voice is croaky from the lack of sleep.

"Good morning, love. I'm just cooking breakfast. Claire is still sleeping, but at least that gives me alone time with you to talk."

I swallow. My happy feeling disappears, now replaced with butterflies.

"Where can I help?" I ask nervously. *What does she want to talk to me about?*

"How about you grab the eggs out of the fridge and make yourself a coffee? I already have mine, and the kettle has just boiled."

I walk to the fridge, then hand her the eggs.

"Thank you."

I finish making coffee, and standing beside her, I help cook.

"Now, I don't want to be rude, but I just need to ask you, how old is Mike?"

Shit! I knew this would come up. "He is thirty-eight."

She nods thoughtfully, then turns to look at me. "You're only twenty-three, Alice. Aren't you in different phases of your life? He must want to settle down soon, and you have only just started your career."

I have thought about this before and when Mike brought it up yesterday, I knew my answer. But I think for a moment before replying, because this is Mom, and she is an important person to me, so her opinion matters more than most.

"Yes, I must admit I wish we were closer in age, but to be honest, I can't walk away. I love him." The feeling of warmth fills my body as I say that out loud to Mom.

"Hmm," she hums.

"Now, don't get me wrong. He is smart, handsome, and clearly makes you happy. I just don't want you hurt due to different life expectations. I will respect your decision and I won't stand in your way if you choose a life with Mike."

I smile back at her.

"I'll set the table and pop some toast on, and then I'll go wake up Claire."

"Good idea, love. Breakfast is almost ready." She finishes flipping the last two eggs, which has my stomach growling in hunger.

I walk to Claire's room and bang on the door before I slowly open it.

I peek around the door and see she is moving. "Claire, breakfast is ready! Come join us. I'll make you some tea."

She mumbles and grumbles and I have no idea what she is saying, but at least I know she is awake, so I walk out, closing the door behind me, and begin making my way back to the kitchen to prepare us tea. We sit around the table and silently enjoy our breakfast.

I hear my phone ring, and I rush to my room to retrieve it. I see my boss' name, Kate, flash across the screen.

"Hello, Kate?" I answer.

"Hi, Alice. How are you? Hope I am not interrupting you."

I sit down on the bed, clutching the phone. "Um, no, you're not interrupting. Is everything okay?"

For a split second, my mind jumps to Mike. *Shit, something has happened.*

She laughs. "Yes, everything is good. Great, actually."

My brows furrow. "Okay?"

"I just wanted to offer you a scholarship for a pre-med course. Doctor Taylor recommended you to the board, and I received the formal offer."

I suck in a sharp breath.

My eyes instantly fill with tears. My throat is dry and constricts. I cannot speak.

He put my name down for a scholarship to study to become a doctor. Prior to our rotation, I would never have thought I wanted to become one, but working with Mike, I have loved every second. But in the back of my mind, I knew I couldn't afford the course. But this would mean I don't pay.

"I can tell you're in shock, but we have seen in the short amount of time the potential. Obviously, it's your decision, and you can say no. It's a long time to study, but you have the best teacher." I hear the lightness in her tone.

It makes me smile, and my mind is racing. I need to speak. I clear my throat as the tears threaten to leak. "Wow, I am shocked. I had no idea. I would love to take the scholarship. Thank you."

"I can't take the credit, Miss Winters. It was Doctor Taylor's idea. But you're very welcome. I will see you when you return to work."

My heart skips at hearing that, and I close my eyes for a second. *He truly is something.*

"Thank you, Kate. I will see you back at work."

"See you then. Bye."

"Bye." I hang up and just sit unmoving.

I need to call Mike. My heart and mind are racing. I have adrenaline coursing through me, and my head is spinning. *I have missed him.*

I want him.

I can hear mumbling in the kitchen, so I toss my phone down and walk to the kitchen. "I just got offered a scholarship for a pre-med course. Mike recommended me," I say.

Mom's eyes instantly fill with tears, and she covers her mouth with her hand.

"Oh, Mom." I stand and move to her, embracing her.

"I'm so proud of you," she mumbles into my shoulder.

"Ally, that's awesome. I'm so happy for you."

"Thanks, I don't have any more information just yet. It's just so unexpected."

"Did you want to head up to the main street, check out some local spots, have a drink to celebrate?" Claire offers.

"I would love that." She smiles.

"We should shower and get ready, so we have plenty of time to walk around." I stand and stack the dishes up before taking them to the dishwasher and lining the shelves. "I'll have my shower first. I take longer than you," I say.

Claire nods.

"Mom, did you want to come?"

She shakes her head vigorously. "No, dear. You two spend some time together."

I take off to get ready and once I am done, I come out of the bathroom, only to find Claire, who is still in her sleepwear with a blanket draped over her knees and a cup of tea in her hand.

"Are you ready?" she calls.

"Yep, your turn." She gets off the couch and heads off down the hall to shower.

Mom joins me on the couch, watching the TV until Claire walks out. "Are you ready?"

"Yep," I say. Jumping up from the couch, I step over to kiss Mom on the cheek. "We will be back soon. We will bring lunch!" I call out.

"Have fun, you two," Mom shouts back.

We climb into my car and I feel Claire staring at me intently. "What?" I snap.

"How is he real? Tell me all the gossip. Right now!"

I crack up, laughing a full belly laugh, and smack her arm with my hand. "Shhh, I haven't left the drive yet."

I begin reversing and driving through the streets.

"I'm waiting, Ally," she huffs.

After shaking my head at her persistence, I answer, "He is amazing, and yes, his body is incredible, but he's even more than that, Claire. He is kind, caring, and fun." I sigh. *The dream boyfriend.* "Don't say anything to Mom, but we are on a small break. But I am so unhappy without him. I miss him so much. I just needed time to think about what I want, whether it was love or infatuation. But I feel miserable without him. I'm so in love with him. I know I don't have much to compare to as I haven't had a lot of boyfriends, but something just clicks with us. He is different." She is sitting up, listening to me.

"I can tell you two were made for one another; the electricity in the room when you're both in it is hot. Like, take-off-my-clothes-I-need-a-cold-shower hot." She fans her face with one hand for effect. *Oh, my God.*

I laugh and feel my face blush red. "How embarrassing."

"Oh, don't be embarrassed. It's just not fair. I need an older, hot, and sexy-as-hell, successful man. Help a sister out, will you?" she begs, and we both fall into hysterical laughter.

We arrive in town and prowl the streets, arms linked. The time off is exactly what I needed.

After a few hours of tasting a variety of food, smelling candles and looking at all the handmade crafts, we pull up in Mom's driveway.

Inside we all eat lunch, and then, I excuse myself and walk to my room to call Mike. I scroll and find his name and decide that I need to give myself another few days. *It's still too early. Give yourself a few more days.* Resisting temptation, I turn my phone off and walk back out.

CHAPTER 36

ALICE

A Few Days Later

Mom and Claire have gone to get some food for dinner. I take the opportunity to phone Mike without being caught.

I hear the ringing in my ear and after only two rings, he answers.

"Alice?"

"Hi, Mike." I hear noise in the background before a door opens and closes.

"Is this a bad time to call?" I ask.

"No, no, no. I just got back to my office after surgery. Are you okay?" His voice is strained.

I feel my heart drop, wishing I was at work, working with him. "Okay, well, I won't take too much of your time. I just wanted to thank you for putting my name in for the scholarship."

"You can never bother me. Call me anytime... You're more than welcome. You deserve it. You would make a wonderful doctor." His words warm my heart, spreading through my body and wrapping me with love.

It's silent for a moment. I can hear his breath through the phone. He is waiting for me. He hasn't bothered me after he left, only sending the one text saying he got home. I appreciate how he listened to me, gave me the space I craved. But I made a decision.

"I'm willing to try, but really slowly though."

I hear a hitch in his voice. "Thank you, Alice. I will take anything. I miss you—so very much."

My stomach is fluttering. "I miss you too."

I hear the door open and know they are back from the shops. "I have to go help my family. Text me when you get home?"

"Sure. Speak to you soon, babe."

I smile and hang up.

A few hours later, I get a text. A warm tingle rises in my body as I open it.

Mike: *I just arrived home. Wish you were with me. I am awfully lonely.*□

Alice: *I wish I was too. It's only a few more days. I'm sure work will keep you busy.*

Mike: *I'd prefer to be busy with you. ;P*

Alice: *Oh really? How?*

Mike: *Yes, very much, and naked, to be specific.*

Alice: *I figured, you crazy man.*

Mike: *Send me a pic.*

Alice: *No way. I am on the couch with my sister and Mom. That's not very sexy.*

Mike: *You are sexy in anything.*

I take a picture of myself smiling and send it to him.

Mike: *You're so beautiful, and I'm so lucky.*

Alice: *Aww, thanks. I feel lucky too.*

Mike: *Well, I need to head out to the gym and get some food for the week. I'll text you when I get back.*

Alice: *Where is my pic? ;)*

Mike: *Soon. ;P*

Alice: ☺

A few hours pass and I'm just getting ready for dinner when my phone chimes. I check it and see it's another message from Mike, so I open it. *Whoa!* It's a picture of him—his gym shorts hang low; his top half is naked; his torso is dripping with sweat, and his wet, dark hair is sticking to his forehead. *How I want to run my hands through his hair.*

I'm rendered speechless for five minutes, staring at this impeccable picture. It's like I just got porn. I am so edgy and hot down in my sex right now. It's begging for attention. *Thanks, Mike, you royally fucked with my head and my pussy with one photo.* I excuse myself and go into my room to text Mike.

Alice: *How are you real?*

Mike: *Is that even a question? Do I need to remind you?*

Alice: *I'm pretty sure I almost died on the spot when you sent that picture. Now, I'm horny and you're not here to help me.*

Mike: *Well... I can help you now.*

Alice: *How?*

Mike: *Dirty texting and pictures, Alice.*

Alice: *Oh.*

Mike: *Yes, oh.*

Mike: *I will help you and you help me. We can get off together.*

Alice: *I haven't done this before.*

Mike: *It's fine. You'll be perfect. Don't worry.*

Alice: *Okay, lead the way.*

Mike: *Send me a picture right now. Don't overthink it. Just send a picture of you.*

I take a picture of me lying on my bed. I have a t-shirt on, and my hair is down and messy, fanning around my pillow. I hit send. Waiting for a reply feels like forever; my heart is beating fast in my chest, but I see the bubbles move within seconds.

Mike: *So beautiful. Now, take off your top.*

I quickly type back.

Alice: *Where is my picture?*

Mike: *It's coming. Give me a minute to take it. For every picture I send, I'm going to ask for one of you. I will send you one back, I promise.*

That makes me feel instantly better. I relax, taking slow deep breaths while I wait.

Mike: *Picture*

Mike is lying on his bed, pillows all around him. He is propped up on a few of them and has his arm behind his head. He is topless and his tanned body, with the light misting of dark hair on his chest, reminds me of how much of a man he really is. His lips are tilted to one side in a smirk. His eyes are a darker blue from desire, and, as usual, his hair looks like he has been running his fingers through it.

I feel hot. My skin has little goosebumps all over it, and my body temperature is rising by the second.

Alice: *You are so sexy. I want to kiss you so badly right now.*

Mike: *What else? Talk to me. Tell me... What else do you want to do to me? Don't hold back.*

Alice: *I would touch your shoulders, smoothing my hands all over them. I'd trace them down your chest, lean forward and take your nipple into my mouth and suck, pulling on it with my teeth. Then I would go back to feeling my way down your abs, enjoying the rock-hard muscles under my palms. Then I'd help take your pants and boxer briefs off. I want you naked ASAP.*

While I wait, I remember he asked to take my top off—so I remove it and throw it on the floor. Do I take my bra off yet? No, I leave it on. He didn't ask for it to come off. I wish I had a sexier bra on, not just a basic white cotton. I need to go shopping for some sexy bras and panties.

Mike: *You are so good at this, and you are making me so hard. I want you here touching me everywhere, taking my clothes off, and I*

*would make you touch my cock. It's so hard
and needy. Send me another pic.*

I quickly snap a picture and send it to him. I'm in the
same position but without my shirt.

Mike: *Beautiful. I wish I could squeeze your
plump breasts in my hands and hear you
moan. Then I would take your bra off and suck
on your nipples, biting them, tugging on them
with my teeth. You have the most perfect tits.
Send me another picture of you. Topless this
time.*

I receive another picture from Mike straightaway. My
eyes nearly bug out of my head. His words are hot, but
seeing him nude? He is covering his dick with his blan-
kets—which is unfair—but I can see his snail trail of dark
hair that leads to the treasure, and his *V* is delicious. I want
to touch him. It's like a perfect arrow pointing straight
down to his cock.

I take off my bra in a hurry and lie back down, sending
him a topless pic, but to make it better, I'm touching my
nipple with my finger. I decide that instead of a picture,

I'm going to send a short video of me squeezing my tit and playing with my nipple. *This will make him crazy.* I can see that he has watched the video, then he responds.

> **Mike:** *Fuck me. You are a natural, dirty fucking girl. It makes me want to jump in my car and fuck you so hard on your bed we will wake your mom and sister up with all the noise. Take off the rest of your clothes because I need to see you naked. Now.*

> **Alice:** *Take off the sheet. It's only fair. I want to see all of you.*

He decides to send me a little video, and it's him removing the sheet slowly off his cock and once it's removed... It ends.

> **Alice:** *Unfair!!!! Send more. Touch yourself. I want to watch.*

> **Mike:** *Send me a pic of you nude.*

I rush to take all my clothes off and grab my little pink clit stimulator out of my bag and snap a picture of my clit up close. I have the toy strategically lying next to my waist.

> **Mike:** *Is that what I think it is? Fuck, you're killing me, babe. I fucking love it. I love you. You're so fucking dirty.*

He sends me a video of him slowly pulling on himself. I see precum on the tip and he takes his thumb and smears it. It's so damn erotic watching him pull on himself.

> **Alice:** *I wish I could taste you, and it be my hands on you. Pretend it's me sending you over the edge.*

That is all I send because I need to touch myself. I decide to video me using my hands to touch my body, and then I grab my clit stimulator and rub it against me. After a minute, I drop it, put two fingers inside, and pump until I'm at the edge. I hit send and continue, because the build-up is climbing. I can feel I'm close. My eyes are shut and I'm leaning back on my bed, envisioning Mike, when my phone chimes.

I open to see a video of him pulling and he comes all over his stomach. His hot sticky white cum covers his abs. The sight has me climbing even higher, and I push harder and faster, dropping my phone as I shiver when I come apart. I haven't come by myself like that—ever, and it takes me a few minutes to recover before I am reaching for my buzzing phone. He's calling me.

"Mike?" I answer.

"I needed to hear your voice. Baby, I miss you so much."

CHAPTER 37

ALICE

A Few Days Later

"What time are you leaving today?" Mom asks.

I glance at the clock hanging on the kitchen wall. "I will probably leave after lunch. I don't want to be too tired for my early shifts this week."

I finish my breakfast and help clean up.

I have been up at Mom's for the whole week now, and it's time to get back home. I want a day to catch up with the girls, get some groceries, and get myself organized for the next week when I'm back at work. I also want to see Mike. We text every day, all day, but it isn't the same. I want to kiss him and hug him and just be with him. The break has been perfect, but I am eager to get back to my life and routine now.

"Please come back sooner next time. I enjoyed hanging out with you again, Ally," Claire pleads.

"Yes, I know. That's my fault. I should have asked for time off way before now. I had so much fun. I miss being home." I sigh.

I say goodbye to Mom and Claire, then I hit the road, listening to music. I sent a text to the girls before I left, letting them know to expect me in a few hours.

When I arrive home, I notice a brand-new sporty black Range Rover parked out front. Wondering who is over visiting the girls in such a nice car, I run up the steps and open the door. I hear the television going as I head inside. Walking into the dining room, I see Tahlia is dusting and Maddison has all her books open in front of her and is writing, so I know she is studying.

"Hey, girls!" I shout to be heard over the TV. I quickly go to my room and throw my bag inside before heading to the dining table and sitting next to Maddison.

"Hey, how was it?" Tahlia wanders over, still holding the duster.

"So good. I'm mad I didn't head back sooner. I miss them."

"I bet. Don't leave it so long next time, and how was lover boy?" Maddison is wiggling her eyebrows at me.

I close my eyes, laughing at her comment. "Amazing, of course, and my family loves him." I roll my eyes.

"And that annoys you, doesn't it?" Tahlia mocks.

I laugh. "Yes. You should have seen Claire! She had a bio on the guy, and when he turned up, he had a bunch of Mom's favorite flowers. Both of them were drooling over him. It was so embarrassing."

"So, they all got along. See? It wasn't so bad, me telling him where you were."

"No, no, no, you're still in big trouble, T! How are you girls? Do anything exciting?"

Maddison points to where her books and papers are sprawled out. "This was my life. I have to hand in an assignment tomorrow."

I noticed Tahlia doesn't say anything. "What about you, T?" I question.

Her cheeks change to a shade of pink. "Err, nothing much, really."

Maddy's head spins quickly up at Tahlia and says, "Tell her."

I frown. "Tell me what?"

"I just went out for dinner. Nothing much. Did you see the car out front?" I know she is changing subjects to divert my questioning off her, but I don't want to push. Tahlia will tell me when she is ready.

"Yeah, but whose is it? No one is visiting us, so which neighbors' visitor parked out front this time?" I ask.

They both look at each other, smile, and stare at me while laughing. My stomach drops. *I don't like the sound of this.*

"What?" I snap. "Tell me what's going on." I lean back in the chair, bouncing my eyes between them.

"Did you look in your room properly?" Tahlia says coyly.

"No, I threw my bag in and came out here. What's in there?" I huff.

I'm suspicious. These girls are hiding shit from me and it's pissing me off.

"Calm down. Just go in there and look around," Maddison says before returning to her studies, dismissing me, and when I glance at Tahlia, she smiles and gets back to dusting. *Bitches.*

I wander back to my room and that's when I see the massive bunch of roses, and as I move over to take a look, they are such a strong smell. It hits me and I instantly know who they are from. I smile and shake my head. It doesn't answer the car question, but it makes me flush that he brought me these. I have missed him this week. I trail over

to my bedside table to where vase is, and I notice the card...
and an envelope. I open the card.

Alice,

*Words cannot describe how much I have
missed you, how far I have fallen for you in
ways I never thought possible. Time really does
make the heart grow fonder.*

*You are my world. You have changed me in the
best possible way. Nothing will ever be enough
to show you how grateful I am.*

Please take my gift as a small thank you.

Love you so much,

Mike X

I grip the card tightly and bring it to my chest. My eyes well up with tears that are threatening to leak out, but I shake myself. He is sweet. One of the few times we managed to speak, he told me he has been back to his therapist this week, and he has said how much she has helped him open up. This card is definitely proof of that. There are no "player" remarks, it's just his heart. This is what I want, his heart to be open to me. I'm in love with him, and these words tell me he feels the same. I put the card back down next to the roses and open up the envelope. This has a set of keys and a note.

Alice,

The thought of you driving that death trap around, especially to your mom's and back scares me. I hope you like the car. It's my gift to you.

I will not take it back, so don't even bother asking. You know I can afford this and keeping you safe is my number one priority.

Someone is due to pick up Lady this afternoon.
You cannot return the Range Rover, but it is
registered in your name.

Mike X

P.S. It just needs a name.

I stare at the note and then at the keys. *What the? He is crazy.* I know my car is becoming dangerous to drive, but I have been saving up for a new second-hand car. I put the note down but keep hold of the keys as I pick up my bag and look around for my phone. Retrieving it, I dial him. I know he is at work, but I need to talk to him. He doesn't answer, so I send him a text.

Alice: *Call me when you can.*

I put the phone in my pocket and walk out of my room. The girls look up at me, waiting for my reaction.

"He is crazy if he thinks I am accepting that," I tell them, pointing in the direction of the front door.

"I don't think you have much choice," Tahlia mocks with a smirk on her face.

"I'll take it if you don't want it, but I'm sure Mike won't allow that." Maddison laughs.

"Let's just have a look at it, and then you can make your decision." Tahlia smiles.

"Okay, come on then. I can see you have been bursting to check it out." I roll my eyes at them.

"Have we ever?" Maddison is bouncing on her heels.

I look at the keys. There is an unlock button, so I press it. The car lights up. We walk toward it and I go to the driver's side. Maddison goes for the passenger side, and Tahlia opens the rear door. *Wow, it's stunning*. It has a cream leather interior, sunroof, and a hi-tech dash. I jump in and sit, and it's so soft. Scanning around, I grudgingly admit to myself that this is so nice. This is a dream car, and I feel like I am living a dream life that will disappear when I wake up tomorrow.

My phone rings in my pocket. I see his name flash. I answer it.

"Hey, babe, I assume this call is about the car?"

"Mike, this is ridiculous. It's way too much. This must have cost you a fortune. It has cream leather seats and a sunroof!"

"You're inside it, so you like it then. I made a good choice." I can hear the smile in his voice.

"Did you not listen to a word I just said? I cannot accept it," I huff.

"You are not driving around in a shitty car when I can easily afford a better and safer car for you. I would feel much happier knowing you are taken care of. Please accept this from me. It would mean a lot to me." The pleading in his tone has me sighing. *How can I refuse? Fuck him and his sweet mouth.*

"Fine, but I don't want you to think you have to buy me expensive things. I love you and that's all I need."

"Okay, I understand, and babe?" He pauses, waiting for me to respond.

"Yes?"

"Thank you, I love you. I do have to get back to work, but I will call you when I leave here. I can't wait to see you. I have missed you," he purrs in my ear.

I flush, knowing I will be driving to his house soon. And if the texts are anything to go by, I will be thoroughly fucked.

"Okay, I love you too. Talk soon."

I hang up and the girls start squealing, but I just laugh and shake my head. "Calm down, it's just a car."

"Take us for a spin! "Maddison squeals.

"I thought you had to study?"

"A quick car drive will be fine." *Of course, it will.*

"Okay, let me run in and grab my purse and lock up."

As I pull up at Mike's house, my palms begin to sweat and my heart skips a beat when he opens the door. I exit the car in a hurry and walk up to him.

"I have missed you," I say.

Mike's eyes turn dark. *He liked that answer.*

He leans toward me, closing his eyes, and I meet him halfway. When our lips join, it's the softest and sweetest kiss. His spicy scent fills my nose, and my stomach is fluttering. My sex is hot, causing the throb to become really uncomfortable. I pull away, glancing down again at our entwined hands. He helps me inside and peers down at me and kisses me again before he pulls away, biting and dragging my lip between his teeth. *Oh shit.*

I feel it in my lower belly, and my sex begins to pulse again.

"Bed," he grunts.

I can tell he is barely holding on too.

Chapter 38

Mike

When we get to our room, I follow her inside and close the door quietly. Standing in front of the door, with my face near hers, I reach out and grab the back of her neck, bringing her close to me until her lips hit mine.

She moans, "Ohhh."

That sound is killing my restraint. I just want to strip her down and fuck her so hard right now, and then again, right after. We still need to make up for all the lost time, but we can't while we're here, so for now I kiss the fuck out of her mouth, forcing my tongue inside and stroking hers. She moans and I smile against her lips.

I kiss her for another minute before pulling away. Her lips are plump and red from the kiss, with my saliva covering them. I gently wipe them with my thumb.

I lean into her ear, and putting my mouth onto her lobe, I bite and tug it hard. When she whimpers, I speak into her ear in a grunt, barely hanging on. "I want you so bad. I want to fuck you right now."

Her eyes are half shut. Looking down at her face with my hooded eyes, I can tell she is falling and wanting to release the built-up sexual tension that I'm sure is rising between her legs. I can smell her scent and it's so delicious. *I want to taste her again.* It's been ages since I tasted her. Her hands are holding on to my waist, and she opens her eyes, bringing her gaze up to meet mine.

"Please..." she begs, and it's turning me on further.

My dick is getting painfully hard, straining in my jeans. I'm too wound up. *Fuck it.* Pushing her away gently so she takes a step back, she opens her eyes and drops her hands.

"Take off your clothes," I whisper. She smiles, a devilish grin as she quickly rips her t-shirt off over her head, which has me quietly snapping at her, "Slowly."

I want to enjoy this. I won't last long, so I want to savor these moments. She stares at me, but doesn't say a word, just begins to remove her jeans slowly until she is standing in front of me wearing only her black cotton bra and pink panties. The vision makes me smile. I love how she goes for comfort, but I still plan to buy her some lacy sets with suspenders and stockings for a touch of variety.

Her body is incredible, and I can't help but wonder if she was made just for me. I take her in, looking her up and down so slowly. Goosebumps cover her skin and I know she isn't cold. She's turned on.

"Take your bra and panties off. I want to see all of you."

She brings her arm around her back and unclasps the bra and pushes the straps off her shoulders, which makes the bra drop to the floor. My cock pulses. Her perfect size breasts and perky, pink nipples are waiting for attention. *Soon*, I think to myself, *I will devour them*. She breaks me from my spell by dragging her pink panties down her legs and stepping out of them.

She is completely bare, and her body is on display just for me.

I take a deep breath, curling my finger toward her. "Come here and strip me now." Her eyes gleam at that and she rushes over, immediately sliding her hands up the sides of my waist. Dragging my t-shirt up, she pulls it over my head and rubs her delicate hands all over my shoulders, pecs, and abs. I glance down at her hands, which are now grabbing at the button and zipper on my jeans.

She tugs them down over my ass, and I have my Calvin Klein briefs on. I chuckle when I hear her whisper under her breath, "Jesus."

My cock springs free when she pushes my briefs down, and without any warning, she grabs my dick with her hand and starts rubbing my precum over the tip with her thumb. I need to pleasure her first because I will not last at this rate.

I pick her up by her thighs and wrap them around my waist. Alice loops her arms around my neck while I walk her over to her bed and lie her down, hovering close and covering her body with mine. I'm breathing hard and heavy, trying to calm myself. My pulse is running a rapid marathon in my chest.

Alice's cheeks are flushed pink, and her eyes are dark, sparkling with arousal. *Fuck*. My dick pulsates. I drop to my knees and open her legs wide with my palms and see that she's glistening with heavy desire. I drag my finger through her wet, slick sex. I spread the arousal up to her clit and rub it in circles. Her eyes close, and she moans. "Mike."

She bites her pillow to prevent sounds from leaving her mouth while I get back to my treasure and start gliding a finger through her slickness. I slide it inside her, which gets me a mumble from under the pillow. I dip my head down and kiss the top of her lower abdomen, bringing my gentle fluttery kisses lower, until I hit her clit and stroke it with my tongue at the same time as I insert another finger in.

Then I pump her harder, pressing my fingers down on her tight wall. She is writhing around so I use my spare arm to lock her hips down so she can't move, which, seconds later, has her coming violently. Once I know she is finished and I've enjoyed every last drop, I stand up and look at her, noticing her closed eyes and very flushed face. When she finally reopens them, her eyes are crystal clear. *Stunning.*

She smiles up at me, then grabs my head and forces it down toward hers so she can kiss me passionately. I'm so hard, and I know she can feel it against her stomach because she is trying to guide me to her wet entrance. I welcome the way her hand wraps around me and guides me inside her. Our lips disconnect when I slide deep inside of her. "This feels so fucking good." I grunt and begin to fuck her hard.

There's no time for gentle.

I thrust repeatedly in the angle that allows me to hit the right spot for her. She whimpers. I continue to pump as hard and as deep as I can. Her fingernails claw at my shoulder as she chases her orgasm.

"Alice, I'm going to fill your tight pussy with my cum," I growl, knowing I won't be able to hold on much longer.

Her lips part and she tips her head back as her body shudders with another orgasm.

"Yes. Mike," she cries out.

I keep moving in and out furiously until I climax.

Laying down beside her, I wrap my arm around her waist and hold her. I smile at her sleepy face, cherishing every second before laying a kiss on her lips. "Sleep well, my love. I love you."

Her eyes spring open and she stares at me with a smirk on her face. "I love you too." My heart constricts in my chest. *She can own me with just one look.*

Now that she is back here, I will never let her go again.

EPILOGUE

Alice

A MONTH LATER

Ever since I got back from Mom's I have been wrapped in Mike's bubble and haven't caught up with Blake and the girls much.

I decide to call Blake on my way in.

"Oh, hello stranger!"

"Good morning. I didn't know if you were on the morning shift, so I thought I would take my chance."

"Yeah, another day, another morning." He sighs.

"Is everything okay?" I ask.

"Yeah, I am just over my ward. I think I need to find something else."

"I know our ward is looking for more nurses. I could check with Kate for you."

"Listen, I wouldn't say no."

I chuckle. "I just parked, but would you be free to meet for lunch so we can chat more? I have missed you." I climb out and walk toward the elevator.

"Sounds perfect."

"I'll catch you at your hospital cafeteria for lunch. Let's say noon, and if you need to change it, let me know. Just send me a text."

"Will do."

I hang up and wander to the ward.

Lunchtime arrives and I have no messages on my phone, so it looks like noon is still on. I see Blake sitting at the table with his head down and buried in his phone. I walk over to the table.

"Hey, what's for lunch today? My treat."

He hits his phone, pops it down, and glances up, beaming. "Hi. No idea. Let's go for a stroll and see what we can find." He joins me in standing and we go over to the buffet, walking along the table.

"This place has way too many choices. I'll stick to what I know."

"Pasta?" I ask.

He nods. "Exactly. At least I know it's good."

"I'm going to grab a sandwich. Meet you at the table?"

"Okay, see you soon." I walk off toward the sandwich station and he heads toward the pasta.

I order my usual chicken sandwich, and once we are seated, we dig into our food.

"Kate said to drop her off a resume. Are you working tomorrow?" I ask between bites of my sandwich.

"Awesome, thanks for asking. I am. There is so much overtime. We are shorthanded every day. Hence why I am tired and over it."

"That's rough." I sigh.

I gaze down and though I haven't eaten much, I feel like I want to throw up. "This chicken must not be cooked properly." I peel back the bread, inspecting the chicken.

"Hmm, why is that?"

"I feel like I want to vomit." Blake eyes me weirdly. "Alice, you have barely eaten anything, and you can't get symptoms of food poisoning that quickly. Have you been feeling off for a bit, like getting sick other days?"

Thinking about it, I nod. "Come to think about it, yes."

His eyebrows rise. "When's your period due?"

"No idea, it's irregular. I think soon, though, like any day now."

"You're pr—"

I cut him off. "No way, no chance." I wave my arms around.

"Only one way to find out for sure," he says with a shrug.

I gaze around and spot a pregnant woman, hand on her stomach, walking hand in hand with her partner through the cafeteria. I have never thought about it before but seeing her, smiling and happy, I let myself think about it for a second and I decide I want that with Mike.

I wander back to work thinking about it, and the longer I think, I slowly realize that the last week I have been extra emotional, had a heightened sense of smell... *Could I be?*

Getting home was like a blur. I hardly remember how I got here. I stopped off at the pharmacy on my way to pick up a test. I feel sick, like I really, really want to be sick. I pull into the driveway at home. Jumping out, I lock the car and run up the path and into the house, bolting to the bathroom as fast as my legs will take me.

I vomit violently into the toilet. My entire body is shaking involuntarily. I pull myself back to sit on my heels and lean against the toilet bowl. I try to calm myself down, taking slow deep breaths, trying to slow down my rapid pulse. I can feel my nerves kicking up. My chest is tight, and panic is flowing through my mind. I count. Ten, nine, eight... but after a few really good deep breaths, I'm slowly calming down. A knock at the door startles me.

"Alice, are you okay?" I hear Mike's concerned voice coming through the door.

"Yeah, I must have eaten bad chicken at lunch today," I mumble back. I hate lying, but until I know for sure, I can't say a word. I don't want to get his hopes up.

"Are you sure? You sound awful. I'll be out here if you need anything. Just call out."

"I'm fine. I'll call you if I need anything," I yell out.

"Okay." I hear his heavy footsteps lead away from the door.

I sigh. I pull open the pregnancy kit box out of my handbag and sit looking at the box. *I don't want to do it. Surely, I can't be pregnant. Surely.* My heart is beating erratically inside my chest. Before I can overthink it, I tear open the box and read the instructions. I know I have to wait three minutes, but I can't sit in here for that long. I rip open the film covering the test strip and once I've done the test, I cover the stick with the lid and lay it flat. I finish tidying myself up and head straight toward the shower.

"Just having a quick shower. I won't be long!" I call out to Mike.

In the bathroom, I put the stick on the counter and turn the shower on. I strip and get under the water. Being in here, I feel so relaxed with the hot water spraying on my back and helping settle my stomach. What will Mike think if I *am* pregnant?

I wash and condition my hair, shave my legs, and with nothing else left to do in the shower, I turn it off. Drying myself off, I know I'm drawing it out because I know I'm close to looking at the test, which has my nerves picking up the speed in my chest again. When I'm dry, I know I can't avoid it any longer, so I wrap the towel tightly around me and step over to the counter.

Those steps feel heavy and long when I finally reach it. I lean forward and look at the little window. *Pregnant.* Instantly, tears fill my eyes and start to stream down my face. Surprisingly, I'm happy and not completely miserable about the prospect of having a baby. I wanted this to go slow, but I'm pregnant now and I want this. I stand up, brush my teeth and finish getting dressed.

I wander out to the kitchen, where I spot Mike sprawled out on the couch, watching football. I walk over to him.

Every step I take I swallow back bile. I have never been this nervous in my whole life.

His head spins and his face falls. Quickly sitting up in a panic, he says, "Babe, what's wrong?"

Warm tears stream down my face. I hiccup and hand him the stick I have been clutching in my fingers. With a shaky hand, I pass it over. His head tilts and his eyes widen. He stares down at the positive stick. I cover my face with my hands and sob.

"Babe, you serious? You're pregnant?" he says, his voice breaking. His heavy steps coming around to me. I feel his strong arms envelop me and I hug him back.

I nod into his chest.

"*Wow.*"

A soft chuckle leaves my lips. "You're happy, yeah?" I lean back to look at his face.

"Fuck yeah, babe." He leans down and pecks me.

I tangle my fingers and pull on his hair, pushing my body up against his. I kiss him and when I eventually pull back, his eyes are closed, and we are both breathing hard and fast.

He opens them, and they are a dark, shimmering blue. "Fuck me, Mama, are you horny?" I don't bother answering him with words. Instead, I grab his top and rip it from his body. "Fuck, this is going to be the best nine months of my life if this is what your pregnancy hormones do."

I smirk up at him, and then my hands are roaming his body, and he is moaning. *I love torturing him.* I drop to my knees and the moment I undo his button, I hear the word, "Fuck" leave his lips. I lick my own and unzip his jeans, pushing them down along with his white briefs. His cock is hard and right in front of my face, so I grab it and lick it. His hands drop to my head and curl in my hair when I take him in my mouth. He is pulling on my hair, but I love that I'm the one taking the power tonight.

"Babe, I can't hold on much longer, so you need to stop, or I'll be shooting down your throat." His voice is gravelly with desire. I smile around his cock and pull him at the base even harder. "I'm coming." I feel the hot liquid hit the back of my throat seconds after his shout.

When he's done, I pull back and look up at him. His eyes are closed, and one of his hands is on his head. His chin is lifted up, and his breathing is fast and uneven. This makes me happy. He is a vision standing there naked while I'm still fully dressed. I slowly stand, which snaps him out of his daze.

His eyes open and he smirks at me, but when I strip my top and bra off, I smirk back, shaking my head. "My rules tonight."

His eyebrows rise. "Is that how it is?" His eyes are focused on me as he watches me remove my clothes and I slowly walk back to the bed.

"Yes." I take my pants and briefs off. He has followed me over while keeping his distance—respecting my rules tonight.

"How am I so lucky?"

"I want you to fuck me hard tonight. I want to scream your name as I orgasm."

That has him grinning wickedly, and he stalks over until he is standing in front of me. "You got it, babe."

He bends down, grabbing my legs and lifting me up so I can wrap my legs around his middle and moves me to the center of the bed. He hovers over me and kisses me, before pulling back and kissing along my neck, working his way down to my nipples, which he licks, sucks, and tugs each one between his lips and teeth. The sensations have me moaning and groaning for more. My hips are bucking up to find release and relief for the pressure building between my legs.

He slowly kisses and licks down my stomach, skipping my sex. I groan, frustrated at his teasing as he lightly kisses up both my inner thighs, one leg at a time and until he finally reaches my sex. He doesn't move, so I push my hands on his head, trying to get him to do something. He chuckles and blows air onto my dripping sex. *This is pure torture; I need release.* He blows one more time and my hips buck again, so he grabs my thighs, holding them down and apart.

He licks and sucks my sex until I can feel myself climbing, and I'm so close to orgasm. *He knows my body so well.* When I'm almost there, he pushes two fingers inside and rubs my clit at the same time as his tongue. I come hard on his fingers. He laps it up even while his hand is still fucking me and stimulating my clit. I knew his hands had won awards for his work as a doctor, but he's even better as a lover.

These hands are perfect. Once he finishes licking up every drop, he moves up to hover over me again and kisses me.

He lines himself up, and he thrusts in hard, exactly the way I asked. I'm building up quickly again. I have never come more than once with anyone else; I didn't think it was possible. But Mike knows how to turn me on and quickly bring me over the edge. He is thrusting into me, but I can tell he wants to go deeper, so he rolls me over until I'm on all fours, then he pushes my shoulders down and re-enters me. This new position hits the spot. One of his hands is playing with my breast and nipple and the other is rubbing my clit.

I feel overwhelmed. The pressure inside me is building up, but I'm not quite there. "Harder." His thrusts become more intense, and he begins to rub my clit, adding even more pressure. "I'm coming!"

"Me too," he groans gruffly.

I come as a powerful orgasm takes over me and I feel his cock empty inside of my body. When he is finished, he pulls out and gently lies me down on my side, cleans up, and then returns to spoon me until we both fall asleep.

EXTENDED EPILOGUE

Mike

MONTHS LATER

I have known since I met Alice that she was 'the one,' but I didn't think I would be lucky enough to be getting to have a baby with her so soon. I still want to make it clear that we are a family and I want to marry her. I want her to have my name. She already agreed that the baby will have my last name, but I want her to have it as well.

Standing in the jewelry store, I'm staring at this sparkling emerald cut ring that I have in the palm of my hand. All I see is Alice, with the unique shape and the sparkle that perfectly matches how I view her. She is going to kill me if she ever finds out how much this ring cost me, but hopefully, she never will. She deserves the best, and this is the best right here.

I glance up at the store manager. "I'll take it."

I hand over the ring and he smiles. "Good choice, sir. She will love it."

He seems kind, but I'm sure he uses that sales pitch on everyone. I don't care, though, because this is Alice's ring. The baby is due tomorrow and even if he or she doesn't arrive, then I'm going to propose. I have waited long enough. I didn't want to overwhelm Alice. The last few months have been hectic: with her moving in, all the renovations, her finishing up at work. She hasn't stopped, but I want this. My heart is telling me that this is the right time to do it.

I pay for the ring and leave the jewelry store. I pick up Alice's favorite smoothie before heading to my car. Her cravings have been the weirdest mix, and I have gone out for food at the most random of hours. But I would do anything for her. I haven't missed a single appointment or scan. I have been there every step of the way. This is my miracle family.

The sex is still crazy. She is hornier than ever, and I hope this lasts even after the baby is born. When I get home, she is asleep on the sofa. I pick her up and carry her to our bed, and set the smoothie down on the bedside table. As I step back downstairs, an idea pops into my head for how I'll propose tomorrow.

I call up Blake, Tahlia, Maddison, Angie, Claire, and my family. I set them all assigned tasks. Everyone is excited and in on the surprise.

I wake in the morning after only a few hours of sleep. I tossed and turned all night, my heart and mind both racing with nerves about today. I'm slightly sweaty, thinking about asking her, but I know she won't say no. *Well, I hope not.* Rolling over, I see she is still deeply asleep, hugging her pregnancy pillow. *That is one thing I won't miss when the baby comes.* I miss us being wrapped around each other, but at the moment, all she wants is to cuddle that massive pillow. I'm glad it's only nine months. Otherwise, I'd need a new bed. I climb out, careful not to wake her, and go get organized.

She still hasn't moved by the time I'm ready to head downstairs. I leave her a note to get ready before coming down. I immediately get started with setting up a special breakfast. I could have taken her to the best restaurant or done something grand, but I know Alice, and she will want all her closest people with her on her special day. Nothing fancy, just love, friends, and family.

The first to arrive is Blake, with Tahlia and Maddison, and a few minutes later, Alex walks into my house. Something is up with my brother; he has been different lately, but I can't put my finger on it. I've no time to dwell on it now. They help me set the table and get the decorations set up. I have already organized everything outside, and once we are finished inside, I tell them to wait out there in case Alice comes down. The rest of our families arrive not too long after, and I'm just in the kitchen making coffee when I hear Alice walking down the stairs. I grab my phone and text Alex.

Mike: *She is on her way down now. Get everyone ready. ASAP.*

When she arrives in the kitchen, I feel so happy when I see her and the bump which holds our baby. She is the most beautiful pregnant woman I have ever seen.

"Good morning, babe."

She frowns. "Hi. What's going on? Why did you ask me to get ready?" She is eyeing me and then looks at the table. Her eyes widen at the setup, and she stares, taking it all in.

"I thought I'd invite our family and your friends over for the baby brunch. They should be here soon."

Her eyes are suspicious, but she shrugs it off. "Ohhh, it will be so nice to see them. Being this pregnant, I can't move much now."

I walk over to her and kiss her. "Not long now." I beam at her.

She nods. "No, any day now."

"Well, do you mind heading outside with me? I want to show you something before they all arrive."

Her brows furrow. "Yeah, what is it?"

"Just come with me. We won't be long," I plead.

I grab her hand, holding it while we walk out the door.

She gasps and tears immediately run down her face. "Oh, my God!"

I've set everything up exactly how it was for our first date, with the projector and cushions. Everything is the same.

"Come here for a moment."

She follows me over to the rug, and grabbing both her hands, I stare directly into her eyes. *This is it.* I take a big breath in and slowly kneel in front of her. She lets go of one of my hands to cover her mouth in shock. Tears are streaming down her face. I have to do this quickly, so I can comfort her.

"Alice, from the moment we met at Luxe to now, you have been nothing but perfect. You are the most beautiful, kind, and generous woman I have ever met. I'm honored to be having a baby with you and I would love it if you would honor me again by agreeing to be my wife. Alice Winters, will you marry me?"

She is nodding and spluttering through her tears, "Yes, yes, yes!"

I pull the ring out of the box and slide it on her finger. She lifts her hand to cover her mouth again and sobs. I stand up and hug her.

Everyone then jumps out, yelling, screaming, and crying out, "Congratulations!" Alice sobs again, and when she notices her mom, she wobbles over and embraces her. Everyone does a round of congratulating us both, and when Alice comes back to stand with me, she wraps her arm around my waist.

For the rest of the day, everyone eats and drinks before leaving.

When there is only Alice and I left, I ask her, "Are you ready to watch the movie now?"

"Yes, please, Mike. Thank you for a wonderful day. It was perfect, just like you."

A few days later, at three a.m., Alice's water breaks in bed. She wakes me up, and I have never been more scared in my life. I forget all things medical and start to freak out like a madman. Poor Alice has to comfort me and calm me down between the start of her contractions.

"Calm down, Mike. Grab my bag and call the obstetrician."

I nod, then walk off and do exactly that.

The obstetrician asks us to come to the hospital so Alice can get the baby monitored and delivered by her doctor and midwife. Half an hour later, we have the car packed and are on our way. I bought myself a "Dad car." Alice thinks it's ridiculous, but I don't. I love it.

Eight hours later, I meet and hold my son, Ethan. I have never cried so much in my life. Alice handled labor like a champion. She is my queen, giving me the most precious gift of all. He is the spitting image of her and that only makes me cry harder. My chest feels like it will combust with love when I finally get to cuddle my two miracles.

The End.

BONUS SCENE

Mikes POV on the night at Luxe

MIKE

The boys want to go back to Luxe tonight. It's only been open for a few weeks, but we all bought memberships and came to the opening party. I'm here tonight with my brother, Alex, and our friends, Ryan and Jackson.

I love the atmosphere of this club. It's sexy, warm, and the crowd is full of like-minded people. It's the perfect place to pick up classy women, and the bonus is that the ratio of women to men is even, leaving plenty of both to go around. It's a great place to come and unwind after a long workweek.

We've only just arrived, and Jackson has already snagged a couch near the back of the club. It's wonderful to be able to sit down, talk, and enjoy our drinks. When it's my turn to buy a round of drinks, Ryan comes with me to help carry them back to the guys. On our way over, I notice this little knockout leaning over the bar, with her dress barely covering her ass. If she leans over any farther, I'm sure I'll come in my pants like a twelve-year-old boy. My walk falters and I'm unable to remove my eyes from her. She is in the smallest, tightest dress I have ever seen, but that's not what has snagged my attention. What I can't tear my eyes away from is her smile. It's captivating and real; she is smiling and laughing so wide it reaches her eyes.

"What's up, Mike?"

I nod in the direction of her with my chin and run my fingers through my hair. Following my line of sight, he scans around until he spots her and smiles in appreciation. "Nice."

I notice she is with a guy who's wearing really tight pants with a peach shirt. *Very strange outfit for this type of crowd.* I watch them interact for a second, noting how he is gazing around at everyone, checking them out from head to toe, but only concentrating on the men around him. I'm pretty certain they are just friends because if he is her boyfriend, then that's pretty fucked up. Ryan and I walk to the bar, joining the queue. Ryan stands beside me, and when it's my turn to order, I lean over the bar to whisper to the bartender.

"I need four scotch on the rocks, please, and do you see the girl there in the black dress and ponytail?" I tilt my head in her direction.

He looks over his shoulder until he spots her and then spins his head back to me. His brows furrow.

"Add all her bills for the night to my tab, but do not tell her it was from me."

I hand over a few hundred-dollar bills, and he takes them, stuffing them in his pocket before smiling back at me. "Deal."

While he sets off to make our scotches, I continue sneaking glances her way. I can't afford to be staring now or she will know the drinks were from me, or her friend will notice and tell her.

The bartender comes back and serves us our drinks. I scoop two glasses up and Ryan picks up the other two. "Let's head back," I mumble to Ryan. He eyes me suspiciously, and I frown back at him. "I'll be able to see her better from where we are."

Ryan nods. "Lead the way."

We walk back to our couch, carrying two drinks each. I stand next to the couch instead of sitting down so I can watch her from afar. I can see her and the guy looking around, no doubt trying to figure out who bought their drinks. Smirking, I raise my glass and take a sip.

The friend leaves her side and moves over to watch the people on the dance floor and finish his drink. She pushes off the bar and follows slowly behind. Watching her saunter toward the dance floor opposite to where I'm standing, I lick my lips, tasting the residue of scotch on my skin. She joins him on the dance floor, still holding their drinks and looking around.

A zap runs down my spine when her gaze finds mine. In that moment, I take a pull of my scotch, letting the burn of the alcohol warm my throat. I continue to stare back, never breaking our intense eye contact. She drops her glass, and it smashes to the ground, sending shards flying everywhere. I watch her squat in her tiny dress and attempt to clean it up. *A born helper.* When her friend stops her by reaching for her arm, she then leaves him while he waits for someone to clean up, and I take this opportunity to go talk to her.

I walk a little too quickly to catch up with her and purposefully crash into her. She steps backward and I reach out to grab on to her arms. "Shit, I'm so sorry."

Her eyes widen under my stare and her cheeks turn a sweet shade of pink. *Adorable.* Her sweet vanilla scent wafts through my nose, causing my pulse to beat erratically in my chest. She nods and I use this chance to take in her beauty. Standing so close, she is even more delectable. I watch as her tongue pokes out and skims her bottom lip, causing my dick to harden inside my pants.

Touching her and standing so close is elevating my body temperature to an uncomfortable level. My mouth is dry, and I need refreshment, but I don't want to leave her.

"Can I buy you a drink?" I blurt.

I stare down at her, watching her pretty pink lips part. Her eyes flutter closed, and she moves her head toward me. I don't hesitate. I bring my lips down to capture hers. I enjoy the passionate kiss, savoring her sweet taste. I am just getting started when she pulls away panting.

She clears her throat, pretending to not be affected. But her body betrays her, and before I can get another word in, she speaks. "I have to go to the bathroom. I'll catch up with you later."

I step back, dropping my hands, and watch as she saunters off into the direction of the bathroom.

What the fuck just happened? Fuck. I take off to the bar and grab another drink before rejoining the boys at the couch. I'm holding another glass of scotch when she spots me again, and I raise the glass to my lips, not breaking eye contact the whole time. The buzz between us is electric. I watch as her friend drags her to the dance floor and breaks our gaze again, so when I finish my glass, I walk around and order another one. *These are going down smoothly tonight.* It's been a long week and going home to an empty house isn't appealing. After I order, I return to the dance floor and scan it for her, still sipping my drink.

"Hello, Mike. Are you here alone?"

I look down my nose and see my ex-girlfriend, Amanda. The music is so loud I have to lean forward so she can hear me. "No, I'm here with my friends." It's simple and blunt, but I'm still trying to spot the one person I do want to talk to tonight.

Amanda continues trying to talk to me, but I only respond with one-word answers. I spot Alex in the crowd, grinding with a woman to the beat of the music, and then he spins *her*, and I freeze. Amanda is still trying to get me to pay attention to her, but I can't hear anything anymore. I shot my drink, the scotch burning my throat with its intense warmth that makes me cough as it burns down to my chest.

A server passes by, and I slam the glass on the tray and shove my hands in my pockets. I'm too engrossed with what's unfolding in front of my eyes to listen to Amanda.

I gasp and grit my teeth as Alex leans down, and I'm forced to watch their lips join. Everything around me seems to fall silent, and I can no longer hear or see the girl in front of me at all.

I watch her with Alex until I'm sure she must feel my eyes burning through her. She glances over and our eyes connect again. Her eyes widen, and she drops her hands from Alex. My hands are firmly stuffed inside my pockets, and I ball them into fists.

Neither of us attempts to look away until her friend breaks our connection, and I watch as she stalks off without a second glance in my direction. A heavy sigh leaves my lips. No longer wanting to talk to anyone else tonight, I storm off and grab a taxi home, alone. *I'm always alone.*

ALSO BY SHARON WOODS

The Gentlemen Series

Accidental Neighbor

Bossy Mr. Ward

White Empire

The Christmas Agreement

Resisting Chase

Saffron and Secrets Novella

Chicago Billionaire Doctor's

Doctor Taylor

Doctor I Do

Doctor Gray

About Sharon Woods

Sharon Woods is an author of Contemporary Romance. Predominantly sexy billionaires. She lives in Melbourne, Australia with her husband and two children.

She drinks a lot of coffee, loves to workout, travel, and has an unhealthy addiction to reality TV.

Follow Sharon:

http://www.sharonwoodsauthor.com

Printed in Great Britain
by Amazon